Adios
to
All the Drama

Adios
to
All the Drama

DIANA
RODRIGUEZ WALLACH

KENSINGTON BOOKS
http://www.kensingtonbooks.com

Acknowledgments

Many thanks to my amazing agent, Jenoyne Adams, for all of her support with this series and for always calming my nerves. I'd like to thank Jenoyne's wonderful team, specifically Candice Smith, Kelsey Adelson, and Taylor Martindale, for their always thoughtful edits.

Thank you to my editor, Kate Duffy. This series truly would not exist if it weren't for her belief in Mariana! And thank you to Kate's assistant, Megan Records, for making the publishing process smoother.

Thank you to everyone in Philadelphia who has reached out to help me promote this series, including: Gail Bower, Jennifer Rodriguez, Jenee Chizick, Bob Mulvihill, Philadelphia Academies, The Lutheran Settlement House, Barnes and Noble in Rittenhouse Square, Head House Books, Mixto Restaurant, and the many school districts in the Delaware Valley including my alma mater, Ridley.

A special thanks goes to all of my Ridley Girls. If I didn't have such great lifelong friends from high school, it wouldn't be so easy to write about those years.

Thanks to the Wallachs for showing such excitement for my work, and a very special thank-you to Paula for being a wonderful editor and mother-in-law.

Thank you to my siblings, Natalie and Lou, for talking up my books to every colleague you meet. I hope I can return the favor someday. And I'd like to give a special thank-you to my parents for everything they've given me, including my drive to pursue this career. Your support and love mean so much.

I'd especially like to thank my husband, Jordan, for all of the work he has done to help make this dream a reality. This includes everything from building my website, to calling reporters, to contacting school districts, to driving me to every bookstore in the Philadelphia area, to being my first editor, to being pleasantly patient while I'm in "writing mode," and for simply believing in me with your whole heart. If it weren't for your love and support, I would not have gotten as far as I have. I love you very much.

Chapter 1

He was arriving in less than a week. When I had left Alex standing on the side of the road in Utuado, waving at my car as it pulled away from my aunt Carmen and uncle Miguel's home, I had truly thought I would never see him again. Sure, we had made plans to keep in touch via e-mail, but there's a huge difference between a few electronic submissions and a half-semester face-to-face visit. Especially when his accommodations were two doors down on the left, next to the hall bath alongside Vince's room.

"So does this mean you're gonna start wearing makeup to breakfast?" Lilly asked as she helped me clear out the drawers in what would soon be Alex's room.

"I barely wear makeup to school. I doubt I'll start caking it on to eat Cheerios." I tossed a bunch of my mom's old sweaters into a plastic storage bin bound for the attic.

"But what if Alex is pouring the milk in your Cheerios?" Lilly raised an eyebrow.

"Well, I may have to brush my teeth . . ."

I grabbed my mom's old cardigan and placed it neatly in another bin. Most of the extra closets in our house held my mom's "overflow" wardrobe. She didn't throw much away out of a belief that it would eventually come back into style—it was a holdover from her childhood growing up in the projects. When you go from Kmart to Chanel in less than thirty years, it's hard to part with those Chanels even when they're dated.

"I still can't believe he's up and moving here to be with you," Lilly stated plainly.

"This has nothing to do with me. He's visiting colleges."

"Yeah, if you believe that. . . ."

"I do!" I insisted, though even I could hear the defensive edge in my voice.

"He's staying in a room down the hall from yours. Is that standard procedure for every kid who wants to tour universities in the greater Philadelphia area? Because if so, your parents need to up their rates. . . ."

"I wouldn't talk, Miss Freeloader."

"Hey, my parents send money!" she tossed a lavender-scented sachet at me.

Lilly had moved here in September to seek a better education. Though her parents were justifiably nervous having their daughter live with distant relatives, Lilly had flawlessly adjusted almost immediately. She was one of the most popular freshmen in our school.

"I'm just saying if you didn't move here from Puerto Rico, maybe Alex wouldn't be so inspired to do the same. It could be *you* he misses." I narrowed my eyes.

"Nice try, but I don't think so."

Lilly carefully lifted one of my mom's formal handbags. Each elegant clutch, leather satchel, or logo-patterned purse was to be individually placed in the fabric dust bag it came in, then nestled into a cardboard box and labeled, then stacked into a plastic bin. Sometimes I thought my mom cared more about those purses than she did her own life.

"So are you guys just gonna pick up where you left off? Have a big smooch fest at the airport?" Lilly blew kisses at me.

"I don't know," I mumbled. "I don't want to act like I expect anything or like I think this trip has more to do with me than it does school."

"But it does."

"No, it doesn't," I said firmly as I locked the lid on the transparent bin.

"You realize your family is single-handedly boosting the Latino population at your school district at an alarming rate," she joked.

"Not exactly. Vince is away at school."

"Ah, but holiday break is just around the corner. The numbers are swinging in our favor."

She was right. My parents' home was quickly becoming a halfway house for Puerto Rican teens looking to migrate from Utuado.

Alex was visiting as part of a mini-exchange program. Somehow his tiny mountaintop private school had arranged to send him to the States for two months to tour American universities. He would keep up with his classes in Utuado online, utilizing Spring Mills High School's computer labs, library, and all other facilities. He'd also be passing me in the halls, eating with me in the cafeteria, and bumming rides from my friends.

I glanced around the yellow-and-green guest room. My grandmother, my mom's mom, used to stay here when she visited. It was decorated specifically for her with the thick plush carpet she preferred, the colors she favored, and an ivy-stenciled border that mimicked her bedroom in Camden. She stayed in the room a lot after my grandfather died. Aside from our maid, hardly anyone had stepped foot in it since she passed away two years ago.

Now it would be Alex's room. Only I couldn't picture him in it. I couldn't picture him here.

Chapter 2

My eyes darted around the cafeteria. Alex would soon be joining the packs of classmates I'd known since kindergarten—the jocks, cheerleaders, band members, mathletes, rockers, and artists. They were all familiar and boring, and now that comforting, predictable dynamic was about to change.

"So you're kinda moody," Emily noted as she swallowed a mouthful of yogurt. "I thought that was *my* job."

I smirked at her. "It's the whole Alex thing."

"Exactly how many Spanish runaways do your parents plan to take in?" Madison asked as she swished her glistening platinum hair over her bony shoulder. "'Cause ya know, for just the price of a cup of coffee they could support entire villages in Africa."

"Very funny," I chirped. "Alex is just visiting. He's not moving here."

"Like the last one," she huffed, examining her manicure. She was referring to Lilly.

Ever since the "Cornell incident" last month, when Emily confessed that her mother was having an affair with my locker buddy Bobby's dad and Madison revealed her secret communications with Evan, she and my cousin had been getting along. Sure, they weren't about to purchase interlocking best friend charms anytime soon, but they had stopped snarling at each other (most of the time). Emily reminded us that we could have bigger problems.

"Well, I'm excited to meet him. At least one of us has a boyfriend," Emily stated.

"*I* have a boyfriend!" Madison squeaked. "Sort of . . ."

"I thought you and Evan were just talking," I pointed out.

"We are. I mean, we haven't labeled it, but he IMs me every night." She gazed across the cafeteria to where Evan was seated with his wrestling buds.

For the past four weeks, Evan had been secretly contacting my best friend via the Internet and text message. But he had yet to ask her on a date, offer any physical affection (they hadn't so much as held hands), or acknowledge their friendship publicly. At this point, I felt he was either embarrassed to be involved with her, or he was keeping his options open to be with other girls. Regardless, I hated him for it.

I watched as Madison stared longingly at the wrestling stud; he was utterly oblivious.

"You know, Mad, maybe you should have 'the talk' with Evan. Ask him what's going on," I suggested, casually dipping a Tater Tot in a mound of generic ketchup.

"No way. I don't want to look all needy and pathetic. Besides, he wouldn't call me if he didn't like me."

"He doesn't call you. He texts you," Emily pointed out before crunching into a carrot stick drenched in ranch dressing.

"It's the same thing," Madison muttered.

"Actually, it isn't," I said.

Madison snapped her icy blue eyes toward me. "At least I didn't have to import some guy from a third world country."

"Puerto Rico is not a third world country! It's part of the U.S. And I didn't ask him to come here," I defended.

"Whatever. Still, not all of us can have guys pining away for us from across an ocean." Madison shrugged and popped a green grape into her mouth. She was eating a Greek salad for lunch, part of her new vegetarian kick (though I secretly wondered if it was just an excuse to eat less calories unquestioned).

"Yeah, well don't get too jealous," Emily stated. "Relationships never last."

"That's not true," I said softly.

The dark circles under Emily's eyes had deepened several shades over the past month. No amount of yellow under-eye concealer masked them, and there wasn't much she could do to prevent them given that she spent most of her nights listening to her mother sob into a pillow. Living with a woman who'd gone from confident college professor to self-destructive mistress had been justifiably wearing on her.

"Try telling that to my dad. Of course, you'd have to speak with the concierge at the Marriott because he never seems to answer his phone. I swear, the woman who cleans his hotel room spends more time with him than I do," Emily muttered.

Madison and I exchanged a look. There wasn't much we could say. We had spent the last four weeks dissecting the situation, listening to her, supporting her, and offering any advice we could find from Oprah to *Cosmo*. We were tapped out. The reality was that her father was now living in a Center City hotel and her parents were probably getting divorced. And as much as Madison and I wanted to take that pain away from her, it didn't look like we could.

"So when does Ricky Martin fly in again?" Madison asked.

"His name is Alex Montoya, and he just e-mailed me his itinerary. I think his flight comes in at 8:00 P.M. on Thursday," I reminded her. "You still driving?"

"Of course. I wouldn't miss the grand welcome of your Latin lover." She smirked.

"Will you please stop calling him that."

"Um, no." She laughed.

I shook my head, smiling.

It's not often that sixteen-year-olds get to play with fire in an academic facility. But today we were in the midst of a chemistry flame test. It was notoriously known as one of the most fun labs conducted all year, mostly because there was an urban legend that a teacher once accidentally singed a student's hair off. As a precaution we were all forced to wear goggles and gloves, and tie our hair back securely.

I fidgeted with my tight ballet bun. I had years of experience tying them, but I usually didn't have to fit the elastic strap of protective eyewear around it. The combination was digging uncomfortably into my skull.

"Okay, the first metal is lithium," Bobby said, reaching for the solid.

"No, wait!" I grabbed his arm.

The skin-to-skin contact made me immediately uncomfortable. I let go and quickly looked down at my notebook. The last thing I needed was a flashback of us getting caught kissing at Cornell—especially not with Alex about to arrive.

"We have to make sure the wire is clean or it won't work," I said.

I dipped our wire into hydrochloric acid and placed it in the flame of the Bunsen burner. The fire didn't change color.

"Okay, it's clean." I handed it back.

In the four weeks since the Cornell trip that wrecked his parents' marriage, Bobby and I hadn't spoken much beyond school-related topics. It was hard to weave, "Sorry your dad was getting down with my best friend's mom," into everyday conversation. This was the same reason we never mentioned the kiss between us—too awkward.

Bobby dipped the wire into the concentrated hydrochloric acid and placed it into the lithium solid. A small amount of the metal chloride formed. Then he held it to the flame. The blaze instantly burned bright red.

"Cool," he said, gazing into the fire.

I recorded the answer onto our worksheet.

"So there's something I've been meaning to talk to you about," he said.

My gut involuntarily sucked in. I said nothing.

"Are you still gonna help out with the film festival? 'Cause we only have two weeks left to plan . . ."

My stomach unclenched.

"Oh," I said, a bit too loudly.

He cocked his head. "What'd you think I was gonna say?"

"I don't know. Nothing." I cleaned off the wire in acid. "Sure, I'll help you. What do you need? Posters? Flyers?"

"Yeah, and we need to recruit some people to showcase their work. So far, the photography club members only have a bunch of amateurish black-and-whites—girls standing in front of boys' urinals and whatnot."

"Seriously?" I asked, my eyebrows squished together.

I had never ventured into a restroom intended for the opposite sex. But I wasn't exactly much of a rule breaker. I'd wait in the women's bathroom line for an hour before ever hopping into an abandoned men's stall across the way.

"I can see if other kids have better pictures. Madison might have some digitals from her family's trip to Rome."

"Yeah, stuff like that would be good."

He dipped the wire coated with potassium into the flame. It immediately altered to a bright lilac hue perfect for a prom dress.

"Wow," I muttered.

"I figure as Thanksgiving gets closer things are gonna get crazy," Bobby said.

"Oh, shoot. I forgot . . ." My brown eyes pulled wide.

"The date? 'Cause you kinda were there when the dean set it."
He dipped the wire back into the acid for cleaning.

"No, it's just . . ." I timidly stared down at our worksheet
and carefully recorded our answer. "I mean, I'm kinda getting
a new house guest in a few days."

"So, is that a problem?" Bobby's blond curls flopped on his
forehead.

"Well, it's just that my guest is gonna be coming to school
with me, *us*. Not to our classes, but I'll need to show him
around. . . ."

"He?" Bobby stared intently at the wire he was cleaning.

"Yeah. He's a friend of Lilly's . . . and mine . . . from Puerto
Rico. He's gonna be checking out some colleges in the area."

"So he's our age?" Bobby interrupted, not making eye contact.

"He's a senior."

My eyes locked on the lab equipment. I didn't know why
I felt so uncomfortable telling him about Alex. Bobby wasn't
my boyfriend, but for some reason I felt like I was confessing
that I had cheated with another guy, and worse, that the other
guy had won.

"If you're too busy, that's cool," he grumbled, shrugging his
lanky arms.

"No, it'll be fine. I'll work it out. I'm a multitasker." I
smiled, hoping to ease the thick tension floating between us. "I
can plan festivals, accommodate guests, leap tall buildings . . ."

"In your case, wouldn't that be pirouette over tall buildings?"

"No, probably split leap tall buildings."

"Ah, even better."

He dipped the wire into the next metal and continued the
lab work. The calcium turned brick red.

Chapter 3

Madison's Audi wove through the narrow city streets. If she moved even an inch to the right, her car would swipe the sideview mirrors of every parked vehicle on the block.

"This can't possibly be a two-lane street," I said from my seat in shotgun.

With all of Emily's family woes, she didn't have much energy to extend to keeping her permanent spot in Madison's passenger seat. We now rotated the position on a regular basis.

"My dad said that all the streets in Philly have two lanes."

Madison's eyes were intently focused on keeping the car straight. She rolled to a stop at a red light, and sure enough, a white cab pulled up to our left, squeezing just a few inches shy of her door. We were so close that, had we wanted, we could have held a conversation with the passenger in the backseat.

"I told you," Madison mocked.

"Hey, this is normal to me," Lilly added. She was seated beside Emily. "Mariana, you've seen how people drive in Puerto Rico."

"Ugh, don't remind me." I flinched, my nose scrunched. "When our cousin Alonzo picked us up at the airport, he sped up this dirt road so fast through the mountains that our tires scraped the cliff. I thought I was gonna die."

"Yeah, well, if I don't pay attention, *we're* gonna die."

Alex was arriving tomorrow, and as a welcome gift, my friends and I were putting together a basket of Philadelphia staples. We were collecting a miniature Liberty Bell, a replica of the Declaration of Independence, postcards from the Constitution Center, a flag from the Betsy Ross House, soft pretzels from sidewalk vendors, water ice from South Philly, and rival cheesesteaks from both Pat's and Geno's famous establishments. My parents swore they'd keep everything preserved until tomorrow night.

"Why don't you guys just run in?" Madison asked as she rolled to a stop.

Lilly and I yanked our door handles and piled out in front of the modern white museum. We darted toward the glass doors of the Constitution Center. An exhibit on the history of baseball was showing inside.

"What do sports have to do with the Constitution?" Lilly asked, staring at a cutout of Babe Ruth.

"I can guarantee you that many Americans know the history of the Yankees and the Red Sox better than they do the Redcoats and the Colonies."

We rushed toward the gift shop. I immediately began swiveling a metal stand of postcards while Lilly swiveled another.

"You know, I could be mildly offended that Alex is getting this big welcome extravaganza when I got *nada*," Lilly huffed as she plucked a photo of Boathouse Row and showed it to me.

"That was different. We all flew in together. What, did you expect Tootsie to put together a grand entrance for you? He can barely roll over for a dog treat." I snatched an image of the Art Museum "Rocky" steps from the display.

"Still, it would've been nice."

"Well, I'll tell Tootsie to get his act together."

I gathered the cards Lilly was holding and spun toward the register. As soon as I reached the cashier, I was stopped by a sight outside of the shop. There, in the atrium of the museum, was Emily's mom. And she wasn't alone.

"Holy shit," I muttered.

The middle-aged sales clerk shot me an angry look.

"No, not you. Sorry." I swatted anxiously at Lilly, pointing. "Look at that."

"Is that Bobby's dad?" Lilly's expression looked horrified.

"Not unless he got major plastic surgery."

Emily's mom rested her hand against the man's chest and laughed, tossing her head back. She looked like she was having a wonderful Wednesday evening, carefree and happy, while her daughter hadn't slept in weeks. The man in the black suit and red tie reached his lips toward Mrs. Montgomery's ear and whispered.

"You know, I can see her four-karat diamond ring from here. She's not even trying to hide it," I spat.

"I take it that's not Emily's dad either."

"Uh, no."

I watched Mrs. Montgomery link arms with the man and casually stroll toward the exhibit. She had no idea her daughter was sitting in a car out front.

I slammed the passenger door shut and stared at the dash-board.

"Did you get what you needed?" Madison asked as she checked her mirrors and prepared to pull away.

I twisted toward Emily in the backseat. Lilly sat beside her silently, glaring out the window as if she wanted nothing to do with what was about to happen. My stomach was already cring-ing and I hadn't even opened my mouth.

"Um, Em," I said cautiously.

She looked at me.

"I saw your mom in there."

Her eyes reduced to slits. "In the museum?"

"Yeah."

Emily quickly glanced at the digital clock on the dashboard. It was 6:00 P.M.

"She should be home by now. I didn't know she was going out."

I stared at her, sucking the Chap Stick from my lips as I squirmed uncomfortably.

"What aren't you telling me?"

I looked to Madison, who was eyeing me carefully. She put her flashers back on as if she realized this might take a while.

"Well, she was with . . . someone."

"Who?" Emily asked in a deep voice.

"I don't know."

"Was it a man?"

"Yes," I squeaked, my shoulders rising defensively.

Emily sighed and stared out the window. "They could just be friends from the college. He might work in her department. Maybe this is some sort of research . . ."

"Emily, he was whispering in her ear," Lilly said bluntly.

"Lil!" I shouted.

"What? It's true."

"You didn't have to say it like that."

"Well, is there a better way to say it?"

Emily took a deep breath, her green eyes closed. Then she clutched the metal handle and swung the door open into on-coming traffic. A monster SUV nearly made Madison's new car a three-door.

"Em! What are you doing!" Madison yelled.

She didn't pause. She stepped into the traffic-clogged street and headed to the museum. I jumped out after her.

"I saw her go into the exhibit," I said when I caught up.

Emily charged toward the museum entrance and was immediately stopped by a ticket-taker at the exhibit doors. She glared at the employee as I ran to purchase two exhibit passes. Emily didn't even say thank you when I handed her the tickets, she just chucked them at the employee and charged into the dimly lit hall. I chased after her as she sped through the maze of documents and memorabilia. It didn't take long for her to spot her mother. It was as if she already knew where to find her.

Mrs. Montgomery was standing in front of a large etched poster that described the room's artifacts, reading every word like the inquisitive professor she was. The man at her side had his body pressed close to hers.

"So is there anyone in Philadelphia you aren't sleeping with?" Emily snipped.

I nearly choked on a gulp of air.

Her mom spun around, her mouth wide and her eyes even wider.

"Emily," she said simply, pushing her glasses up the bridge of her nose.

"Bobby's dad wasn't bad enough? You're just adding more men to the list? What, do you guys draw numbers?"

The guy coughed awkwardly and stepped back.

"Do *not* speak to me that way," her mother warned, moving closer toward her daughter.

Museumgoers around us craned their necks to eavesdrop, while I tried to melt into the background. (If I had the ability to develop a superpower, at that moment I would definitely have made myself invisible.)

"Why shouldn't I? What, do you think you deserve my *respect*?" Emily barked.

"I am your mother."

"And you used to be someone's wife. Clearly those roles don't mean much to you."

"Listen, little girl, think what you want of me, but your father is no saint."

Her mom glared at her without an ounce of sympathy. She didn't even look embarrassed. She smoothed her indigo cotton dress over her hips, which flowed casually to her leather boots. She looked more concerned with her hippy-esque appearance than her family.

"Maybe he's not. But I'd take a workaholic over an adulteress any day."

"Don't speak to your mother that way." The man of the hour stepped forward, resting his hand on Mrs. Montgomery's shoulder.

"Oh, please! Are you blind to the wedding ring on her finger, or do you not care?" Emily snarled at the two of them, her green eyes flaming with fury.

"You don't understand," he started.

"Well, don't bother explaining."

"Emily, I am not going to take this behavior from you," her mother warned.

"Behavior from *me*!" she shrieked, shaking her head. "You know what, I'll make it easy for you, Mom. I'm moving out. I wanna live with Dad."

My palm shot to my mouth as I gasped. Mrs. Montgomery's apathetic eyes turned toward me as if she'd just realized I was present.

"Fine, go ahead. See if he *wants you*."

Her mom's final words hung in the air. The entire exhibit room had cleared out, thankfully decreasing the audience to catch the tears clinging to my friend's eyes. I stepped toward her, but she waved me off.

"Well, at least Dad's not an embarrassment."

And with that, Emily charged out of the exhibit room. I hurried behind her, past the cases of Americana history, hardly comprehending the spectacle that had unfolded. When we got back to Madison's car, Emily broke into sobs.

"Take . . . take me to my dad's. I-I wanna go home."

Chapter 4

I stood at Madison's locker waiting for Emily. We'd left her in the lobby of the Marriott after a tearful call to her father. She said he would drive her to school in the morning. It was the first time since school had started that we didn't all carpool together.

"You know, maybe it's better she's not cooped up with her mother anymore," Lilly offered as she leaned against a locker adjacent to Madison's.

She was showing her support by waiting with us.

"I don't know what to think," I muttered, staring down the hall for my friend.

"It's like her mom is turning into *Fatal Attraction*. I'm waiting for her to boil some guy's bunny," Madison mocked as she dumped the books out of her bag.

"At this point, I wouldn't be surprised. Look at my family. It's been thirty-five years and my uncles are still pissed that my grandfather had an affair."

"True, but the rest of your family did kinda get over it," Lilly pointed out. "Your grandparents stayed married."

"Yeah, but I don't see that happening in this case . . ." Before I could finish the thought, I spied Emily trudging down the hall alone. I nudged Madison's arm.

"She looks pissed," she whispered.

"She looks sad."

"Hey," Emily said as she approached with a weak smile. "How was it?"

"Not too bad. My dad has a suite, so I kinda have my own room."

Her face was pale and her hair was wet from her shower—this from a girl who owned more hair products than most beauty salons. I'd never seen her leave the house without her maple locks perfectly flat-ironed, let alone with them soggy and in a ponytail.

"He dropped you off this morning?" Madison asked, slamming her locker shut.

"No, his work's car service did," she grunted. "How pathetic is that?"

"Well, is it better than your mom's?" I asked, trying to sound helpful.

"Right now, Folsom Prison would be better than my mom's. I can't believe her. You know, she didn't even call me last night to see if I was all right? I could be lying in a ditch somewhere for all she knows."

I stared at Madison. I didn't know what to say. I couldn't imagine my parents ever treating me that way—but then again, about a year ago I bet Emily thought the same thing.

"Well, I'll drop you back at the hotel after school," Madison offered.

"Oh, you're forgetting the big event," Lilly pointed out as she tossed her book bag over her shoulder. The bell was about to ring to start first period.

"That's right! The Puerto Rican prince arrives!" Madison teased, her glossed lips gleaming. "Smoochy, smoochy!"

I giggled, before catching the fake happiness Emily was forcing across her face.

"You know, Em, you don't have to come tonight if you don't want to. I totally understand."

"No, it's cool. I wanna go. I need to get out. And please, one of us deserves to have something good happen."

Just then the bell rang to start the day. It was odd to think of how differently I would be ending it.

We stared at the arrivals board. Dozens of planes from every destination I could think of lit up the black electronic monitors at Philadelphia International Airport. Lilly, Madison, Emily, and I were meeting Alex in the baggage claim area.

"It says his plane landed." Lilly pointed to the board.

"Why do I feel so nervous?" I ran my fingers through my auburn hair.

"Because we're finally gonna meet your Latin lover," Madison teased.

"I dare you to call him that to his face," I challenged.

"No, don't," Lilly said quickly. "He'll take it as a compliment. It'll only pump his ego further."

The airport was cold, with stark white corridors, glass panels, and a PA system buzzing with the latest information. Dozens of travelers whisked around us with wheeled carry-ons dragging behind them. Babies cried as families hugged good-bye, teens passed by with headphones plugged in their ears, and middle-aged men carrying laptops hollered into cell phones as they rushed toward their destinations. It reminded me of when Vince and I left for Utuado. It felt so long ago.

I scanned the baggage claim monitors and finally caught a flash of Alex's flight number.

"Are you sure you remember what he looks like?" Emily asked as she tightened her short chocolate-colored ponytail.

After weeks of misery, I had thought I was finally getting

my friend back after the secrets that broke at Cornell. But as it turned out, I only got a glimpse of her. She hadn't smiled in a long time.

"Of course I do. I remember him exactly." And I did. I was just hoping he still looked the same, with no major haircuts or facial hair changes to alter the comfort between us. I wanted him to stay the same.

About fifteen minutes later, I glimpsed Alex's face emerge in the crowd. His black hair was trimmed a bit shorter than when I saw him last and his face was a bit tanner. But it was him. His dark eyes frantically surveyed the masses as my heart thumped in my chest. I nudged Lilly.

"There he is!" Lilly yelped, gesturing to Emily and Madison.

It took every bit of self-control I had not to run to him like a madwoman. I willed him to see me with every fiber of my being, and it only took seconds for our eyes to catch. As soon as he saw me, his dimples flashed. I'd missed him.

"Here he comes," Lilly whispered.

He rushed over and hugged me tight, lifting my feet off the ground. A whiff of his citrus shampoo hit my nostrils, and a chill flooded my skin. It was like I was back in Utuado and no time had passed.

"I missed you, *mi amor*," he whispered.

"Oh, you're just delirious with jet lag," I teased as he slowly pulled away.

"Well, it's good to see you haven't changed. Still not accepting compliments?"

"You've been here for thirty seconds and you're already making character judgments?"

"Well, I think I'm particularly skilled to make this judgment," he said with a grin.

I stared into his eyes, oozing with happiness.

"What am I, invisible?" Lilly teased, breaking the moment. "Old friend here! Known ya forever, *recuerda*?"

"Of course, *mi otra amor*." He hugged Lilly.

I glanced at Emily and Madison standing awkwardly beside us, fidgeting with their hair.

"So these are my friends," I pointed out, raising a chin. "Emily and Madison."

"*Hola.*"

"Hey." Madison nodded. "You know, if you're gonna live with Mariana, you better get used to us. We come with the package. Just ask that one." Madison curled her lips in a cocky grin and peered at Lilly.

"Yeah, we go way back," Lilly groaned, pumping her eyebrows.

"Let's get you home," I said happily, grabbing his hand. "We've got school tomorrow."

Chapter 5

Alex appeared even more stunned by the sight of Spring Mills than Lilly had. As we roared through the streets, crammed in Madison's new car (another detail that made his jaw drop), he stared out the window blinking uncontrollably. I sat next to him in the backseat, my fingers laced with his and my eyes glued to his dimples.

"Just normal people live here? They're not movie stars?" he asked, shaking his head as a gated stone mansion with acres of property whizzed by.

"That kid's family actually owns the beach house next to mine in Avalon." Emily paused. "Well, I guess it won't be mine for much longer. . . ."

Alex looked at me. I shrugged. I didn't want to explain Emily's saga at the moment.

"His dad's a lawyer," Madison explained.

"For who, the president?" Alex asked.

"No, even better. Big pharmaceutical." Madison grinned into the rearview mirror.

We roared by another house so large that it looked like a luxury hotel. It was a massive brick estate, swelling across half the block with a grand lighted fountain in the circular drive. It was locked away behind an iron fence with pillars.

"These kids go to your school?" Alex asked.

"No, a lot of them go to private schools. My parents are sticklers for public education," I explained as I gazed at the familiar Main Line Philadelphia homes.

"My dad said he's not paying all this money in property taxes so I can go to boarding school in Connecticut," Madison added.

"My mom's a professor. She's all about not raising a 'sheltered, spoiled brat.' But apparently serving as a role model for meaningless sex and betrayal is perfectly fine in her book," Emily snipped.

Alex looked at me again, his eyes curious at Emily's tone.

"Is she all right?" he mouthed.

"It's a long story," I mouthed back.

Lilly grabbed Alex's shoulder. "Isn't this crazy?"

"Loco," he repeated.

Then he turned his face away from me and whispered to my cousin. *"Is their house like this?"*

"Sort of, but not as bad," she replied softly.

"Hey! No secrets!" Madison yelped. "It's my car, and I get to hear everything."

He looked at me. "I just can't believe your dad grew up in Utuado, *my* Utuado, and now he lives . . . *here*," Alex muttered.

"Why, is Utuado that bad?" Madison asked.

I bit my lip. I had told her that I had lived in a cement house, sleeping on a moldy twin bed for two summer months, but truly I didn't think Madison was capable of picturing the scene. To her, staying at a Holiday Inn was roughing it.

"It's not *bad*!" Lilly squeaked, offended. "It's my home."

"A home that you couldn't wait to get away from," Madison added.

"It wasn't like that . . . exactly."

"Uh-huh." Madison nodded.

Just then, the car rolled to a stop in my spacious driveway. Alex scanned the monster white house artfully lit by a landscape designer. The black shingles and shutters glowed in the dusk above the expansive white porch that encompassed the front façade. The lawn, illuminated by floodlights in the grass, had not even the hint of a dry blade.

"This is home," I said, raising my eyebrows with a wide grin.

"I love it already."

When we got inside, my parents had rolled out the red carpet. The cheesesteaks were heated, our Philadelphia-themed souvenirs were arranged in a toile-wrapped basket, a collection of collegiate brochures littered the kitchen table, and they were standing like the welcoming committee—with Teresa and her fiancé Carlos beside them.

"Wow, Teresa. I didn't know you were coming," I said, my tone sounding more surprised than I had intended.

"It was a last minute thing," my mother explained with a gentle smile. "We figured why not surround Alex with as many familiar faces as possible?"

"*Gracias.*" Alex nodded at my mom. "This is *increíble.*"

His Spanish accent made my insides flutter.

"Good to see you again, Alex." Teresa stepped out to greet him, her hand extended.

Alex shook it politely and kissed her cheek.

"So, *bien-ven-i-do,*" my mom welcomed slowly, with horrific Spanish pronunciation.

"It's good to have you here," my father added, loosening his red power tie.

"No, thank *you.* It's so generous of you. *Gracias. . . .*" Alex nodded to my father.

"Well, when Uncle Miguel called and told me your situation, how could I refuse? It's the least I could do after he let my kids spend the summer in his home. Any friend of Miguel's is a friend of mine," my dad explained.

"Um, Alex is my friend too," I pointed out.

My father coughed awkwardly as if to block out my statement. We had yet to have any real discussion about what Alex's moving here meant to *me*. Of course these are the same parents who skipped over the birds and the bees speech and never bothered to discuss the menstrual cycle that debuted when I was twelve. A box of pads and tampons just miraculously appeared in my bathroom closet. (I'm still not sure if our maid or my mother put them there.)

"So come, eat," my mom ordered as she herded us into the formal dining room. My friends shuffled behind. I could see they were being careful not to interfere. Teresa added an awkward element to most situations.

The cheesesteaks were being served on a stainless steel tray along with my parents' wedding china. I don't think chipped beef ever had it so good. I plopped down on a polished highback chair and grabbed a sandwich.

"Ever have one before?" I asked, handing Alex his meal on a white porcelain plate with a silver-patterned trim.

"No, what is it?" He pushed his chair closer to mine.

"A local delicacy. Try it."

Alex glanced at Teresa and they both took tentative bites into the foreign substance, grease dribbling down their chins.

"*Está bien,*" he mumbled, reaching under the linen tablecloth and squeezing my knee.

My eyes immediately shot to my father, who was staring at Alex's stretched arm like it was an automatic weapon. I discreetly brushed his palm away and Alex furrowed his brow. I pulled my eyes wide, hoping to telepathically inform him that he was not to touch me in my parents' presence. He didn't catch on, but Madison and Lilly did. They both glared at me and then at my dad. He was stroking his black mustache and frowning, his dark eyes pointedly focused on our house guest's hands.

"So, Alex, I'll have to give you the low-down on the Ruízes," Lilly joked, subtly nodding at my father.

"Oh, please, if you want the real truth, come to me," Madison said. "I'm practically a member of this family."

"Well *I* actually am," Lilly added.

"Wow, two teenagers fighting over how much they *want* to be part of this household. I'll have to film it and send it to Vince," I joked.

"That's enough," my mom warned. "We have guests."

"No, I like how your family interacts," Teresa said as she delicately placed her cheesesteak back on her plate. "It's like you have your own language."

No one said anything.

"It's nice," she reiterated.

All I could think of was how she probably never had this for herself. She didn't have siblings growing up to annoy her. She'd only had her mother, and from what I'd heard, that wasn't much of a consolation prize. The woman had had an affair with my grandfather and a very public falling-out—she ran my family off the island. No wonder Teresa was seeking a bond with her half-brothers, no matter how late in life.

"Well, I'm sure you and Carlos will have your own language with your kids," I said.

"Manny will be here soon," she said, referring to her two-year-old terror. "I can't wait for Carlos to spend time with him."

"Neither can I." Carlos kissed Teresa on her nose.

"There's actually something I've been meaning to ask you girls." Teresa's brown eyes darted nervously between Lilly and

I as she brushed her dark red hair behind her ear. "It's about my wedding . . . I was wondering. You see, I don't have any sisters and all of my friends are in Utuado. And with everything coming up so soon, I was hoping . . . that maybe . . . and this is entirely up to you . . . that you'd like to be my bridesmaids?" She bit the inside of her cheek and glanced at the table.

"Totally!" I cheered. "How cool is that?"

I looked excitedly at Lilly.

"I've never been a bridesmaid before," Lilly said.

"Only if it's okay with you, Lorenzo." Teresa peered at my father, who didn't look nearly as thrilled as Lilly and I.

He rubbed his scalp as he sighed, assuming his thinking face. I knew it well, and I was betting he was weighing the reaction of his brothers versus ruining his new half-sister's big day. My mother silently stared at him, saying nothing.

"Sure, if it's fine with the girls, then it's fine with me," my father stated.

"So when's the date?" Madison asked, whipping out her cell phone. "Because I have the greatest event planner."

"We're thinking New Year's Eve. To start the year off right. . . ."

"That's perfect!" Lilly said.

"I love it," Madison added, her fingers flying over her phone. "You'll probably get some great discounts because the winter is off-season. Do you have a location yet? I'll see if Gayle can put something together. And don't worry about the budget, I can work with anything."

"And we'll help . . . with the reception," my mother offered, subtly referencing my aunt's low finances.

"No, really. It's okay. I want to do it on my own." Teresa looked at Madison.

"Are you sure? Because I know every ballroom within a thirty-mile radius. You should have seen the number of places we visited before I booked my Sweet Sixteen." Madison's finger was poised above the "send" button, itching to make the call to Gayle.

"No, *está bien*. I think this would be a nice project to get me acquainted with my new town."

"Your new home," Carlos corrected.

"Seems to be a new home for a lot of us," Alex said.

"You got that right," Lilly stated.

"All thanks to you." Alex leaned in and kissed my cheek, holding the kiss a moment longer than was typically considered friendly.

"I think we all need to go over a few things," my father bellowed in a deep tone, glaring at Alex.

"Well, why don't we show Alex his room first?" I suggested, rapidly changing the subject. "Wanna check out your new digs?" I asked him.

"I'd love to. And you'll have to show me *your* room," Alex said.

We stood up from the table and headed toward the spiral stairs just before I heard my father grumble, "Remind me to put a padlock on her bedroom door."

My friends, cousin, and I flopped onto the floor of Alex's yellow-and-green room as he collapsed on the bed with jet lag.

"I don't think I've ever slept on a full-size bed," he said as he tested the springs.

"Actually, it's a queen," Madison noted. "Hey, did you tell him about your grandma?"

"Mad!" I shrieked.

Alex peered at me.

"It's nothing. This used to be her room," I explained.

"She was here all the time . . . before she died," Madison said ominously.

I shot her a look but she kept going.

"The final heart attack happened right here, in this room."

"Not in this bed?" Lilly cried, her face twisted.

"No," I said quickly. "My mom gave that bed to Goodwill. This is a brand-new, never-been-slept-in model."

"Well, if you don't count her ghost."

"Madison, shut up!" I warned.

"What? She's right and you know it!" Emily joined in. "You've heard the bed squeak in here when no one was in it."

"I don't know what you're talking about," I said a bit too quickly, not making eye contact.

"Yes, you do! Grandma Gryzbowski is still chillin' in here." Madison snickered.

"Mariana, you never told me that," Lilly said. "We cleaned out this whole room together!"

"See, there are some things you gotta go to the real source for, Alex. You wanna know about the bastard aunt from Utuado, ask Lilly. But if you wanna know about the Ruíz family from Spring Mills, I'm your girl."

"Bastard aunt? When did you start calling her that?" he asked.

I nodded. "You missed a lot."

By the time I finished catching him up on all the family drama I felt unfit for sending him in an e-mail, from the verbal rumble between Uncle Diego and Teresa at my Sweet Sixteen to Teresa's mother's—my grandfather's mistress—plans to attend her daughter's wedding with my family, it was almost midnight and we all had school tomorrow.

"All right, Em. I think it's time I take you home. Which lovely abode will you be going to this evening?" Madison asked.

"Back to Philly, definitely. But first I need to stop by my mom's and pick up a few things," she said sadly. "Isn't it weird that in a month my house has gone from being my 'home' to being 'my mom's place'?"

None of us said a thing, and soon the girls stood and showed themselves out. Lilly retired to her own room, and we were finally alone. I inhaled the silence.

"So, you glad I came?" he whispered.

"Absolutamente," I teased.

He placed his hand gently on my chin and raised my face toward his as he lowered his lips. It was the kiss I had been waiting for all night. As soon as our lips touched, everything flooded back: the tingle down my spine, the tickle in my belly, the dizziness in my head. I absorbed the familiar sensations.

"Now *that's* what we need to talk about," my father roared as he stormed through the doorway.

I quickly pulled away.

"I think your friend and I need to have a little discussion." My father's beady eyes shot bullets at Alex.

Alex sucked his lips under his teeth and flinched. He didn't protest when my father dragged him into his den, insisting I not follow. I figured I'd give it ten minutes and then tiptoe down anyway (after all, the man was humiliating me, so I had a right to know how bad).

I flicked on my laptop and checked my e-mail as I waited. There was a message from Vince.

Hey, Mariana!
Is your Puerto Rican fiancé there yet? I can't believe Dad's letting this dude sleep in our house. He's clearly delusional. But never fear, I'm totally going to take advantage. I'm thinking of bringing this chick I've been seeing home

over Thanksgiving. Her name's Mali, she's from Malaysia, and the flight back is crazy expensive. So I told her she could stay with us for the week. Like Mom and Dad can say no now! Suckers. I can't believe I spent eighteen years breaking them in and you're reaping all the benefits.

Also, do you know anything about Shakespeare? I have this paper coming up over break that I might need to talk to you about—my frat brothers are no help. They actually threw a brother's desk out a window yesterday. It was, like, 2:00 A.M. and everyone was tossing stuff out the house's third floor windows. I launched this old typewriter and it exploded into a zillion pieces—springs, keys, everything. Then we took this kid's IKEA desk and torpedoed it an hour after he put it together. The dude woke up this morning and was all freaked out because he couldn't figure out where his desk went. It was toast! Freakin' hysterical!

Anyway, see you in a couple weeks! You're gonna love Mali!
—Vince

Just then, I heard my father's voice carry from downstairs. I could not believe he was hollering at our guest on the first night. I shut down my computer and crept down the steps.

Chapter 6

The next morning, Madison could barely concentrate on the road. All she wanted to do was extract every possible detail from Alex about his mortifying conversation with my father.

"So did the words 'sexual relations' ever come up?" she asked giddily, while staring at him in her rearview mirror.

"Uh, no. He wasn't that blunt," Alex said, staring at the roof of the car as if envisioning the horrific scene in his mind. "I believe his exact words were 'do not even think of laying one finger on my daughter as long as you're living under *my* roof . . . or God help you.'"

"He's being ridiculous," I muttered.

I was sitting on the hump in the backseat, nuzzling next to Alex. For the first time in the history of the Audi, Lilly was sitting shotgun. With Emily commuting in from Philly with her dad's corporate driver, a vacancy opened up front. Madison wasn't thrilled with her new driving partner, but with Alex added to the mix I would much rather sit in the back with him than in the front with her.

Despite my free ride, I still often found myself missing Vince's BMW. I liked being able to leave when I wanted and to sit where I wanted. I wouldn't have that luxury again for at least another year—my father insisted his children were not "mature enough" to drive until our seventeenth birthdays. Apparently, he knew more than the government. And he was also quite certain he knew more than me, especially when it pertained to my own life.

When I had woken up this morning, for a second I had forgotten Alex was even here. I trudged into the shower like I did every day, pulled on my bathrobe and let my soppy hair drip down my back as I headed to the kitchen for breakfast—that's where I saw Alex, sitting across from my father, eating toast. It was an odd scene given the unbearable conversation they'd had the night before.

"My daughter will go to college and have a future, and you are NOT getting in the way of that." My body recoiled at the thought. *"This is my house and you will follow my rules. If you don't like it, leave."* My fists clenched. *"You better hope you came here to visit colleges, because if I find out you have other ideas, you're gonna wish you'd never met my family."* For the love of God, I was sixteen years old and Alex was my first kiss. I wasn't exactly headed down the road of a hardcore porn star. He didn't have to be so, as he would say, "dramatic."

"Mr. Ruíz can get pretty intense," Madison offered.

"Yeah, I noticed." Alex sighed.

"But he's really generous. He let both of us move here," Lilly pointed out.

"Yeah, but he also pretty much accused Alex of being some dirty pimp bent on corrupting his daughter," I snapped.

"Well, what'd you expect? He caught you guys making out in a *bedroom* in his own house," Madison said plainly. "Not too many dads would say, 'Oh, how sweet.' It's all about respect."

Alex nodded, saying nothing.

We pulled into Spring Mills High School's parking lot moments later. Alex didn't have the same reaction to the sprawling campus as Lilly had. He nodded with a look of satisfaction, but he was in no way in awe of the facilities. Maybe it was because his situation was only temporary, or maybe it was because he was preparing to tour college campuses that were much more expansive than this. But he simply smiled as we strolled through the front doors. He didn't even look intimidated by the students, no matter how many designer purses and phones they carried.

Unlike Lilly, he didn't want to go straight to the school's front office to kick-start his new life. He said he wanted to see my *"mundo"*—my "world," so I led him to my locker as the first stop on the Mariana Ruíz World Tour.

"So this is my home away from home," I said, swinging the door.

He carefully scanned my organized shelf of books arranged by subject and size in a color-coded system. His eyes breezed from the locker mirror adhered to my door to the old black-and-white dance calendar photos pasted below it. Then he eyeballed me from head to toe. I couldn't help but squirm.

"I'm happy I'm here," he said. "And I'm sorry about your dad. I'll be more *respectful*."

"*Please*, Vince had them very used to a constant stream of disrespect. If you spoil them with politeness now, you'll ruin all his hard work."

"Vince was that bad?"

Alex took the books I had collected for first period out of my arms, as if he intended to carry them for me. If he did, it would be a first in the history of Spring Mills. Most of the girls in my school were lucky if they could get their boyfriends to call them let alone engage in sincere acts of chivalry.

"Vince argued with my father like it was an Olympic sport," I explained. "Seriously, there should have been judges and a medal ceremony. It was that impressive."

"What would your dad do?"

"He argued right back. Where do you think my brother gets it from? I thought it was a weird recessive gene. But after the crap they pulled on Teresa recently, I somehow dug deep and found my own inner 'drama queen'—As my father likes to say."

He reached out and brushed a lock of wavy auburn hair from my face. As his finger grazed my forehead, I shivered. "So what's the situation with Teresa?" he asked.

"Well, pretty much everyone but my dad treats her like a leper. Just wait till you meet my uncle Diego. He pretty much blames her for driving his family out of Puerto Rico. Like she had any control over being born. Seriously, the man should be fitted for a padded cell and drool bib."

Alex laughed, leaning toward me. I could feel energy buzz between us.

Just then, a heavy book bag slammed on the ground beside me. I slowly swiveled, already knowing who I'd find. My body instantly tensed as I spied Bobby, focused on his locker, refusing to catch my stare.

"Oh, hey, Bobby. This is my friend . . . Alex."

I gestured anxiously between the two of them. Alex extended his hand, but Bobby didn't look over let alone return the handshake.

"Hey," Bobby muttered, aggressively stacking his books on the shelf.

"*Hola,*" Alex said, his accent squeaking through.

Finally Bobby's head turned, his eyes scrunched and his lips taut.

"So, you're from Puerto Rico?" he asked, curtly.

"*Sí,* but I'm thinking of going to college here."

"Why? Aren't there any colleges in Puerto Rico?"

"Bobby!" I interrupted, stunned at his overt rudeness.

"It's just a question. I honestly don't know much about your island." Bobby cocked his head at me. "Actually, I didn't know that *you* did either until school started."

"Well, I didn't until this summer. But things change. You should know that."

"You got that right." Bobby shot me a smug smile and snapped his head back toward his locker.

I shook my head at Alex as if to apologize for my friend's behavior, but he immediately brushed it off. It didn't seem to bother him.

"Wanna show me to the front office?" Alex asked, lightly placing his hand on my lower back.

"I'd love to." I clutched my purse as Alex continued to grip my books with one hand and the small of my back with the other. "See you in Chemistry, Bobby."

"Yeah, can't wait," he spat.

And with that, I led Alex to the same office I took Lilly to on her first day of school. Only, unlike my cousin, Alex wanted my help.

I couldn't stop staring at the periodic table. Anything was better than looking Bobby in the eye. Given how rude he was to Alex, I at least expected an apology. But not only did he refuse to offer the olive branch, he was grunting and sighing the entire class period as if *he* were annoyed with *me*.

"So as we all know by now, the periodic table is arranged according to the periodic law," Mr. Berk droned from the front of the classroom, pointing to his rolled-down chalkboard-size diagram. "And the periodic law states that when elements are arranged in order of increasing atomic number . . ."

I started to tune him out. We had covered this topic already, yet somehow teachers felt compelled to repeat themselves constantly as if we were all too stupid to catch the lesson the first time. It's why most of my honor's society classmates aced their classes while only doing half the required reading.

My mind drifted to Alex and me on the beach in Utuado, his tan skin peeking out from his board shorts, the way my body tingled when his arm brushed against mine. It was like I could feel a force sizzling between us when he was close. Now *that* was a type of chemistry worth discussing; forget atomic numbers.

"I need your homework," Bobby grumbled, tapping the table for my attention.

I jumped slightly. "What?"

"Your homework? From last night? We need to turn it in." He rolled his eyes.

"What's with you?" I asked, pulling my typed assignment from the proper folder.

"Nothing." He snatched the sheet of paper from my hand, wrinkling it.

"Clearly, there's something."

"What, do I have to discuss every little thing with you now? Because Emily's mom slept with my dad?"

Mr. Berk looked over from the front of the classroom. I smiled politely and nodded to the assignments floating through the class.

"You're acting like a jerk."

He flicked his head toward me. "Well, maybe I'm not as fickle as you."

"What's that supposed to mean?"

"Nothing. Forget it. Go have fun with your boy, *Alex*."

I exhaled loudly through my mouth. "Alex is a friend from Puerto Rico. I told you that."

"He looked like more than a friend this morning. What, are you too embarrassed of him to say he's your boyfriend?"

"No, I'm too *polite* to say he's my boyfriend," I snapped, shaking my head. "Why do you have to make things weird between us?"

"Because they are!"

Mr. Berk coughed from the front of the room as he collected the assignments.

"Bobby, I wanna be your friend. I wanna help you with the film festival. If that's not enough . . ."

"Fine," he said softly, in a defeated tone. "Are you coming to the meeting today?"

"What meeting?" My eyebrows bunched.

"I sent you an e-mail weeks ago! All the students participating in the festival are meeting after school today. I thought you could talk about the flyers and stuff?"

I dropped my head and stared at the lab table. I knew if I said I couldn't make it because of Alex that would solidify the end of my friendship with Bobby. But I also couldn't ditch Alex on his first day in Spring Mills.

"Do you think it would be okay if I brought Alex?" I mumbled.

Bobby's shoulders immediately squeezed his neck. "I guess."

He flung his attention back toward the worksheet we were supposed to complete. It was the end of the discussion. We both finished the lab in silence without offering each other any help.

Chapter 7

We trudged toward the auditorium. I thought it would be hard to convince Emily to join the meeting—she was avoiding spending time with Bobby for fear she might have to discuss their parents' bedroom activities. But when we met at Madison's locker after school, she merely shrugged.

"I can drive you home after," Madison offered.

"No, it's okay. My dad's car service is on call."

"Is it bizarre living in a hotel?" I asked, Alex at my side.

He was waiting at my locker before the bell even rang. He'd spent the day strolling the grounds with Dean Pruitt and then checking in with his Utuado school via the Internet. His teachers from back home already had sent him three new assignments. When I mentioned that I had a meeting after school, he didn't bat an eye. He seemed happy to be included. He grabbed the messenger bag from my shoulder and tossed it over his. It was nice to have someone to carry my stuff.

"Well, our room is cleaned every day with fresh sheets and towels. They put a mint on my pillow each night, and I get room service twenty-four hours a day. Plus, my dad's never there."

"But don't you kinda miss being around other people?" Lilly asked.

"I have a hotel full of people. If I go down to the coffee shop, I can read a book surrounded by a random group of business travelers and college students."

"But they're not your friends," Lilly insisted.

Emily said nothing.

"Well, I think it's great that he's letting you stay." I squeezed Alex's hand hoping he'd join in the conversation. I wanted him to get to know my friends better.

"I have a friend whose parents got divorced. In the end, they just screamed at each other. It's good that your parents aren't doing that to you," Alex said, trying to be helpful.

"I almost wish they would scream at each other. At least then they'd be talking. Right now, each acts like the other doesn't exist. My dad won't even mention my mom. This morning he asked, 'Are you going over *there* this weekend?' Like it's some foreign place he couldn't remember the name of," she muttered.

"He's trying. Cut him some slack. His wife cheated on him in his own bed," Madison stated.

"Don't sugar coat it or anything," I snipped.

"Well, I wouldn't get over it." Madison pushed open the auditorium doors.

About two dozen students sat huddled in the front seats. Bobby was sitting on the edge of the stage facing them, his long lanky legs dangling off the end. Even from the back of the auditorium, I could hear his voice perfectly projecting the theme of the documentary he'd be debuting.

"Ireland is an amazing country. The people are so friendly. And they're so passionate about family and religion and . . . beer." He chuckled.

The metal doors slammed shut behind us and everyone turned.

"Hey." I waved, my other hand still tightly clasping Alex's palm.

We marched down the aisle. The crowd was silent and their faces looked as though we were interrupting a State of the Union Address.

"Guys, these are some of the people who helped me put this together. They're gonna be doing the posters and stuff. Ya know, the grunt work." Bobby's tone was insulting.

My forehead clenched. He still sounded angry with me.

"Yeah, um, we saw the film," I spoke up. "It's incredible, really. . . . Oh, I'm Mariana. These are my friends Madison, Emily, Lilly, and Alex."

"Well, I don't actually go to school here," Alex explained with a sultry Spanish accent. "I'm just visiting."

"Where you from?" a blond, doe-eyed girl asked.

"Puerto Rico." He released my hand and leaned toward her seat.

"That's so interesting," said a curvy brunette.

"Did you live on the beach?" asked a dirty blond.

"No, in the mountains. Lilly and I are from the same town."

"Oh, I didn't even know Puerto Rico had mountains," said an Asian girl.

"I did. My family went there two summers ago. It was very . . . hot," said a redhead, her eyes gazing prettily at Alex.

I reached out for Alex's hand once more. These girls were acting as though they didn't notice that we were together, that he was clutching my palm as we walked in and that he was holding my school bag. Did I really need to buy a sign that said "girlfriend" in blinking pink letters (though that probably wasn't a bad idea)?

"Anyway," Bobby interrupted, "this meeting is about the film festival."

My friends and I took seats in the front row. I yanked a notebook out of my bag.

"So as I was saying earlier, we need to get more photography. We want 8x10s or larger and everything will be displayed in the front lobby." Bobby pointed to where we had entered.

"Well, I have my black-and-whites from the photo club last year," one boy said.

"And I have my submission to the *Felt Pen* magazine," another kid added.

"Those are great, but I think I'd like to add more travel photos. Since the film is based on my travels, I wanna continue that theme." Bobby looked at me. "Mariana, were you able to put anything together?"

I flicked my eyes toward Madison. "Well, I tried . . ."

"Unless you want pictures of me trying on leather boots in Rome, I don't think I have much to add to your exhibit," Madison said. "But they are awesome boots."

Bobby smacked his lips. "I can add my Ireland photos to the mix, but I don't want the entire thing to be about *my* trip."

"Well, I have Disney shots from the summer," one kid suggested.

Bobby groaned.

"Jersey Shore photos?"

"Are they artistic?"

"Is *Jersey* artistic?" the kid rebutted.

The room fell silent. I focused on my blank paper. Despite owning an expensive digital camera, I wasn't much into the art of photography. All of my pictures included at least one friend or relative making a silly face. I never tried "capturing the light" or "showcasing the moment." Ballet was my strong suit and I saw no need to attempt any other activity that I couldn't perfect.

"Well, I have some photos," Alex spoke up.

Bobby's head jerked back, the skin on his face pulled tight. "Um, what?"

"Of Puerto Rico. I have a lot of images on my memory card that I could print."

"Look, don't take this the wrong way, but we're not looking for your basic beach scene," Bobby said with a condescending stare.

"Actually, most of the photos are of the mountains, a lot of nature shots, some images of the rain forest—"

"What did you take them with?" Bobby interjected.

"A Nikon Digital SLR. I won it in a photo contest in San Juan last year."

"I remember that!" Lilly shrieked. "Your photos kicked butt. That one with the green bird sitting on the leaf! And the beer can floating near the waterfall."

Alex nodded.

"He has an *awesome* camera," Lilly added. "That thing is *huge.*" Lilly held her hands wide.

"Well, you know what they say about guys with big cameras . . ." Madison joked.

We all giggled—except for Bobby, who was grinding his teeth.

"Well, I'd have to see the photos first. And since you don't really go here, we'll have to clear it with Dean Pruitt . . ."

"Please, Dean Pruitt's the one who set up this whole faux exchange program. I don't think he'll mind," Madison said. "Mr. Ruíz will just *make another call.*"

Bobby blew out a puff of air. "I guess that settles it."

About an hour later, after I had filled three pages of college-ruled paper with notes on flyer layouts, fonts, wording, and e-mail formats, we headed to the parking lot.

"So the festival's in a week and a half. That's not much time. Between that and ballet, we're gonna be zombies," Madison said as she unlocked her car.

"We have this huge ballet performance around Christmas," I explained to Alex.

"So I'll get to see you dance?"

"If you play your cards right," I teased, nudging his shoulder.

"Hey, will Vince be here for the festival?" Lilly asked.

"Yup. He comes home next weekend. He already has plans for me to help him with his homework."

"How sad is that? An Ivy Leaguer needs academic help from his sixteen-year-old-sister?" Emily asked candidly.

"Hey, don't knock it. At least we know we'll have one person in the audience," Madison noted.

Emily stopped alongside the car as we all piled in. "I'm just gonna wait out front for my ride."

Everyone groaned. "Em! This is ridiculous!" I whined.

"I'll give you a ride!" Madison insisted.

"No, it's cool. Ken is already on the way."

"You're on a first-name basis with your driver?" Lilly asked.

"You kidding? Ken's one of my closest friends."

"Em!" Madison and I shouted.

"No, seriously. It's no big deal. He already sent a text saying he was down the street."

"Fine," I muttered begrudgingly.

"You want us to wait?" Madison asked.

"No, don't. I was gonna go grab something from my locker anyway."

We nodded and Madison slowly pulled out of the parking lot. As we rolled away, I twisted back to wave and saw Emily saunter through the school's front doors. For a moment, it looked like someone stepped out of the shadows in the vestibule. Like someone was waiting for her.

Chapter 8

We spent our Saturday strolling down Market Street, scouting every hotel ballroom along the way. So far we weren't having much luck with our price range. Most of these locations had marble lobbies full of high-end business travelers with plastic name badges clipped to their lapels. They were used to a clientele that could plunk down more cash than my *tía* from Utuado. These hotels didn't need our business. Our only bright spot was that Teresa's guest list was small, only sixty people (and that was after she agreed to add my friends to her list).

"You know, we could also try restaurants," I suggested as we walked toward City Hall.

The white decadent structure with marble statues and European-style pillars loomed before us. At one point in history, it was one of the tallest in the world—odd considering it now sits in the shadows of modernistic glass skyscrapers.

"I really like the idea of having the reception in a hotel," Teresa explained. "A restaurant makes it feel like just another dinner."

"I understand." I nodded. "Of course I had my Sweet Sixteen in my backyard where my parents also hosted my first holy communion reception."

"Don't knock it, so did I," Lilly added.

I was trying to be polite and play along with Teresa's plan to host the wedding in Center City. It was a beautiful urban location and I couldn't blame her for having her heart set on it, but the prices these hotels commanded were significantly higher than those in the surrounding suburbs. She could probably plan the entire wedding in South Jersey for a fraction of the cost, but my *tía* was stubborn (a Ruíz family trait that apparently was embedded in our DNA). At this point, I was determined to work out a deal with one of these hoteliers. I knew it could be done. Madison could talk circles around these people. If she were here, she'd have them slashing the per-head prices and negotiating upgrades before they could say "open bar."

"Okay, here it is. Last one," Teresa stated, stopping in front of another hotel.

Its façade was impressive and looked as if it had been on that street for quite some time. A bellman in a dark hat helped us push through the antique revolving door. The marble lobby, with its arching glass windows and antique metal trim, looked more like a train station than a fancy hotel. It was oddly funky in an historic kind of way.

"It says here that it used to be part of City Hall," Teresa read from the travel guide where she had selected all of the hotels on our wedding reception tour (at this point, if *Fodors* didn't like it, neither did she). "It's an historic landmark."

"Isn't everything in this city historic?" Lilly sighed.

"Hey, don't knock it. It's our 'thing,' " I said.

"I thought cheesesteaks were your thing."

"They're our other thing."

Teresa stopped at the concierge desk to locate the event planner, who would be showing us our fifth room of the day. I briefly closed my eyes; they were starting to glaze over from all of the floral carpeting and crystal chandeliers.

"Hi, I'm Suzanne," chirped a petite blond as she hurried out from a back room. She held out her navy-suit-covered arm to shake Teresa's hand. "You must be the bride."

"*Sí*," Teresa said. "I mean, 'yes.'"

"No problemo." The woman giggled with an awful South Philly accent. "I can't wait to show you the space we have available. Now, you spoke to Richard on the phone, right? Because he said you're only looking for space for about fifty to sixty people. And let me tell you, you're in luck."

The woman whisked us into a copper-trimmed elevator without pausing to take a breath between sentences.

"We have a room that just opened up. It's not a ballroom." Suzanne grimaced as if it were a painful thing to say. "It's one of our smaller party rooms. Now, Teresa, I know what you're thinking . . ."

She looked at us all with a serious expression as she held up her palms.

"You're thinking, I wanted a ballroom for my wedding. But let me tell you why you're wrong. While a ballroom is great, I really think that for the size of your affair a smaller room would really create a more intimate setting. You don't want your guests getting swallowed by the room."

Suzanne laughed loudly at what she thought was a joke as we all stared blankly.

"Teresa, this room has everything you're looking for. Beautiful décor, elegant chandeliers, plenty of windows, and enough space for a dance floor and several round tables. Plus, you wouldn't have to overpay for a giant ballroom you don't even need."

The elevator stopped and Suzanne sped out, shuffling us down the wallpapered hall.

"Now before we go in, I want you to picture this: night-time, candlelit tables, the smell of fresh flowers, the sound of a string quartet . . ."

Suzanne pushed open the doors and we were pleasantly greeted by a stylish room half the size of the others we'd seen, but perfect for Teresa and her small collection of guests.

"Teresa Mendez, welcome to your wedding," Suzanne whispered.

Graceful wallpaper with gold accents perfectly matched the crystal chandeliers and chair-frame detailing. The carpet was floral but not as tacky as those in other hotels we'd seen. The linens were crisp, the ceiling paint was fresh, and the windows looked directly onto City Hall. I turned to Teresa and her face was glowing. Of all the rooms we'd seen, this was most like the vision she had described: elegant yet modest enough to fit her budget. Now it was time to work some negotiating magic.

"So, you say this room just became available." I approached Suzanne, who was busy pulling the wedding package portfolio from her briefcase.

"Yes, you're very lucky."

"Well, the holidays are just around the corner." I walked to a table and sat down, smiling pleasantly up at her while trying to channel my best Madison Fox (or better yet, Madison's father, who taught his daughter everything she needed to know). "I'd imagine it would be hard to find another group to book this space on such short notice."

Lilly snapped her head toward me. After years of being sur-rounded by corporate-level, Main Line–living negotiators, I realized that quite a bit of knowledge had sunk into my brain. It was now time to dig it out on my *tía's* behalf.

"Well, this is a very popular hotel and we have a great lo-cation," Suzanne told me.

I nodded toward the massive windows. "I noticed. Right below William Penn's hat."

"Yes, and we can offer you a discount on hotel rooms for your guests."

She sat down across the table as Teresa and Lilly stood behind me.

"I'd imagine the Mummers Parade on New Year's Day presents a lot of logistical problems," I stated.

"We could offer a discount at our parking garage." Suzanne pushed the wedding portfolio toward me.

I flipped open the folder and scanned the prices. The per-person costs were at least twenty percent above Teresa's price range. I turned the pages carefully, absorbing the information.

"I see." I nodded casually.

"You'll notice our prices are very competitive given our location and superior amenities. And our food is spectacular." She tapped the page before me, pointing to the entrée choices. "We can set up a free tasting."

"Mmhmm." I hummed, examining the page slowly before passing it to Teresa and Lilly who were still hovered silently behind me.

When I spun back around, the smile was lost from my face.

"You see, Suzanne. The prices on that sheet are rack rates, which while they are very reasonable"—I tossed out a fake, hollow chuckle—"they don't really reflect the situation we're in right now. Do they?"

Suzanne coughed slightly as she turned her attention back to her briefcase.

"Because, Suzanne," I stated firmly, "I know you're in a bit of a pickle. Losing a booking only two months out usually means a big dent in revenue. Most groups, and definitely most weddings, book months—even years—in advance."

I stood up from the table and waved my hands around the

room. "All of this beautiful space could be left vacant. And that really would be a shame, wouldn't it?"

I smiled at her, my head tilted.

Suzanne huffed, then leaned back in her evergreen upholstered chair.

"I see what you're saying," she said simply. "And you're right. I can't believe I didn't mention it sooner. Of course, we'll offer a discount."

I plopped back down at the table and met her hazel eyes dead on.

"We can probably knock ten percent off the cost per head and maybe offer an extra appetizer."

"You know, I'm looking at this." I snatched the paper back from Lilly. "And I can see you already offer a choice of six appetizers. I really don't think we need more than that. Maybe instead we could get twenty percent off the per person cost?"

I pulled my lips tight.

"Uh, I'd love to." She winced. "But my boss would have my head!"

We both pretended to laugh.

"But, and I really shouldn't be doing this," she offered. "I could probably do fifteen percent off."

"How about fifteen percent, a free bridal suite and free valet parking?"

"Fifteen percent, the bridal suite and half-off valet parking."

"Deal." I nodded, extending my hand.

Suzanne shook it without even glancing at Teresa. Finally I swung my head toward my *tía,* remembering this was actually her wedding not mine.

"Oh, is this okay with you?" I asked, smiling awkwardly.

"Es perfecto." Teresa nodded, her dimples denting in so far that I thought her cheeks must hurt.

"Okay, I'll go drum up a contract. We'll need a deposit

within two weeks—it's ten percent to hold the date," Suzanne explained as she rose to her feet, collecting her briefcase. "I'll be right back with everything."

She rushed out, the heavy banquet-room door slamming behind her.

"You were unbelievable!" Lilly practically tackled me in my chair.

"Mariana, I don't know what to say. I can't believe I'm going to get married in a place like this." Teresa's eyes twinkled as she gazed around the room.

"I know it's still a little bit over your budget . . ."

"No. It's perfect. It's better than perfect."

"Who knew you were such a negotiator?" Lilly shook my shoulders once more.

"Well, thank Madison. You can only watch a girl talk down a sales clerk so many times before a bit of those skills rub off." I turned to Teresa. "She negotiated the price of her eighth-grade dance dress. The saleslady was actually sweating. She gets it from her dad . . ."

"And apparently, so do you," Teresa cheered. "I could never have done that."

Suddenly, Lilly broke into an impromptu salsa sway. I popped to my feet to join her, moving my hips and envisioning the room on Teresa's wedding day: me and Lilly in shiny bridesmaid dresses with horrific fluffy butt bows in front of all of our family and friends.

Suddenly, I stopped and glanced at my watch. "Hey, Teresa, do you think we could make a pit stop before we go home?"

After the paperwork was signed and Teresa had officially staked her claim on the reception space for New Year's Eve, she dropped Lilly and me off at a familiar downtown hotel.

"I'll pick you girls up in about an hour. I'm going to swing by a few florists," Teresa told us as we climbed out of Carlos's beat-up sedan.

"Good luck with the flowers," Lilly said cheerfully as she slammed her door closed.

"Remember, it doesn't have to all be roses," I said.

Teresa pulled away as Lilly and I strolled into another shiny lobby. It was one of the few hotels we didn't look at for reception space (it was just too weird with Emily living there). But our friend's new home was only a block away from Teresa's chosen venue.

We walked past the lobby bar to the reception desk.

"Emily Montgomery's room please," I said to the clerk, who didn't look much older than we did.

She smiled as she tucked her blond hair behind her ear and checked her computer screen.

"Oh, she's a resident," the girl said. "I'll let her know that you're here."

"No, please don't," I said quickly. "We want to surprise her. We're her friends."

The girl tilted her head. "I really should call first."

"Please, we're not ax murderers. We're just her friends. It's a surprise."

The clerk grinned and looked the other way. "It's room 1405. I didn't see anything."

Lilly and I swiftly darted toward the gold-trimmed elevators and sped up to the fourteenth floor. When we stepped into the cold, impersonal hallway, I was hit with a wave of sadness. I couldn't believe Emily lived here. This wasn't a home. There was no front porch or family photos, no fireplace or smell of cooking. Lilly glanced at a sign near the elevator.

"Her room's this way." She pointed.

I followed Lilly down the generic corridor past the identical beige doorways until we stopped at 1405.

"Home sweet home," I muttered before knocking.

I could hear someone moving inside.

"Em? Em, it's Lilly and Mariana," I said as I knocked again.

I heard a door slam shut inside and then the hurried sounds of footsteps. Finally, the handle turned.

"What are you guys doing here?" Emily asked nervously as she opened the door, her forehead beaded with sweat.

"Gee, great to see you too," I said, rolling my eyes as I pushed past her and into the room.

When she told us that she was going to live in a hotel with her father, I assumed it would be something akin to a condo with a full kitchen and a dining area. But their suite simply looked like a large hotel room. Sure, there were two bedrooms and a common sitting area, but that was it. There was nothing it in that resembled a home. It even had the same blue patterned carpeting as the rest of the hotel.

"So this is where you live?" Lilly asked in an equally shocked tone.

"Um, yeah," Emily said, grabbing a towel off the wingback chair so we could sit down. "It's only temporary. My dad's looking at apartments."

"Has he found one?" I asked, my eyebrows raised.

I would think getting his daughter into a more suitable living situation would be a father's top priority.

"He's trying. But he works a lot. His assistant found a couple places."

"Well, thank God for the assistant," Lilly muttered as she plopped down on a small couch.

"Em, you know you have to live in Spring Mills to go to Spring Mills High School," I pointed out as I sat down.

"Well, my mom's house is still there. As long as she 'claims' me, I'm fine." Emily put finger quotes around the word and rolled her eyes.

"Em, look, I realize things are bad with your mom right now, but this can't be much better." I waved my hands around the room, which was littered with old newspapers and wet towels; clearly the maid service hadn't arrived yet.

"I can take care of myself," Emily huffed.

"How? By calling room service? By having a corporate driver take you to school?"

Emily grunted. "Beats the hell out of my mom's place. And now I can do practically anything I want."

Just then, something crashed inside the closed bathroom door. My head jerked as I rose to my feet.

"What was that?" I asked.

I could feel Lilly breathing right behind me.

"Is there someone in there?" Lilly asked.

"No," Emily said quickly as she jumped between us and the door. "I'm sure something just fell."

"What, from all the wind swirlin' around in here?" Lilly mocked.

"Em, what's going on?" I stepped toward her.

She moved back, protecting the door. "Nothing. There's nothing going on. And you know, you guys really should have called first."

"Uh, obviously. Looks like you've got someone hiding in your bathroom." I squinted my eyes as if I didn't recognize the person standing before me.

"I do not. It's just that the place is a mess. I would've cleaned up if I knew you were coming. And I just got out of the shower a second ago, so I'm sure the shampoo just slipped. The ledges in the shower suck, they're really tiny . . ."

Emily was talking so rapidly it was hard to follow her train of thought. But one thing was clear: she was lying. If she had recently showered, then she a) wouldn't have been sweating when we showed up and b) her hair would be wet.

I stared at Emily, not moving and not saying anything.

"It's just kind of a bad time right now. But I'm really glad you guys stopped by. It was very cool of you. Why are you here anyway?" Her gaze shot rapidly between Lilly and me.

"We were looking at reception sites with Teresa," Lilly explained, as she grabbed my arm and yanked me toward the hotel room door.

"I think it's time for us to go," Lilly said under her breath.

"I'm sorry you aren't able to stay longer. Maybe we can set something up for next time," Emily said as she hurried us to the door.

I stopped abruptly and stared at her. "Do I want to know who's in that bathroom?"

"There's no one in there," she lied. "Seriously, there's nothing going on."

"You know you're getting really good at that," I noted, my tone flat.

"At what?"

"At lying."

Chapter 9

After we got home, Lilly and I decided to forget about Emily. While we had waited for Teresa's return, we sat in the hotel lobby for nearly thirty minutes theorizing that our friend was hiding everyone from a secret lover to Jimmy Hoffa. By the end of the talk, we still had no real answers. If Emily insisted on keeping her new boyfriend a secret, so be it. It's not as if I were going to strap her to a water board and torture the truth out of her. I'd already learned from experience that she'd tell us when she was ready. I just hoped that it wouldn't be after her whole world was shattered and she was left sobbing in a puddle of desperation like she was at Cornell.

The car ride home with my *tía* was devoted entirely to discussing which shade of flowers best matched the carpeting in her reception site and whether it was possible to get spring flowers in January. My brain was on overload. From Emily's drama to Teresa's wedding, I was ready to shut down the minute I walked through the door. Only that wasn't an option. As soon as I got home, I received a group e-mail from Bobby reminding everyone to have their festival "tasks" completed by Monday.

So, with barely a brain cell functioning, Lilly and I switched gears. We were currently spending our Saturday night designing posters and editing photos from Alex's digital camera. Not exactly a wild evening of booze and salsa like Alex was used to in Puerto Rico, but he said he didn't mind.

"So you think I should design it with the school colors?" I asked as I stared blankly at the layout on my screen.

I was utterly void of inspiration.

"I think you should go with shades of green," Lilly pointed out as she scanned the photos in Alex's camera. "That's what I think of when I think 'Ireland.'"

"Good point."

"Wow, these photos are amazing," Lilly whispered.

"Gracias."

Alex was seated on the floor at the foot of my chair, his hand resting in my lap as he watched me design text boxes and word art.

"So do you just take photos of birds and frogs? Or do you have any of *us*?" Lilly asked as she clicked through the images.

Alex's eyes suddenly shot toward her with a glint of panic. "*Ay, Dios mio.* Lemme see the camera," he ordered.

A smile quickly spread across Lilly's freckled face.

"You *do* have photos of us, don't you?" She laughed, darting toward the bathroom, the camera in her hands.

Alex chased after her, reaching desperately, but she swiftly slammed the door shut and locked him out.

"Lilly! *Por favor!*"

I swung around and saw him pounding on the solid wood panels. Lilly was silent on the other side. I had no idea what was on that camera, but I was suddenly very intrigued.

Then, I heard her gasp through the wood. *"Caray,"* she cursed.

Alex slumped against the wall and slid down to a seated position. He rested his head in his hands and folded his knees to his chest in an act of defeat.

Slowly, the doorknob turned and out walked Lilly, beaming from ear to ear.

"Are you ready for your close-ups, Mariana?" she teased.

I popped up and snatched the camera from her hand. As soon as my eyes met the digital two-inch screen, I sucked in a quick breath. There I was—a tight shot of my brown eyes, a stray lock of hair dripping in front of them. I flicked to the next image; it was me standing in front of my uncle's hotel in Utuado. I moved to the next photo, and it was me looking over my shoulder, not realizing a camera was present. There had to be at least a dozen more images like this. All when I wasn't looking.

"But I don't even remember you having your camera out," I said, my forehead wrinkled with confusion.

Alex sighed, closing his dark eyes tightly.

"When could you've possibly?" I murmured, shaking my head.

I flicked to the last image. It was taken through a pane of glass. The image was blurry, but almost artistically so. My eyes appeared focused and serious. Behind my left shoulder, I caught a fragment of a familiar sign.

My fingers immediately flew to my lips. It was the Internet café at UPR. I stared at the tiny patch of T shirt exposed in the frame. It was exactly what I was wearing the day Alex found me in the Internet café with Javier. When we hadn't spoken for two weeks. When Lilly had manipulated us to stay apart.

"Oh, my God," I whispered, blinking at the screen. "You took these when we weren't together . . ."

"It's not how it seems," he said quickly, rising to his feet.

"Were you . . ."

"I think the word you're looking for is 'stalking,'" Lilly joked.

I glared at her, not finding any of this nearly as funny as she was. She immediately wiped the grin from her face.

"No, I wasn't. It was just, I don't know. I wanted to see you. . . . But Lilly told me to back off." He snapped his eyes toward her. She quickly looked away, flushed with guilt.

"So why didn't you say 'hi'? Why didn't you call? You just followed me . . ."

My mind was whirling. On some level, I was flattered. To think that he liked me so much after knowing me for such a short period definitely filled me with a surge of confidence. The idea, however, that I was being watched and I hadn't noticed, scared the breath out of me. I watched enough *Law & Order* to know those stories don't usually end well.

"I wanted to talk to you. I wanted to go up to you. But I thought it wasn't what you wanted. . . . And, sometimes, I would just see you around . . ."

"And take my picture!"

Lilly closed my bedroom door quietly so my parents wouldn't hear. Thankfully, she had the good sense to realize that if my father heard a word of this conversation, he would lose it in a way that made Uncle Diego seem passive.

"I missed you, and I wanted to see you. And I was too scared to tell you how I felt."

I paused, bewildered, staring at the photo of me in the café one more time. I remembered how I felt at that moment. I was consumed with sadness over the fact that I hadn't seen Alex, that he had possibly lost interest. My mind was crammed with constant images of him, never-ending questions about what had happened between us. It took every ounce of self-control I had not to talk about him every second of the day.

"I shouldn't have invaded your privacy. I'm sorry if I made you uncomfortable—"

"No, I understand . . . sort of," I interrupted. "I missed you too. Not enough to stalk you like the paparazzi, but still . . ."

Alex rushed over and hugged me tight.

"Lo siento, mi amor," he whispered.

"Your first fight, how cute," Lilly cooed from across the room.

He leaned down and kissed me. I tried to kiss back, my mind still reeling. Then Lilly coughed loudly and reopened my bedroom door.

"Okay, now that that's settled," she said at maximum volume.

Alex slowly unwrapped his arms from around my waist, and I quickly turned back to my computer. I didn't think I should spend any more time helping him edit his photos. I'd leave that up to Lilly. I doubted the images would disturb her as much.

Later that night, I curled into my fluffy white bed. The room was dark and the house was still. I closed my eyes, but snapshots of my face kept skipping through my mind. I liked Alex. I had from the moment I met him. The idea that he had missed me filled my chest with warmth, but the fact that he'd photographed me without my knowing, made my gut wrench.

I tossed under the covers, trying to find a comfortable position that would settle my mind. But before I could relax, I heard my doorknob turn. Instinctively, I shot up and reached for my bedside lamp, only I couldn't find the switch. Then a familiar image appeared in the shadows. It was Alex.

"Shh," he whispered.

I nervously yanked my comforter up to my neck. I was

sleeping in shorts and a ballet camp T shirt, but somehow the fact that I was lying in bed made me feel naked.

"What are you doing here?" I asked in a hushed voice.

He sat on my bed. "I heard noises in my room."

"What?"

"And I remembered those stories about your *abuela* . . ."

"Alex, my grandmother's ghost is *not* in your room," I whispered sternly. "Seriously, you have to go. If my dad finds you here, he'll kick you out of our house."

He brushed his hand against my auburn hair, which was loosely tied in a low ponytail.

"I'm worried about the photos. About what you think . . . of me," he said softly, still stroking my hair.

"Alex, we can talk about this later."

He ran his hand softly down the side of my cheek. My body tingled. I closed my eyes.

"I don't want you to be scared of me. I'm not *loco*," he whispered.

"I don't think that." I opened my eyes and peered at him timidly.

He lowered his face abruptly and kissed me, clutching my jaw in his palms. He dug his fingers into my hair and he tried to shift his weight on top of me. I immediately stiffened and shoved him away.

"Alex, you have to go," I said firmly.

The look in his eyes was almost desperate. I didn't want to hurt his feelings. If I were an eighteen-year-old boy and my girlfriend was sleeping down the hall, I might think there was a chance of midnight romance as well. But this was *my* house, with *my* father. And this was not the way the Ruíz family op-erated. For as much as I liked Alex, he was only going to be here for two months. And I had to live with my parents forever (or at least the next two years). If my dad found him in my room in the middle of the night, he *would* ship him back to Utuado and he would never, ever look at me the same again.

"I'm sorry. It's my dad. I don't want to get you into trouble. Not during your first week," I whispered quickly, lightly pushing him out of the bed.

I scrambled to my feet and tugged at my shorts.

Alex smiled. "I understand. I'm sorry."

"I'm not mad at you," I whispered.

"Good."

He leaned over and kissed me again, softer this time. My shoulders relaxed as I clasped my hands around his neck. For a moment, I wanted him to stay. Then reality set in.

"Go," I said again, pushing him toward the hall.

He tiptoed out of my room, and I carefully closed the door behind him. I stared at the clock on the far side of the wall. It was 1:00 A.M. on a Saturday night. I knew at least one person who'd be up at this hour.

I plucked my cell phone from my desk and hurried into my bathroom.

The phone rang three times.

"What up!" Vince shouted into the receiver.

"Vince, it's Mariana," I whispered loudly.

"What are you doing up?" He didn't wait for me to answer. "Man, it was one of the brother's twenty-first birthdays. He actually kicked twenty-one shots, including a blow-job shot with all this nasty whipped cream. It was freakin' hysterical! The stuff was all over his face! And you do not want to know what that looks like coming back up," he said, laughing.

"Vince, are you wasted right now?"

"Not completely. The after-hours parties haven't started yet. We're doing an eighties theme. I tore up a pair of jeans and got this bandana for my head. I *so* look like *Bruuuuuce*," he joked in a deep tone. "Too bad I can't grow a good beard. . . ."

"Vince, focus. I've got issues with Alex."

"Holy shit! I forgot all about him. You a child bride yet?"

"I'm serious."

"You're not knocked up, are you?"

"Vince, come on. It's just—"

"Is he trying to get in your pants?" Vince yelled.

"I don't know, I mean—"

"Oh, my God! That freak's been there what, two days? And already he's—"

"Vince, it's not like that . . . exactly. It's just . . . weird."

"What'd he do?" Vince sounded dead sober, all humor lost from his voice.

While he wasn't the type of brother to listen to my problems and offer sound advice, it was nice to know that he would step up if any guy tried to hurt me.

"This summer, in Puerto Rico, he took pictures of me . . ."

"You let him take pictures of you naked! Are you retarded? Do you know how many websites they could be on? Oh, my God! I mean, I have some pictures of chicks like that—I didn't take them, but they're crazy hot. . . . Anyway, you do not want to end up on an e-mail forward!"

"Vince, no!" I interrupted, shaking my head (it was amazing where his mind went). "He took pictures of me without my knowing. Of my face. Fully clothed. When we weren't together those two weeks. Apparently, he was kinda, like, following me. Like, everywhere."

"Ew."

"And then, he came into my room a few minutes ago, while I was sleeping—"

"Just stop. Dad needs to boot this tool back to the island."

"I don't know what to do."

"First, tell him to keep his little stalker fantasies to himself. And second, *lock your door!*" he yelled. "Dude, I'm comin' home next weekend. I'll straighten this freak out."

"Yeah, you're gonna take time away from Mali to deal with my drama."

"Ah, man, wait till you meet Mali. She's smokin'! I have a total Asian fetish right now."

"That is beyond offensive. Do you say that to her face?"

"Not usually. But whatever, I'll take care of Alex."

"No, it's okay. It's just, I don't know. Things aren't exactly going the way I expected."

"You mean that perfect little bubble Alex existed in during your vacation on a tropical island didn't follow him here? Gee, I'm so surprised," he snipped. "Mariana, there's a reason they're called 'summer flings.' They're not meant to be pushed past Labor Day."

I frowned. "I'll see you next weekend."

"Yeah, and brush up on *Macbeth* if you can. This paper's gonna kick my ass."

I smirked as I hung up the phone. I thought college was supposed to be hard. Right now, Vince's biggest worry seemed to be which party to go to and which class to blow off. I couldn't wait to graduate.

Chapter 10

I had never been so happy to have ballet practice in my life. My house was getting a bit crowded lately, and I desperately needed a break. When I woke up the next morning, I found Alex seated at the breakfast table with my father. A wave of embarrassment flushed over me. I couldn't believe I had called Vince—now he was going to hold everything I said against Alex. (Is it possible to take back an overreaction?)

I sat down at the glass table and bit into my sesame bagel.

"Sleep well?" my father asked, folding down a corner of the paper he was reading.

"Of course," I grumbled through a mouthful of dough. "Madison's picking me up in an hour."

My father hummed cheerily. Ever since my friend got her license, she had become my personal driver, a task my father was happy to relinquish (though it didn't seem to inspire him to let me get my license).

"Can I come with you?" Alex asked.

"To ballet? Not really," I said honestly.

I wasn't about to mention that I was rather happy for the reprieve. Two hours of nothing but body crunching practice was enough to wipe any awkward situation from my mind.

"I'm sure Lilly will keep you occupied," I added.

"Don't count on me," Lilly said as she bounded down the steps in a pair of my designer jeans. "I'm going to the movies."

"Well, take Alex with you," I insisted, my eyes pleading.

"Can't. Betsy already ordered the tickets online. Show's sold out."

"Gee, thanks for thinking of us."

"She just called this morning."

"And that's when you decided to borrow my jeans?"

"They look good on me, right?" She spun on her toes.

I rolled my eyes.

"Mariana, let Lilly go out with her friends," my father commanded.

"Well, what about Alex?" I didn't think I would have to argue with Lilly about hanging out with her own friend from home.

"Actually, Alex, I thought we could spend the day together," my father stated. "I spoke to Vince this morning, and he thought maybe you and I should go to the driving range. You play golf, right?"

I coughed, pieces of bagel flying out of my mouth. I couldn't believe Vince called my father. It was only 10:00 A.M. My brother slept until noon as if it were a personal commandment.

I looked to Alex. His pupils had swollen to the size of walnuts.

"Um, I've never played before."

"No problem. I'll teach you," my father said with a grin as he smoothed the edges of his mustache.

My dad rarely smiled, and usually when he did, there was a lot more going on behind that expression than simple happiness.

Alex turned to me, fear in his eyes.

"You guys'll have fun," I lied, choking on my bagel.

As soon as I swallowed my last bite, I dashed upstairs to call Vince. But after more than a half dozen dials, he still wasn't answering. Finally, following my seventh message threatening death if he dared mention last night's late-night activities to our conservative Catholic father, I received a text on my cell phone.

> I didn't tell dad about ur BF. Just that he's Ted Bundy mixed w/Hugh Hefner. GL! BTW Bruce costume wuz a hit till I fought w/a guitar. Guitar won, lol!

There wasn't much I could do to save Alex at this point. I had to go to my ballet practice, and Lilly had no intention of breaking her plans. I was left to trust that my father was a rational man who never listened to a word Vince said in the eighteen years he lived in our house (why start now?).

Madam Colbert wanted me to perform my solos for the company. I had been receiving private lessons for the past month to perfect my celebratory dances, and this would be the first time the rest of the production would see my progress.

I took my position on the floor and waited for the music. As soon as the first note hit, my body took over. My muscles remembered every move instinctively, and I flowed from beat to beat. The light danced above me as I soared like Princess Aurora on her sixteenth birthday, turning and leaping across the floor with perfect lines and pointed toes. In a way, I did feel a bit like her at my own birthday party, only substitute the Tchaikovsky with the Gipsy Kings.

I hit my final pose and finally focused my eyes on my fellow ballerinas who all clapped riotously, nodding with approval. Madison rose to her feet.

"Woohoo!" she cheered.

Even Emily stood, graciously patting her hands together. It was nice of her to support me given how badly she'd wanted the role. She hadn't shown any signs of resentment since the day the parts were announced. Maybe it was because the dark emotions of her character were more in tune with her reality.

"Miss Ruíz!" Madam Colbert gushed. "You were brilliant! Absolutely brilliant. It was as if all of the lights and music gathered on you. You *are* Princess Aurora."

My shoulders instinctively rose as I smiled meekly. I was probably blushing, though I couldn't tell given all the sweat and heat collected on my face.

Finally, a few hours later, after all of the ballerinas were dripping in sweat, our instructor called it a day.

"That was brutal," I noted as Madison's Audi rolled into my driveway.

She and Emily nodded, and almost instantaneously, a car pulled up to drop off Lilly. My cousin popped out of the passenger side of Betsy's SUV, smiling and waving.

"You girls wanna stay for dinner?" I asked, tugging at my door handle.

"My dad's taking me out to eat," Emily said as she politely waved to Lilly. "It's the benefit of living within walking distance of every major restaurant in the city."

"I'm busy driving her home." Madison nodded to our friend. "Plus, I'm mastering my ability to handle I-95. You should see me fly into the left lane!"

I giggled.

"Hey, girls," Lilly said cheerfully as she approached.

I still hadn't told any of them about Alex's midnight visit. The fact that he thought he could just roll into bed with me reflected as poorly on me as it did him, like he assumed I was some "slutty American." It's not like I actually believed he was scared of a fictitious ghost, but in a way it was also a bit excit-

ing to have someone *want* to crawl in bed with me. Still, if I
brought it up now it would turn into a big thing—and I didn't
have the energy.

"See you guys later." I waved.

Lilly and I darted through the front door, and before I took
a step toward the kitchen, the hair rose on my forearms. Something was wrong. I grabbed Lilly's arm.

"What?" she asked.

"Don't you feel it?"

"What are you talking about?"

I wasn't sure if I believed in ESP, but I was certain that my
family exuded a physical energy that only we could feel.

"Something's up."

"You're crazy," Lilly muttered.

But the minute we walked into the kitchen and I saw that
it was empty, I knew I was right. My mom wasn't cooking and
it was six o'clock. My eyes instinctively swiveled toward the
back porch. The scene almost reminded me of the day I had
learned that I was being shipped off to Puerto Rico, only this
time the players were different. My dad, my uncle Diego, my
uncle Roberto, and Alex were seated silently. My uncles and
my father were smoking cigars—my dad never smoked—
while Alex stared at them, sweaty and panicked.

"Whoa, what is this? A *Godfather* remake?" Lilly mocked.

"If so, then I guess I should be thankful the death scene
hasn't happened yet."

I slid the glass doors open. Four black-haired heads immediately spun around.

"Mariana, glad you're home," my father said with the tone
of an executive.

My uncles nodded while Alex's eyes darted frantically, search-
ing for an exit.

"What's going on?" My facial muscles twisted in confusion.

"Oh, I just took Alex out with the guys." My father patted Alex's leg.

Alex flinched like he thought my father might hurt him.

"Since when do you hang out with 'the guys'?" I peered at my uncles.

"We went to the driving range," my uncle Roberto explained as he blew out a thick puff of smoke.

"And a firing range too." My uncle Diego sneered.

"You took him shooting?" Lilly blurted.

"Of course. It was fun. Wasn't it, Alex?" My uncle Diego grabbed Alex's leg and squeezed it. His knuckles whitened.

Alex nodded obediently, ignoring the death grip.

"That's what I thought."

"You know, Diego and I are excellent shots," my uncle Roberto added. "We go hunting every year."

"My wife calls it 'killing.' " My uncle Diego chuckled hollowly. "But I guess it's the same thing."

He stared at Alex as he laughed, a cigar held to his lips.

"Okay, um, I don't know what you guys are up to," I said, flicking my gaze at each of them. "But I think Lilly, Alex, and I are going inside. Where's Mom?"

"She's at the museum," my father answered calmly. "She said to take you guys out for dinner. Like a whole big happy family."

My father and my uncles burst into a roar of laughter that sounded a tinge like the wicked witch. I glanced in the sky but didn't see the flying monkeys.

I sat at McCormick & Schmick's in Philadelphia inhaling the fresh scent of costly seafood and wondering when my father joined some sort of Puerto Rican mafia.

"Alex, you wanna drink? Maybe a little rum?" my uncle Diego asked as he sipped his bloodred wine.

Alex's dark eyes darted in all directions in the dimly lit dining room. I could see he didn't know how to respond. He was eighteen, which was the legal drinking age in Puerto Rico (though the boy probably had his first drink before his age had hit the double digits). He was used to having the freedom to drink what he wanted, when he wanted. Only he wasn't in Puerto Rico anymore.

"Um, I think . . . I'm fine," he said carefully.

His eyes squinted, a wrinkle forming above his nose. It looked as if every syllable that passed through his mouth required the same amount of concentration as the SATs. Apparently, it had been like that all day.

From what I had gathered, the four men arrived at the driving range around noon where they "hit a bucket of balls." Alex didn't display the same skill as the three men who shot a round every Sunday when the sun was out, so my uncles took to calling him "Kitten," as in the anti-Tiger (Woods). Alex smiled and pretended to laugh every time they said it. But I could see his eye twitch with each condescending reference.

At some point, my uncle Diego decided it would be fun to go to a shooting range. Given that my uncles have deer heads mounted on their walls and basement freezers full of venison, this would not have been an odd suggestion if it were just the two of them. My father, however, vehemently hated firearms and prior to this afternoon had never fired a weapon (at least not to my knowledge).

Only this didn't stop them from dragging my teenage visitor off to some crazy gun club. Nope, my uncles joked all night about how they'd "never seen a guy's hands shake like that, Kitten!" And how he'd better "man up" or he'd "find himself on the wrong side of the rifle one day." Then they'd all laugh as if they weren't making veiled threats to end his life.

"So, Kitten, ever been to jail?" my uncle Diego blurted, snapping me back to the conversation.

"Oh, my God!" I shrieked, my mouth wide.

"What? I got arrested once. It was for a bar fight in college. Nearly beat the guy senseless," he said in ominous tone. "Got off on a technicality though."

"Gotta love lawyers," my uncle Roberto added.

"And we can afford plenty of 'em." My uncle Diego laughed in Alex's face, spit splashing.

"This is hysterical," Lilly mumbled under her breath, barely trying to mask her laughter.

"Dad, when are you gonna stop this?"

"Stop what?" he asked, brushing me off. "I want to get to know your new boyfriend."

"I never called him that," I muttered, staring at my tiger shrimp.

"Oh, that's right. You already have a boyfriend, don't you?" my uncle Diego announced in a loud voice as he leaned back in his chair.

My face pulsed with heat as my heart drummed in my throat. I felt like every wealthy suit in the restaurant was staring at me over their surf and turf. I did not want to discuss Bobby, and if I could have melted into the polished wood table, I would have.

"Oh, that boy from your party," my uncle Roberto added to my misery.

"Yeah, you guys looked great dancing together."

I dropped my chin to my chest. I hadn't told Alex about Bobby. I thought it was a non-issue. We only shared one kiss and then the Emily-bomb landed. There was no hope of Bobby and me being together, at least I didn't think so (plus, I kind of felt that my kiss with Bobby might be construed as a betrayal to Alex and I really didn't want to risk it).

"What is he talking about?" Alex asked, peering at me.

"Here it comes," Lilly whispered.

"It's nothing. I did not have a boyfriend at my Sweet Sixteen," I said diplomatically. (That wasn't a lie.)

I tugged at the cloth napkin on my lap, twisting it in my fists.

"So what would you call him these days?" my uncle Diego asked. "Your fella? Your *novio*? Your boo?"

"Did you just say 'boo'?" Lilly giggled.

"What? That's a word, right?" My uncle looked offended that he may have misused his slang terminology.

"It is, but . . . 'boo'?" She shook with amusement as if this scene were nothing more than a means for her entertainment.

"Forget it!" I interrupted. "I do not have a boo."

Lilly burst into laughter, and I couldn't help but join her. I knew I shouldn't be giddy, but the tension at the table was driving me to the tip of insanity. I had to release it somehow, and I figured a fit of giggles was better than a fit of rage.

"Mariana? What's going on? Who's he talking about?"

Alex looked concerned. I tried to contain my giggles, but I couldn't stop picturing my uncle Diego in a rap video singing about "being with his boo" and pouring champagne on a hoochie momma. The laughter spewed in waves.

"Alex, I'm sorry." I snorted.

I got up from the table and placed my napkin on my chair, still laughing. Lilly immediately followed my lead. I needed some air. I held my hand up to Alex, signaling I'd be back, and took off toward the restroom. Lilly's clogs clicked right behind me.

"Oh, my God. That was hysterical," Lilly said as she pushed open the bathroom door.

I looked in the mirror at the tears streaking my cheeks and plucked a soft cloth from a wire basket.

"How does he even know that word?" she asked

"Maybe he's a closet MTV freak?" I suggested as I reapplied a layer of Chap Stick.

"What are you gonna tell Alex?"

"About Bobby? Or about my uncles turning into mob lords?" I asked.

"Either one. I mean, where is all this coming from anyway?" she asked.

"Well"—I paused, focusing on the shiny chrome sink—"Alex climbed into my bed last night."

"What!" she shrieked.

"Nothing happened. I kicked him out but . . . I told Vince."

"What? Are you *loca*? Of all people!" she yelled, dropping her lip gloss onto the granite counter.

"I know, but I figured he was the one person who wouldn't do anything about it. He's never cared about my life before—"

"He's your brother! Do you think he wants to hear about some guy in your bed?"

"He tells me about the girls in *his* bed!"

"It doesn't matter. That's different. What do you think he told your dad?"

"Enough to turn my family into gun-toting nutcases."

"Well, I think this has been a very entertaining evening. And I'll have to send your uncles thank-you cards." Lilly's freckled cheeks puffed as she grinned.

"I'm glad you're enjoying yourself."

I headed out the door of the ladies' room and looked around the restaurant. It was filled with older couples utilizing their corporate cards as they sipped martinis and bottles of wine while dining on high-end shellfish. It actually looked like fun. The fancy clothes, the PDAs, and the hushed conversations.

I scanned the tables briskly before my eyes suddenly locked on a familiar face. There, seated by the window, lit by candlelight was Emily.

And she wasn't dining with her dad.

Chapter 11

I didn't approach her. I had no idea who she was sharing an expensive meal with in a fancy restaurant, but I had a feeling it was the same guy who was hiding in her hotel bathroom a few days ago. The guy looked older than Vince, and from the way he stroked her hand, I was guessing he was more than a friend.

"Um, she's your best friend. Why are we pretending we didn't see her?" Lilly asked as we rushed back to our table.

" 'Cause she lied to me yet again and I want to find out why. Plus, if I go over there, I'll just embarrass her."

"I will never understand you people. Wouldn't things be simpler if you were straight up with each other?"

"Like she is with me?" I scoffed. "Anyway, like I said, welcome to Spring Mills."

When we approached our table, Alex was gnawing on his thumbnail. His bites made horrible clicking noises, and I couldn't imagine the sensation felt pleasant. His eyes lit up the moment he saw us.

"Great! You're back!" he squeaked.

"I was just telling Alex some old war stories," my uncle Diego stated proudly.

"You're telling 'Nam stories over dinner?" I gasped.

My uncle Diego was drafted into the Vietnam War when he was eighteen (my father and my uncle Roberto were still underage). He worked as a radio operator for a search-and-destroy unit, and he often shared stories—and not just about the missions.

"Don't worry. I was just talking about my R&Rs in Bangkok. Man, it was crazy there. The drugs, the booze . . . the women. But you wouldn't know anything about that, would you, Alex?"

My uncle Diego punched his arm in jest, only I caught Alex wince slightly.

"Okay, enough tough-guy talk," I told my uncles. "Can we give Alex a break?"

"I don't know what you're talking about," my dad said, shrugging with innocence.

"Uh-huh. Sure."

I sat down and yanked my cell phone out of my purse. For as much sympathy as I felt for Alex, I felt even more confusion at having caught my fifteen-year-old best friend on a romantic date with a secret lover. I concealed the phone under the table and frantically flew my fingers over the keys.

In Philly w/fam. Wanna meet up? Where R U?

I hit send and waited.

"Did she reply?" Lilly mouthed, glancing at my hands.

I shook my head and stared at the screen. I could hear my uncles grilling Alex about the colleges he would be visiting and why. The poor kid had spent the day in an endless game of twenty questions. If he gave the wrong answer, they'd launch into another informative joke detailing exactly how skilled they could be at ending his time in Philly (and on the planet).

My phone beeped and I immediately opened the text message.

W/Dad @ dinner. Cant leave. C U 2morrow.

I blinked at the two-inch screen. Emily was blatantly lying, *again*. Dazed, I handed my phone to Lilly. She quickly read the text, then glared at me, her eyebrows shoved high.

"What the heck is this?" she mouthed.

"Don't know," I grumbled, the feeling of betrayal ripping through me.

"Mariana, you said the University of Delaware was a good school, *verdad*? You said I should visit?" Alex asked loudly, clearly begging me to save him.

"Oh, uh, yes. It's a good school." I nodded, still a bit stunned. Then I peered at Alex; his eyelids drooped with exhaustion and his shoulders slumped forward.

"You know, Alex is very smart. His school gave him time off because his grades are so high. They *trusted* him to complete his classes online." I confidently raised my chin toward him. "And he's a great photographer. He's gonna have photos displayed at our film festival."

It was time for me to step up. Nothing that happened last night was worth what my uncles were putting him through now, and I didn't want to lose him over a misunderstanding (or a mafia-linked hit ordered by my psycho family).

Alex gazed at me and smiled weakly. He looked exactly the way I'd remembered him in Puerto Rico: confident yet innocent. I think he served his time. I doubted I needed to worry about locking my bedroom door.

★ ★ ★

Lilly and I sat with Alex in the living room. My uncles had left right after dinner and my father drove us home in silence. I thought it was safer not to push an argument about embarrassing me in front of my guests. My dad might call my uncles back for more.

"I'm so sorry about today," I apologized as the TV hummed in the background.

I popped in a DVD, mostly to drown out the sounds of our conversation. Not that I thought my parents could hear us— their bedroom was upstairs on the other side of the house. But I didn't want to risk it. Given the scene today, I couldn't really say I knew how they'd react to anything anymore.

"No. *Está bien,*" he said softly.

He was seated on the opposite end of the sofa as if he were afraid to come within three feet of me.

"I've never seen my uncles go this over the top."

"You were right to tell them. I shouldn't have gone into your room. . . ."

"I didn't tell them!" I shouted.

The last thing he needed was to think I had ordered this fiasco.

"You didn't? Then how?"

"I sort of . . . talked to Vince. I didn't tell him anything, not really . . ."

"Oh, please. Vince called your dad, and he had your uncles lay the smackdown," Lilly stated bluntly.

"Well, my dad never cared when Vince dated."

"Vince never had his girlfriend living in your house," Lilly stated plainly.

"Your dad must hate me." Alex stared at his hands.

"No, he likes you. Or he wouldn't have invited you here." I inched closer to him, but he jerked back. He was either scared of me or no longer interested in putting up with my drama.

"I disrespected him."

"I actually thought the whole thing was pretty funny," Lilly joked.

Alex glared at her, his nose scrunched.

"What? It was! You should have seen your face—"

"Speaking of faces," I interrupted, giving Lilly a wide-eyed stare. "What do I do about Emily? Should I call her out? Tell Madison?"

"Let it be. So she's dating some college dude with cash to burn? Let her have her fun. If anyone needs it, it's that girl," Lilly said as she stared at the action on the TV and patted my poodle's head. He was curled up in a curly black ball beside her.

"She'll tell you all about it when she's ready," Alex advised.

I had told him the whole story the minute we got home, mostly out of a desire to turn the conversation toward anything other than my uncles. I was surprised he was even listening.

I thought about Emily seated at that candlelit table for two. The way that guy's hand reached for hers. It was intimate and special. Even if he were too old for her, if he made her happy then I should be happy, right?

Only something about it felt wrong, and it was more than just the age difference. I couldn't pinpoint the problem, but my stomach had rippled when I saw the guy. I swore I almost recognized his face.

Chapter 12

It was hard to stare across the lunch table at one of my best friends without wanting to blurt, "Who were you with last night?" Add to that Madison not knowing I was keeping a major secret about Emily and the fact that I couldn't glance at Alex without feeling embarrassed for what I had put him through, and I was understandably gripped with tension. I could hardly swallow a french fry, the cafeteria was so suffocating.

"So, Alex. Would you like a rifle to go with your fries? I'm sure Uncle Diego could hook you up," Madison teased.

She loved every second of my family-turned-*Godfather* saga. She didn't even care that I hadn't told her earlier about Alex's attempted bedtime booty call, because she found my uncles' reactions so hysterical. The only detail I left out was which restaurant the final torture took place in—I thought it safer not to tip Emily off to our sighting.

"Very funny," he muttered as he ate his hot dog. "I hate guns."

"I would too if I had one nearly pointed at my head," Madison joked as she ate a pita and hummus.

"They didn't hold him at gunpoint." I sighed, humiliated.

"They almost did," he added.

"Alex, I'm so sorry."

"No, it's *my* fault." He hung his head.

Madison looked at me as if she finally realized that he didn't find the situation nearly as comical as she did.

"Alex, Mr. Ruíz is kinda strict, that's all," Madison offered, before gesturing to me. "Remember how he freaked out when my mom and I took you shopping for a bikini? He literally accused my mother of corrupting you. I thought he was never gonna let me see you again."

"This was, like, a year ago," I added to stress her point. "Trust me, it's not you, it's him."

He grinned, and I saw his shoulder blades release the invisible walnut they were crushing.

Just then, Evan strolled past our table. He released one arm from the tray of food he was carrying and brushed the back of Madison's chair. She quickly turned as he walked away, and for a brief second he gazed back. I could practically see the lust drifting off her.

"So how are things?" I asked carefully.

Her face beamed as she finally looked away from him. "Good, I guess."

"Did you hear from him this weekend?"

"He IMed me Sunday."

"Mad, I'm sick of this IMing crap. You waited around Saturday night for him to call!"

"No, I didn't!" she gasped, putting down her pita. "I just didn't feel like going out."

"Uh-huh." I cocked my head at her, pumping my eyebrows.

"Leave Evan be. He'll come around," Emily said quietly.

I snapped my face toward her. "What, you got some insider knowledge you wanna share with us?"

She shrugged. "No, it's just, things aren't always as simple as you want them to be."

"Boy meets girl. Boy likes girl. Boy *calls* girl. How complicated is that?" I asked.

"I just want him to ask me on a date. One date," Madison whispered as she pushed away her half-eaten meal (though half a pita didn't seem all that filling to me).

"He will," Emily stated. "But really, where would you guys go? He doesn't have his license yet."

"So? I do."

Emily shook her head. "Guys wanna be in control."

"What is this, 1950?" Madison huffed.

Emily didn't respond, which was enough to push me to the edge. I couldn't hold it in any longer. It seemed like she was being talked into a secret relationship by some control-hungry college guy.

"So how was dinner with your dad?" I asked in my sweetest voice. "It sucks that we couldn't meet up."

"Oh, it was good," she mumbled.

"He talking to your mom yet?" Madison asked, not realizing she was interrupting the trap I was setting.

"Nope. Neither am I."

"Em, she's your mother." Madison's tone was heavy.

"So? If she doesn't care about how her extramarital love life affects me, then why should I care about her?"

I bit into a french fry. I didn't have it in me to finish my manipulation. Emily had enough to deal with.

We had a test in Chemistry, so I barely glanced at Bobby the entire period. With how tense things had gotten with Alex over the weekend, I didn't have much energy to commit to Bobby's awkward feelings. But as soon as the bell rang and the papers were collected, my locker buddy grabbed my arm.

"I saw the flyers you e-mailed. They're perfect," Bobby said kindly.

"Thanks. It was nothing." I snatched my messenger bag off the floor.

"Do you think you could pass them out tomorrow? We've barely got a week until the festival."

"No problem."

I started to walk away, but he blocked my path.

"I also saw the photos that . . . *your friend* took. They're really good," he said softly. "I'm sorry I was kinda rude before."

"No, it's cool. Everything's crazy right now . . ."

"No, I'm just freakin' on everybody these days. Things are weird at home . . ."

He ran his hand through his blond curls and let the strands float back onto his forehead. It was a gesture he made a million times a day, but for some reason the deep look in his eyes made my heart lurch.

"How are your parents?" I asked, trying to brush off the sudden rush of feelings.

"Still in separate bedrooms." He offered a fake grin.

"Well, Emily's living at the Philadelphia Marriott, so it could be worse."

"I know. I heard my father screeching that my mom ruined the one good thing in his life."

"Oh, my God! Seriously?"

Bobby nodded, the sad smile on his face softening to a frown.

"I guess he and Emily's mom broke it off?"

He shuffled his feet. "My parents don't believe in divorce. But my mom said that if he even so much as thought of *that woman*, she'd plaster both their campuses with all the 'adulterous details.'" His fingers formed air quotes around the last words.

"Ouch." I winced.

He scooped his books off our lab table, prepared to head to his locker.

"Well, at least it's over. It has to get better from here, right?"

He tilted his head at me. "How long ago was your grandfather's affair? Thirty, forty years? I think we have some time before this blows over."

It was the first time Bobby ever mentioned what happened at my birthday party. He stood beside me during the whole scene with Teresa and my uncle, but he always acted as if he hadn't paid attention. Of course I knew he must have heard, but it was easier to pretend that he hadn't than to deal with the humiliation of the situation.

"I'm sorry you've gotta go through this. But if it makes you feel better, things are getting more normal with us. Teresa's getting married. I'm even a bridesmaid."

"That's good." He nodded, his face genuinely pleased. "Maybe by the time I have a kid in college, my parents will be speaking again."

"See, now that's the spirit," I teased.

We walked toward our lockers, through the rush of students darting out of the building. Everyone always seemed to move faster at the end of the day.

"Do you think your parents will come to the film festival?" I asked as we pushed through a crowd of students.

"Of course. It's Spring Mills. They'll stand side-by-side like Bill and Hillary."

"And just gloss over that whole Monica thing."

"Exactly." He chuckled.

"Two more years and you'll be at NYU," I offered optimistically.

It was the same advice Vince gave me when I fought with my dad. There was a light at the end of the tunnel, and that light was college.

"Yeah, if my dad doesn't have me kidnapped and chained to a fraternity wall at Cornell first." He chuckled, resting his palm on my shoulder. I glanced at his fingers. They felt warm.

"Just think of all the torturous things they could do with beer until you broke down and applied," I said.

"You kiddin'? Those guys wouldn't waste beer on me."

We both laughed just as Alex stepped out from the crowd hovered in front of our lockers. I quickly brushed Bobby's hand off, and he straightened his frame away from me, clearing his throat.

"Hey, Alex," I said. "You remember Bobby?"

"*Sí.*" He raised his chin politely, but his eyes were beady.

"Hey," Bobby muttered as he swung his locker dial.

Alex wrapped his arms around me as I opened my locker. It was the first time he'd touched me since he'd crept into my room. His grip was tight.

Chapter 13

With the performance of *Sleeping Beauty* looming, we now had ballet practice every evening, which was making it hard to entertain two house guests and help my *tía* plan her wedding. She had been begging Lilly and I to go dress shopping, and while I wanted to feel excited to watch my half-aunt try on fluffy white gowns, I couldn't seem to draw enough enthusiasm to actually make the time. It also wasn't helping that my father had yet to tell my uncles that Lilly and I would be standing up for the woman whose birth ruined their parents' marriage. I was starting to feel a bit like the family's Judas (only minus the life-and-death scenario).

I plopped down on the ballet studio floor and changed out of my dance shoes. It was only Wednesday and my feet were already covered in blisters. It was hard to wear anything other than sneakers anymore.

"Ms. Ruíz, you did excellent today," Madam Colbert commented as she popped her CD from the sound system.

"Thank you," I said with an exhausted sigh.

"Hang in there. You're doing great."

Madison and Emily dropped beside me.

"My back is killing me," Emily groaned as she leaned over her legs to yank off her pointe shoes.

"Tell me about it." I stretched as I pulled a pair of knit pants over my leotard.

"Me too," Madison added.

I grinned at her.

While Emily and I were justifiably exhausted, Madison practiced about half as many hours. Her solo was brief and her role in the chorus was not very challenging (at least, it wouldn't be for the rest of the dancers).

We all stood up from the hardwood floor to head to Madison's car when the front door to the studio flung open. In walked Lilly.

"Hi girls." She smiled. She was dressed in my beige dress pants and a red sweater, which were way too done up for after-school attire.

"What are you doing here?" I asked, narrowing my eyes.

"Well, tennis practice was cancelled 'cause of the rain." She gestured out the window. It was pouring, and I hadn't even realized it. "So I called Teresa, and we thought we'd go dress shopping. We're here to pick you up."

"Are you kidding me? I just finished a two-hour practice!" I flung my dance bag off my shoulder. I was so tired its weight was crushing me.

"So? It's only five-thirty and the dress shops don't close until eight. Teresa was able to make an appointment."

Lilly clearly saw no flaw in her plan, never mind that I was soaked in sweat from head to toe, that my feet were practically bleeding, and that I could hardly hold my head up I was so hungry.

"Lil, I can't go right now."

"Mariana, Teresa's outside. She borrowed Carlos's car. You can't say no now."

"Well, when exactly could I have said no? Because I don't remember anyone asking me."

I rolled my eyes at Madison and Emily, looking for sympathy.

"Mariana, you agreed to be a bridesmaid," Madison stated plainly. "Now you have to do what she says. It's her day."

"Her day isn't for two months!" I whined.

"I'm gonna have to side with the bride," Madison continued.

For a second, I got a glimpse of what it would be like when Madison wore the veil. She'd probably run her wedding like a boot camp.

I turned to Emily.

"Don't look at me. I'm the last person to be giving advice on family situations." She held her palm toward me.

Without a word, Lilly strutted over and grabbed my dance bag.

"Don't worry. You look fine," she said. "You just have to watch her try stuff on. I'm sure the place has a couch."

"You're getting me something to eat first," I groaned.

"There's a sandwich in the car."

And with that, she clutched my hand and dragged me out the door.

The dressing room was the size of a small hotel suite. Since Teresa didn't have enough time to order a wedding gown to her specifications, she had to settle for either a dress off the rack from a bridal shop or a sample dress from a pricey boutique. She had done her research, and Lilly and I were currently seated on an elegant white couch in one of the most luxurious bridal boutiques in the Main Line.

We spent nearly thirty minutes combing through the racks

of sample dresses squished within clear plastic garment bags. Teresa was probably a size six, which was excellent given that the majority of the dresses were a size ten. With alterations, anything could be made to fit her. Only she had no idea what she wanted and thus, was going to make us watch her try on every gown in the store.

"She has at least ten dresses in there," I moaned, burping up my turkey sandwich.

"Like you have room to talk. You tried on way more than that for your Sweet Sixteen," Lilly stated as she leaned back on the crisp white fabric.

"I didn't have a choice. You guys piled them in."

"And we watched you zip up every one without a complaint. So smile, and be happy."

"That's not so easy. I swear, even my cheeks are sore." I dropped my head back.

"Oh, stop complaining. Poor Mariana, forced to dance. Woe is you."

I pursed my lips.

Just then Teresa emerged from the dressing room, and I quickly wiped my expression clean. An elegantly dressed Indian woman with shiny black hair halfway down her back stepped out of the room with my *tía*. She was her "bridal associate," and apparently it took at least two people to put on every gown. When I saw the pleats and ruffles on Teresa's first choice, I could see why.

"What do you think?" she asked as the strapless gown hung lazily from her small chest while the massive ballgown engulfed her lower half.

My first reaction was that the dress looked like a Cinderella remake and was probably more appropriate for a blushing twenty-something bride whose silver-haired father would be walking her down the aisle. It just didn't seem age appropriate for a woman with a kid.

"It's very poofy," Lilly said, rising from the couch.

Teresa climbed a pedestal to examine her figure from a half-dozen angles. The dress was too big and clipped in the back with a giant plastic clothespin, not exactly offering the full effect.

"Do you like it?" I asked, smiling forcibly.

"It looks kinda heavy." Lilly lifted the fabric.

"The silk is very light. And the look is just stunning." The bridal associate adjusted the gown to better fit Teresa's small bosom.

"I think I look *gigante*," Teresa muttered. "I need something simpler."

The associate immediately whisked Teresa off her pedestal and rushed her back into the dressing room.

I slumped farther into the couch. "How long do you think this'll take?"

"As long as Teresa wants it to take. It's her wedding! Can you perk up a bit?"

"This coming from a girl who wanted so little to do with her *Quinceañera* that I had to pick out a dress for you . . ." I cocked my head.

"That was different. It was a stupid birthday party I didn't want to have. But this . . . this is her wedding." Lilly lifted one of the sample veils from a nearby rack and placed it on her head, spinning in front of the mirror.

"Oh, God. You sound like Madison."

Lilly gasped. "I can't believe you said that!"

"If the tiara fits . . ."

Lilly sneered at me as Teresa emerged again, her bridal associate carrying the Princess Diana–worthy train behind her.

This dress offered off-the-shoulder sleeves that seemed more fitting for a bride in her mid-thirties, but the bodice was so heavily beaded that she looked like a Miss America reject.

"Mejor?" she asked as she hopped on her perch in front of the mirrors.

"Do *you* like it?" I asked.

Teresa shrugged.

"It's got a lot of sparkles," Lilly said, gesturing to the bodice.

"You're right. It's still too much." The associate again helped her off her stool and whisked her away.

"What do you think we'll look like when we get married?" Lilly asked as we watched another bride emerge from her dressing room in a strapless lace gown.

"Can't say I've thought about it much."

"I don't think I'll ever get married," Lilly said, watching the bride and her mother smile into the mirror at her gorgeous reflection.

"Why?"

"I don't know. Guys just don't like me in that way," she said softly.

"Are you kidding me? You practically have to beat them off of you."

"Yeah, they wanna *get* with me, but they don't want to take me home to meet their mothers. . . . I've never had a boyfriend."

"So? You're fifteen! Not eighty. Besides, I've never had a boyfriend either."

"Oh, please! You've got Alex crossing an ocean to be with you and Bobby practically begging for your attention."

"Yeah, right!"

"I'm serious. Guys meet you and see a girlfriend, guys meet me and see a hook-up. Why is that? We practically look identical."

I glanced at my cousin's chest, which was currently stretching out my cashmere sweater. "Well, there's one glaring difference," I joked.

Suddenly, the door to the dressing room opened and out walked Teresa. A slender ivory dress clung to her curves, dipping low in the back to show her flawless skin. Thick straps twisted in a sweeping scoop neck before landing on the outer edges of her shoulders. There wasn't even a clothespin holding it up. It looked as though the gown was made for her.

"It's perfect," I whispered, awestruck, as I watched my *tía* glide toward the bridal pedestal.

"Wow," Lilly murmured.

Teresa placed her foot on the stool and rose to admire her reflection. She turned in every angle, her pearly white teeth glinting in a hue that matched the gown.

"Me encanta," she whispered.

Her bridal associate beamed with pride. "You look amazing. Truly spectacular."

There was something about a wedding gown that truly inspired awe. Maybe it was because it was white, or maybe it was crafted differently, or maybe it was because the woman wearing it was so confident and radiant in a way that could never be replicated in another dress. I didn't know what it was, but I knew that Teresa sparkled in that gown.

"Es magnifico." I smiled at her.

She stood there twirling for another few moments. I knew there were several more dresses in the room for her to try on, but they wouldn't matter. The search was over. She had found "the one."

Chapter 14

Life was finally returning to some sense of predictable order. Ballet practices were still in full swing, and Alex spent the rest of the week touring college campuses with his academic advisor. Without the added pressure of seeing each other at lunch, in the halls, and in the carpool, Alex and I were able to get past the debacle with my uncles and return to a more relaxed flow of conversation. For the first time since he'd arrived, I felt at ease around him, so much so that by Friday he managed to smooth things over with my dad and even persuade him to borrow the family car. Alex was taking me on our first real date.

"So you decided to go with jeans?" Lilly noted as she strolled into my bedroom decked out in a short skirt and a tight sweater with knee-high boots.

She was going to a party with Betsy and her friends. I already had her under strict orders to keep an eye out for Evan. If he so much as spoke to another girl while not picking up the phone to invite Madison, I would hunt him down myself (okay, maybe I'd hire my uncles to do the hunting).

"I feel more comfortable when I'm not dolled up. And I think Alex and I could use a little comfort." I smoothed my black boat-neck top over my low-rise denim.

They were my going-out jeans, primarily because they were the only ones I had that actually clung to my barely there curves rather than hiding them under folds of baggy fabric.

"Your butt looks great."

"Hey! Don't stare!" I shrieked, covering my rear with my palms.

"What do you expect? Those are booty pants. Alex is gonna be checkin' you out."

"Should I change?" I asked nervously, staring at my backside in the mirror.

"God, no! You *want* him to look."

I rolled my eyes.

I had never been on a date before. All the times that Alex and I saw each other in Puerto Rico usually involved groups of people. We didn't go to restaurants or to the movies. We went to cafés and rain forests. Now he was going to drive me into the city to eat at a downtown location (as yet unknown to me) like a real couple. Maybe he was my boyfriend after all.

A subtle knock tapped on my bedroom door.

"Mariana, your date is waiting in the living room," my mom said.

Everyone was treating it like prom night. I half expected a video camera and a corsage to await me.

"Have fun tonight, sweetie." She hugged me.

"Mom, it's no big deal."

"Oh, it's your first date. Let me have my moment," my mother whispered, her expensive floral-scented perfume floating into my nostrils.

"Knock 'em dead," Lilly teased.

When I glanced back, she pointed to her butt and wiggled. *"Work that ass,"* she mouthed.

I shook my head and sauntered down the stairs, my high-heeled boots clanking on the wood steps. Alex was standing in the living room with my father. His sleek dark hair was perfectly styled and his strong frame looked stunning in a blue button-down and khakis. He pulled a single yellow rose from behind his back. The color of friendship. It was perfect.

He stopped the car in the South Street lot where Vince always parked. It made me wonder who gave him the directions.

Alex turned off the ignition of the Mercedes, quickly hopped out, and dashed around to my side. He opened my door like a gentleman.

"Why, thank you. I'm impressed," I said with a nod.

He smiled and clasped my hand.

"So where are we going?"

"The best place in town," he said.

"And it's on South Street?" My forehead wrinkled with confusion.

We strolled over the colorfully lit pedestrian bridge and gazed at the mass of people before us. I yanked my jacket closed as a brisk breeze swept over us.

"You cold?" Alex quickly took off the black leather coat he had bought specifically for his trip. There wasn't much need for winter outerwear in Puerto Rico.

"No, I'm fine. Really."

He graciously smoothed the coat over my shoulders as we hit the packed sidewalk. A family in plaid sweaters pushed their daughter in a stroller in front of us. A pack of teenagers in flannel smoked cigarettes across the street. Twenty-something professionals laughed loudly from the balcony of a nearby bar. And a thirty-something guy in leather pants kissed his fishnet-wearing girlfriend, gripping her spiky hot pink hair.

We strolled hand-in-hand, weaving through the crowd, passed the piercing shop where Vince had threatened to im-pale his tongue before we were shipped off to Puerto Rico—before I met Alex. It was amazing how much had changed since the last time I stood in this spot. Suddenly, Alex stopped.

"We're here," he said, waving to the corner restaurant.

"The Famous Fourth Street Deli?" I laughed.

"I hear it's the best restaurant in town." He grinned.

"For a sandwich, maybe."

He pushed the chrome and glass doors open. A counter full of pastries greeted us as a waiter in a black-and-white uniform led us to a table. I looked out the massive row of windows and onto the glistening dark street as couples strolled by historic town homes and cars circled the block for parking.

"I must admit, I wasn't expecting this," I said, placing a paper napkin on my lap. "Are there many Jewish delis in Puerto Rico?"

"Not that I know of," he said, staring at the menu. "What's brisket?"

I giggled. "It tastes a little like roast beef, but not really."

He nodded as the waiter quickly darted over to take our order.

"I'll have a hot corned beef sandwich and water." I handed him my menu.

"I'll have the brisket."

As soon as the waiter left, Alex reached over and gently placed his hand on mine.

"I'm surprised you brought me here, considering you didn't know what brisket was." I smiled at him suspiciously.

"Well, it's good to keep you guessing."

"Don't worry. People seem to be very adept at keeping secrets from me these days."

"You still haven't talked to Emily?"

"You kidding? She's on lockdown. And even if I did confront her, she'd probably lie."

He squeezed my hand. "You're a good friend. A lot of people would force her to come clean."

"That's why I'm not telling Madison."

The waiter appeared with a tray of food that looked like it weighed more than I did. He plunked a heavy plate in front of me; the sandwich was at least six inches high. Alex's was even bigger.

"Enjoy," the waiter said, before rushing off.

I opened my mouth as wide as I could and bit down. I loved that he didn't take me to a pretentious restaurant where I'd feel uncomfortable ordering anything that cost more than his entrée. I didn't have to worry about him not knowing what fork to use (my mother taught me proper table manners when I was five), and we didn't have to feel like the youngest couple in the restaurant.

"Good?" I asked, gesturing toward his pound of beef.

"Mmhmm," he mumbled as he chewed.

As soon as we finished our meals, we headed out onto the street. Alex strolled through the blocks as if he knew exactly where he was going, which I found rather impressive given that I barely had any sense of direction in this town and I had lived within a fifteen-mile radius of it since birth.

He led me across South Street and onto the cobblestone roads that run down Second. My ankles twisted with every step.

"I like Philadelphia," he said suddenly.

"I'm glad. You think you'll go to school here?"

"Hopefully. But I haven't found the right place yet."

"I understand. Vince visited tons of schools last year, and he mostly picked Cornell because of the baseball coach."

"Yeah, well, I don't really have a sport to fall back on."

"What, Latin ballroom dancing isn't considered a sport?"

"Uh, no. Though I could have a promising future in reality TV."

"Hey, those dark good looks could take you far. I wouldn't vote you off."

"Good to know. But I think my parents expect me to pursue something not so centered around a semi-bare chest."

"Just a waste of a God-given talent." My tone was teasing.

"Like your ballerina legs?" He stared at my jeans and I squirmed, tugging at my waistline.

"Yeah, well, my chances of getting a ballet scholarship are about as good as you getting a free ride for salsa."

"I guess we'll just have to settle for dancing together."

He pulled me toward him and flung me into a ballroom hold. Before I knew it, he spun me out in a rapid turn and drew me back with ease. I'd forgotten how fun it was dancing with him. He could lead anyone. Then he pulled my body toward his and swiveled his hips, dancing me down the sidewalk.

"Now that's how you treat a pretty lady!" yelled a homeless man in a wheelchair, shaking his cup of change.

We smiled and stopped dancing. Alex reached into his pocket and dropped a handful of coins in the tape-covered plastic cup.

"Thank you, sir," said the gray-haired man as he accepted the donation. "Now you treat her right. Pretty girls like that don't come around every day. Trust me, I know!"

My freckled cheeks flushed with embarrassment.

"You can't even accept a compliment from him?" Alex asked as he re-clasped my hand and strolled beside me.

"Well, you did pay him for it," I teased.

"Ah, you'll never change, *mi amor.*"

A few minutes later he led me through the door of a trendy coffeehouse. Couches and art deco chairs filled the loft-like space, and the air was thick with the scent of espresso (one of the best smells on earth). Older couples sat together on lush sofas enjoying the full bar, while younger groups sat in booths sipping nonalcoholic foaming beverages.

"Another surprise. What, did you study a travel guide or something?" I asked as we plopped down.

"You'll never know."

He grabbed the menu and ordered as soon as the waitress popped over.

"We'll have the s'mores and two peppermint hot chocolates." He handed her the menu as she briskly walked away.

"All right, now I know you're getting inside information."

He offered an innocent grin.

"That's my favorite drink in the whole world. There's no way you would know that. I didn't drink anything that wasn't iced the entire time I was in Utuado."

"A lucky guess," he said, staring at the ceiling as he spoke.

"Uh-huh." I squinted my eyes with suspicion. "I'll find out who tipped you off."

"You'll have to beat it out of me."

"That can be arranged. You met my uncles."

As soon as the waitress returned with our graham crackers, chocolate, marshmallows, and a tiny silver Bunsen burner, Alex dove in. I stared at the blue flickering flame as he skewered a marshmallow. The burner reminded me of chemistry labs and Bobby. I was half-tempted to record the color of the fire as Alex plunged his glob into it.

"What are you thinking about?" he asked.

"You," I lied.

He squished his melting white goo onto a cracker with a bar of chocolate and held it out for me to bite. As soon as I leaned in for a nibble, he reached his face across the table and kissed me. This time the only thing I felt rippling through my stomach were butterflies. I closed my eyes and gave in to the warm feel of his lips. When he pulled away, I didn't want him to stop. I opened my eyes and caught him smiling at me.

"Tus ojos son muy bonitos, pero tu boca es perfection," he purred in Spanish.

Normally a guy complimenting the beauty of my eyes and mouth would make me groan at the cheesiness, but somehow hearing it in Spanish made it the most romantic sentence ever uttered. I parted my lips to thank him, but before I could, I caught a memorable face out of the corner of my eye.

"Oh, my God." I froze.

"What?" Alex twisted his neck to follow my gaze.

There across the room sat the guy from the restaurant—the guy who'd stroked Emily's hand and whispered to her over candlelight. Only this time he was with friends clad in button-downs and baseball caps, like they'd just stepped off a college campus.

I stared at Emily's date, frantically trying to place his face. I thought he might have graduated from Spring Mills, but if he had it was long before my time. I watched as he rested his arm around an elegant blond in a crisp white shirt and sharp black, wire-framed glasses. She looked significantly older than Emily as she sipped her red wine and laughed breezily with his friends.

I didn't know what this guy was doing with fifteen-year-old Emily or why he was hiding in her hotel room, but it looked like she wasn't the only girl he was romancing.

Chapter 15

Our date was perfect. After I got over the shock of having caught Emily's secret date with his arms around what appeared to be his twenty-something girlfriend, Alex paid the bill and led me out of the restaurant. While we didn't dance back to the car, he did do his best to steer my mind off the Emily situation. And when he stopped the car in front of my house rather than pulling into the drive, I knew the date wasn't over.

He leaned in and kissed me before I could thank him for the evening. My mind quickly emptied of everything other than the feel of his lips moving with mine. I didn't know how long we kissed, but when I finally pulled away I noticed he was sweating. He didn't want to go in and neither did I, but I knew my father was probably waiting in the living room for us (and his car) to return home.

We both retired to our separate bedrooms and I spent the night dreaming about the tingly sensation of his touch. Only when my eyes popped open the next morning, it wasn't Alex that flung to my mind. It was Emily. Apparently, Lilly awoke with the same thought—only for a completely different reason.

"You are *not* gonna believe what happened!" Lilly spat as

she bounded into my room and kicked Tootsie off the mattress. She dove beside me.

"What?" I rubbed the crust out of my bleary eyes.

"Okay, so I went to that party with Betsy. And you know how you said I should keep an eye out for Evan?"

"You saw him?" My mind felt instantly awake.

"Sort of," she said, with one eye squinty. "As we were leaving, this black car pulled up. It looked like a fancy taxi cab. So I was staring at it. I mean, how weird is it to have a driver take you to a high school party?"

I nodded, my brow furrowed as I tried to guess what she was getting at.

"Anyway, sure enough the driver got out and opened the back door. Out walked . . . Evan."

"All right, well, I guess that's kinda weird, but his dad does run a law firm. They probably have a fleet of corporate cars. Still, why wouldn't he come with his friends?"

"But he *did* come with a friend." Lilly's eyes almost bulged out of their sockets. "When the driver opened the other side, out came . . . Emily."

"What?" I screeched.

Tootsie raised his head off the floor and barked.

"Sorry," I mumbled, before shooting my gaze to Lilly. "Are you serious?"

"I'm telling you that Emily came to that party with Evan Casey."

"That's impossible. She would never do that."

"She did."

"Well, did you talk to her?"

"No. Betsy was leaving, and she was my ride. She literally dragged me out. And when I asked her about it, she brushed it off. Like she knew that they were friends." Lilly shook her unbrushed hair.

"Did she say that word, 'friends'? Or did she act like they were something more?" I asked carefully.

"She said 'friends.' And she wouldn't volunteer much else."

I closed my eyes and flopped back onto my pillow, my hands dug into my sweaty red hair. My mind swirled. I had already caught Emily on a date with a college guy; I already knew she was keeping a secret; was it possible she was seeing Evan, too? What if it wasn't the college guy in her hotel bathroom that day? What if it was Evan? What if he was the secret she was keeping all along?

"But I thought she was seeing that guy from the restaurant?" Lilly stated as if reading my mind.

"Yeah, well, maybe we were wrong. 'Cause guess who *I* saw last night?" I moaned. "The mystery man with his mystery girlfriend. And they're, like, old. Like twenties."

"Huh," she huffed. "Do you really think she could be seeing Evan?"

"I don't know any more when it comes to Emily. But I do know that if she is, she'd lie about it."

"Well, this will make for an interesting afternoon."

She, Madison, Emily, and I were set to hit Suburban Square for some advance Christmas shopping. Only so much deception buzzed between us now that part of me wanted to curl into a ball and not get out of bed.

I wandered through Suburban Square with a soft pretzel. Dark-speckled mustard dripped from the thick doughy knot. I needed comfort food—anything to take my mind off the giant pink elephant that was strolling beside us, unspoken. It was getting harder and harder to pretend it wasn't there.

"So you totally made out with Alex!" Madison cheered. "How was it?"

"It was like we were back in Puerto Rico. Comfortable and normal." I smiled as I chewed.

"Is he a good kisser?"

"I don't know. I think so. It's not like I have much to compare it with," I admitted.

"I wonder what it would be like to kiss Evan. I bet he's an awesome kisser," Madison said in a dreamy voice as she gazed into the cloudless sky.

"Well, I'm pretty sure he's got more experience under his belt," Lilly muttered, the insinuation obvious.

I elbowed her.

"You're just jealous," Madison chirped, hiking her designer purse higher onto her shoulder.

"Of what? Your cyber relationship?" Lilly asked. "Yeah, I just wish I had a guy to e-mail."

"It's more than that," Madison mumbled.

"Did he call you last night?" I asked, staring at Emily as I spoke.

"He texted me this morning." She grinned as she dug through her bag for her rhinestone-studded cell phone.

"He did? What he say?" Emily asked, her green eyes flashed with concern. Madison didn't notice, but I did.

Ever since I had gotten back from my summer vacation, Emily had turned into a virtual stranger. She kept more secrets than the federal government, and I was somehow manipulated to believe that I couldn't confront her on any of them. I felt that if I pushed too hard, she would drop me as a friend, the same way she had dropped her mother. We used to roll our eyes at Madison's drama queen antics, now it seemed like Madison was the levelheaded one.

"Hey, babe. Sleep well?" Madison gushed as she read from her cell phone. "I had a killer dream last night. You were in it. Then he added a smiley face with a wink."

I watched her read the message once more. Her enthusiasm concerned me.

"Well that *is* suggestive," I noted as I bit into my pretzel.

"Did he tell you what he did last night?" Lilly asked, glaring at the back of Emily's shiny chocolate hair. I could see she was not planning to let this go.

"No. He said he'd call me if he was gonna go out. So I guess he stayed in." Madison tucked the phone back into her purse as she strolled into Urban Outfitters, shop bells tinkling above us.

I swallowed hard, a mass of pretzel sticking in my throat as I rushed in behind my friends. Something told me we weren't going to walk out of this store as carefree as we were walking into it.

"Mad, are graphic T shirts still in?" Emily asked casually as she lifted one from a round table, switching topics.

"Totally. I think they're universal." Madison nodded as she scanned a pile of perfectly folded tees.

"What about one with zebras?" Emily lifted a top.

"What about Evan?" Lilly asked bluntly, steering the conversation back to last night's activities.

"What about him?" Madison asked as she held up a white short-sleeved shirt covered in faded butterflies.

"He didn't tell you he went out last night?" Lilly asked.

Emily briefly shot a look through the corner of her eyes.

"No, why? Did he? Do you know something?" Madison dropped the clothes she was holding.

I grabbed Lilly's arm, but it was too late. She glared directly at Emily.

"I went to Chris Hoffman's party last night. And I saw Evan show up around midnight when Betsy and I were leaving."

Emily's lashes blinked rapidly, her gaze flickering between Lilly and me.

"Omigod! Are you sure?" Madison asked, her eyebrows bunching.

"Yup, I saw him pull up." Lilly cocked her head at Emily, who shoved the T shirt she was holding back on the circular table and snorted.

"Lilly, I don't think you should get Madison all freaked out over nothing. He may have just popped in for a second," Emily said, her tone cool.

"Still, he didn't call *Madison* to go to the party," Lilly said sternly.

"Maybe it was a last-minute thing," Emily defended.

"Or maybe there was something going on that he didn't want her to know about."

I jumped between Lilly and Emily and glued a fake smile across my face.

"Hey, who knows why Evan does anything, right?" I said breezily.

"Wait, it sounds like Lilly knows something," Madison insisted. "If you do, just tell me."

Her blue eyes softened, pleading with Lilly. It was one of those situations where I almost felt it would be kinder to lie, but then I knew if I did I would lose my best friend—and besides, the truth always comes out.

I shot my head toward Emily, whose expression looked bored. I squinted my dark eyes. At that moment I hated her for putting me in this situation. I didn't care how bad things were with her mother, she could just as easily self-destruct without stealing Madison's quasi-boyfriend.

"I don't know why you're staring at me," she lied, her eyes wide and threatening.

"Did you go out last night?" Lilly asked.

Madison scoffed. "What are you guys talking about? I don't

care what Em did last night. No offense, Em." She waved at her. "I wanna know what's going on with Evan."

I glared at Emily once more but she refused to meet my stare. Lilly clutched my biceps and dug her nails in. I knew she was about to blurt out everything, and to be honest, part of me wanted to let her. I was sick of protecting Emily's secrets.

"Evan showed up at that party last night. And he arrived with a girl," Lilly stated simply.

"Omigod." Madison shook her head, dazed, as she stared at the rainbow of T shirts. "Do you know who?"

Lilly stared at Emily with enough anger to start another cold war. Emily clicked her tongue in annoyance and turned her head in the opposite direction. She was so confident we wouldn't reveal her secret that she looked almost smug.

"She goes to Spring Mills," Lilly added. "I recognized her."

"But you don't know her?" Madison pushed.

"No, I definitely don't know her at all."

A lull fell over the conversation as Madison absorbed the information. I could see the feeling of betrayal in her pale eyes and sunken chest, only I knew she had no idea how badly she was being betrayed.

We left the shop without saying another word. Except for Lilly, who continued to mutter quietly into my ear.

"I can't believe her," she hissed. *"How could she keep her mouth shut? What's wrong with her? She should be locked up . . ."*

I needed a moment to reason with Emily, to convince her to come clean on her own. I had no desire to be the messenger of her misdeeds.

"She's a piece of work, you know that."

I brushed Lilly off and cleared my throat loudly.

"So you know, Vince'll be home tonight," I announced. "And he's bringing his *girlfriend.*"

I smiled as wide as my mouth would permit, hoping to buy time by flipping the conversation to something more neutral.

"What's her name?" Emily asked, relieved at the new topic.

I scrunched my nose, then turned toward Madison who was strolling aimlessly past every cosmetic and shoe store she normally visited religiously.

"Her name's Mali and she's from some Asian country."

"Ohhh, exotic," Emily said.

I rolled my eyes. The girl seemed to have perfected a phony insincere act when I wasn't looking. I wondered what else she was faking.

"Yeah, well she's just gonna be here for the week."

"She's staying for Thanksgiving?" Madison asked, finally joining the conversation.

I perked up. "Yup, it'll be the fam plus Lilly, plus Alex, plus some random foreign girl, my mafia-esque uncles, and my bastard aunt. Should make for an interesting holiday."

Everyone laughed.

"Well, it beats a turkey sandwich with my dad from the room service menu," Emily added sadly.

"Oh, I'm sure he's not the only person you've got in your life," Lilly snipped.

"Yeah, like your mom," I added quickly, nudging Lilly.

"Who knows which guy she'll be spending her holiday with," Emily grumbled.

Lilly huffed unsympathetic.

"Shoes. I need shoes," Madison said with certainty as she walked toward a pair of red designer pumps displayed in a store window.

Emily started to follow her in, but I clasped her arm. "Em, you need to go to the bathroom?" I asked, squeezing her arm tightly.

"No," she grunted as she tried to yank her arm away. I wouldn't let go.

"Well, then just come with me anyway. We'll meet you guys back here."

Before she could protest, I dragged Emily off toward the public restrooms. I didn't even let the door slam shut before I started my tirade.

"What the hell is wrong with you?" I shrieked, the scent of stale urine assaulting my nostrils. "How could you possibly go out with Evan Casey? You know she likes him! And don't tell me you don't have any other guys to date . . ."

"Oh, please. Like you have room to talk. My date with Bobby sure didn't stop you from going after him." She thrust her face at me.

"This is not the same thing and you know it," I challenged, stepping forward to tighten the gap between us. "You swore up and down that you weren't interested in Bobby. How was I supposed to know what was going on with your parents? You didn't tell me. You don't tell me much of anything!"

I slammed my hand on the sink's Formica countertop, and she swiveled her head away from me.

"You know Madison likes him. It's all she's talked about since my party," I stated, trying to reason with her.

"I'm not going out with him." She rolled her eyes as she turned back to face me with an almost bored expression.

"You went to a party with him last night. I call that going out."

"Yes, we physically went to the same party at the same time, but it wasn't a date. It was a carpool."

"Since when are you carpooling with Evan Casey? Since when are you even friends? And when did you start going to parties and not telling us?"

"What, do you think you know everything about me?" She waved her hands in the air, her lips puckered.

"I *used* to."

"Well, things have changed."

"Yeah, I noticed."

"Why do you have to make a big deal out of this?"

"You *went out* with the guy that your *best friend* is obsessed with and you lied about it. This makes me wonder what else you're lying about."

"Oh, please," she huffed.

"Was Evan the guy in your bathroom that day?"

Emily's eyes flicked toward me, dark and serious. "I can't believe you're gonna bring that up again."

"Answer the question."

"No, 'cause it's a ridiculous question."

"Actually it's a pretty logical question given all the lies you've been spewing lately. *Was it Evan?*"

"I'm not answering that. I can't believe that's what you think of me."

She rested her hands on the sink and hung her head. I stared at her through the dirty mirror. Her reflection appeared far away, fitting given how distant she felt.

"Look, I'm not gonna get into Evan with you," she said calmly. "We're friends, that's it. If you wanna know more, ask him."

"What do you mean, 'ask him'? *You're* my best friend!" I thrust my manicured fingers into my auburn hair and tugged with frustration. I felt like I was fighting with my father.

"Evan and I are not dating. And I don't need to explain myself further."

She stood up straight and pulled back her thin shoulders with an air of arrogance.

"Fine, you wanna keep your secrets and hurt your friends? Do it. But don't expect any favors from me." I shrugged, thinking of the blond at the café draped all over Emily's secret restaurant date.

"What's that supposed to mean?"

"I'm sure you'll find out. But I know I don't think I need to explain myself further to *you*."

And with that, I spun toward the exit and pushed open the door. When it crashed behind me, she was still standing inside, alone.

Chapter 16

His Beamer was in the driveway. Vince was home.

Madison roared her Audi to a stop and the four of us piled out. After I'd left Emily in the restroom, I returned to the shoe store to find Madison plunking down her father's credit card for another pair of pumps she didn't need. I didn't speak to Emily for the rest of the day, though I doubted she'd noticed. She was so absorbed in her own mind that I didn't even think she realized she was walking alongside us. Frankly, her constant mood swings were getting rather old.

I opened my front door and heard my brother's bellowing laugh drift from the kitchen.

"Be careful or I'll ship you back to wherever you came from!" he shouted between giggles.

"Wherever I came from? Is that what you're calling Malaysia these days?" said a spunky female voice with an odd British accent.

"You never know, he may have been talking to me," I heard Alex respond.

My breath halted. I couldn't see them from where I was standing; I had no idea what was really going on in the kitchen. But hearing Alex's voice mixed with hers made my forehead tense. Maybe it was the tone he used or maybe it was my utter paranoia, but something about their easygoing conversation perked the hairs on the back of my neck.

I stepped into the kitchen, my friends grouped behind me. Alex was resting on the black granite counter beside a tiny, tan-skinned Asian beauty. All one hundred pounds of her (if that) were nestled in a seventies punk T shirt layered atop a white long-sleeved tee. Her spiky black hair was styled in an intentionally messy formation that looked like it took hours, and skill, to create. Her cheeks were sharp, her lips were full, and her face was perfectly symmetrical. But it was her bright gray eyes that stopped me cold. They pierced through the air with a sultry vibe I had never before encountered outside of a Hollywood film. They had to be contacts because if they weren't, I might as well have resigned myself to a life of vanilla cream and saltine crackers, that's how bland I felt in comparison.

Alex immediately straightened his torso away from her and she likewise stood up, though that barely added a difference to her height (she couldn't have been more than five feet tall and perfectly petite). I pulled on the waist of the baggy jeans covering my long, knobby legs.

"Hey," I said.

Vince spun around from the fridge where he was digging out sodas.

"Is that all you gotta say? Come on! The big man on campus has returned!"

He rushed over and hugged me. Vince and I never hugged. I awkwardly tapped his back.

"Have you been drinking?" I asked as he pulled away.

"Not yet! God, I just got here. Gimme a few hours." He strutted over to his Malaysian beauty and wrapped an arm around her slender shoulders. "Mariana, this is Mali. Mali this is my sister . . . and all of her friends."

He waved to the girls, who were standing silently behind me. I turned and caught a brief glimpse of Madison's horrified reaction. And I couldn't blame her. Mali was so beautiful, you wanted to dislike her even before she opened her mouth.

"These are my friends Madison and Emily. And this is our cousin Lilly." I gestured toward the girls.

"I told you about Lilly," Vince added, giving her shoulders a slight squeeze. "She's the cousin we met in Puerto Rico."

"And she's *my* friend." Alex's dimples deepened as he leaned in to speak to Mali.

My fingers tightened.

"So where are Mom and Dad?" I asked as I pulled a stool out from the island.

Madison immediately sat beside me while Lilly and Emily stayed in the doorway.

"They went to pick up dinner. Only the best for our guests."

Mali curled her dainty pink lips. "It's very nice to meet you," she said with her slightly-off British accent (which I found odd considering she was Asian; shouldn't she have an Asian accent?).

I nodded at her.

"Where are you from?" Madison asked bluntly.

"Kuala Lumpur."

Madison blinked back oblivious to the locale.

"Malaysia," Mali reiterated.

"That's near China, right?" Madison squinted, still unclear.

"It's in Southeast Asia."

"So the people are Chinese?"

"No, we're 'Ma-lay-sian,' " Mali said slowly, as if she thought Madison was mentally handicapped. (I really couldn't blame her at this point.)

"Only people from China are Chinese," I whispered to Madison. "She's 'Asian.' "

Madison tilted her head.

"So then why do you have a British accent?"

Vince laughed and patted Mali's back. "See, I told you!" He chuckled.

"We learn English in school when we're very young. I guess you can say we learn British English, not American English." Her perfect teeth glowed between her lips.

"So your family lives there, like, right now?" Madison asked.

She nodded, again with a look like she thought Madison might be retarded.

"And you just decided to up and go to school here? Why? What's wrong with your country?"

"Madison!" I said, horrified. "Excuse her."

Madison swatted my arm.

"No, it's okay." Mali nodded patiently. "I'm a gymnast. I was recruited by the coach at Cornell."

"Mali's freakin' awesome!" Vince said happily. "You should see her, like, flip around."

She giggled at my brother as his brown eyes oozed devotion. I had never seen him look at a girl the way he looked at Mali. It was as if all the joy in the world was being expressed through his face. And what concerned me was that when I turned to Alex, he had almost the same glint in his eye. And he wasn't looking at me.

I shoved a forkful of baked ziti into my mouth. I could barely choke it down. Madison and Emily left not long after my parents returned home. There was more than enough food for them to join us, but I think Madison rapidly lost her appetite the more she looked at Mali.

"So, Mali, Vince tells us you're involved with gymnastics," my mother said sweetly as she nibbled on her Caesar salad.

"Yes. I specialize in the uneven bars and the floor. I've been doing it since I was a kid." Mali nodded as she rearranged the food on her plate, barely eating a morsel (it was a move I saw Madison execute on a regular basis).

"She's amazing. She wins, like, every meet," Vince gushed through a mouthful of pasta.

"Not *every* meet." She peered at him through her thickly coated, jet-black lashes.

"So what do your parents do?" my father asked as he dabbed at his mustache with a crisp cotton napkin.

"My father owns several newspapers in Malaysia and my mother plays first violin in the Malaysia Philharmonic Orchestra in KL."

"That's Kuala Lumpur. She calls it KL," Vince added, grinning at her.

"Yeah, I think we got that, Vince." I crunched into my garlic bread, irritated.

"Wow, so your family must be loaded," Lilly said, burping up her veggies.

"Lil," I grumbled, embarrassed by the mention of money. We didn't normally discuss such things.

"No, she's right. They are," Vince said proudly. "They make us look ghetto."

"Vince, that's not true," Mali insisted, with her perfect manners. She turned her exotic eyes toward my mother. "You have a lovely home."

"You should see my parents' place in Puerto Rico. The whole thing could fit into a guest room here," Alex noted.

"Try a guest bathroom," Lilly snipped, pursing her lips.

"Like your parents' house is any better. You live with your grandparents."

"You live with five siblings!"

"I don't have any siblings," Mali stated softly.

"Ah, you're not missing anything," Vince joked as he tossed a green bean at me.

"Very funny. Don't think I wasn't more than happy to see you pack up in September," I huffed.

"So happy you had to call in replacements." He pointed to Alex and Lilly.

"Hey, we're not replacements!" Lilly hollered, her mouth agape.

"Well, he's not." Vince elbowed Alex. "He's my sister's boyfriend."

"Vince!" I shouted, my face burning pink.

When I looked at Alex, his gaze shot down to his plate in an unusual act of shyness. It was almost as if he didn't want to acknowledge our relationship. And while that was typically my reaction, it felt painful seeing it from him.

"Oh, so she's your girlfriend," Mali said sweetly, peering at Alex with her brilliant gray eyes. "You didn't tell me that before."

In that moment, I wanted to stab her repeatedly with my stainless steel fork. I speared a wad of noodle and cheese instead (but I swear I could see her face in the mozzarella).

"Um, well, we didn't really get to that . . ."

"Does anyone need more water?" my mother interrupted, as if on cue.

She was always adept at halting awkward moments. She gracefully rose from her dining room chair, flipped her blond hair over her shoulder, and grabbed Mali's glass.

"I'll get you some more water," she said as she headed off to the kitchen.

"So what are you guys doing tonight?" Lilly asked as she chomped on her pasta.

"I was thinking I'd show Mali around Spring Mills. Take

her down Main Street, maybe go to that new ice cream place. You guys wanna come?" Vince asked.

"I'd loved to," Alex answered, before I could respond.

Mali smiled at him.

While I knew that she was my brother's girlfriend and that Alex was kind of, sort of my boyfriend and that in no way could I possibly have anything to worry about, I still couldn't stop from cringing every time she looked at him. The chick needed to keep her smoky eyes to herself.

Chapter 17

Lilly and I licked our cups of homemade ice cream. With so many flavors to blend, I felt like choosing my dessert was more complicated than choosing a college. In the end, I went with vanilla ice cream, topped with oatmeal, chocolate-covered raisins, and cake batter. Lilly tossed in almost every candy on the menu.

"Wow, this is good," she gurgled as she slurped. Chocolate stained her lips.

We were sharing a booth while Vince, Mali, and Alex waited for the cashier to finish her latest ice cream–related ditty. The poor clerk, a junior at Spring Mills, had to sing candy-coated tunes every time a customer ordered the "flavor of the day." (There wasn't enough money in the world you could pay me to do that.)

I watched as Mali held a plastic spoonful of dripping dark chocolate out for Vince. He licked his lips before slowly caressing the morsel (it was a decent attempt to look seductive while eating—I'll give him that). Then Mali dug her spoon back into her dessert and turned toward Alex. My stomach lurched.

"Oh, no, she isn't," I hissed, gawking at her.

Lilly's eyes shot toward the line just as Alex playfully bit at her spoon and removed the lump of ice cream. She giggled in response.

"So she's friendly." Lilly pumped her eyebrows.

"Who does she think she is?" I screeched, as quietly as I could.

"She's your brother's girlfriend. Isn't it obvious?" Lilly chuckled.

"This isn't funny."

I drummed my nails nervously on the white plastic table.

"Do you really think Alex is gonna try to hook up with your brother's girlfriend?"

"He hooked up with me when you didn't want him to."

"But he also backed off when I asked him to."

"So ask him to back off now."

"You want me to go over there and tell him that Mali's presence is making you so insecure that you'd rather he ignore her until she hits the road next week?"

"Yes," I said with a straight face.

"Yeah, well, I'm not going to." She shook her red hair. "Psycho."

I swiveled my head and watched as Mali took a bite out of Alex's waffle cone.

"Come on! That's weird!" I gestured toward the line where the guys were paying.

Lilly giggled. "Well, Vince doesn't seem to mind."

"That's because he's too busy staring at her chest to notice what she's doing with her mouth."

Just then Alex, Vince, and Mali sauntered over to our booth. Vince and Mali squeezed alongside Lilly, leaving Alex no choice but to sit beside me.

"Hey, wanna bite?" Alex asked, moving his cone toward my lips.

I could see the kissy-mark from where Mali had taken her suggestive nibble.

"No, thanks," I snipped, staring at Lilly.

I didn't bother to offer him a taste of mine. I doubted it was my spit he was interested in sharing.

Mali was supposed to be sleeping in the guest room on the first floor, near my father's den. But from the way Vince was sliding his hand up her thigh as we sat on the living room sofa, I doubted they would immediately separate to individual sleeping quarters. Lilly lounged on the brown leather chair closest to the TV as Alex nestled next to me. The more mischievous Mali and Vince got, the more he tried to move his lips toward my neck. I was brushing him away at every touch.

"So did you guys enjoy your date the other night?" Vince asked, finally taking his eyes off Mali.

"Yeah," I said, peering at him suspiciously. "How'd you know about it?"

Vince chuckled. "Wasn't it obvious?"

I snapped my face toward Alex.

"Vince may have given me a few pointers," he muttered softly.

While I knew someone must have helped Alex with his sudden Philadelphia know-how, especially when it came to ordering my favorite hot chocolate concoction, I was almost disappointed to learn the truth. I liked believing that Alex went to all this trouble to please me, not that he just shot my brother an e-mail.

"What? Were you feeling guilty after sending the Puerto Rican mafia after him?" I accused, glaring at my brother.

"Yeah, I heard Dad and the uncles went nuts." Vince laughed.

"I can't believe you told Dad!"

"Oh, I barely told him anything. You were the one who got caught making out in Alex's bedroom."

"We were hardly kissing when Dad walked in."

"Yeah, well, that was enough."

"What's going on?" Mali asked, apparently disappointed all the attention wasn't focused on her.

"Alex and Mariana . . ."

"It's nothing," I snapped, cutting Vince off.

I shot him a scrunch-faced look.

"What?" he mouthed.

I shrugged. I was already sick of Mali. I really didn't need to hear her perfect little opinions about my imperfect love life. I was guessing she always knew just what to do to keep a guy interested.

"So, Mali, you're gonna be around for Thanksgiving dinner?" Lilly asked, interrupting the awkward silence.

"Yes. It's my first Thanksgiving. I feel like such an American." She smiled.

"Well, we should have a full house," I said.

"I can't wait to see all the Teresa drama for myself," Vince noted.

"Be careful what you wish for," I warned.

"The uncles don't know we're bridesmaids yet," Lilly explained.

"Oh, this is gonna be classic!" Vince bellowed.

"Who's Teresa?" Mali asked softly, while giving my brother a sexy stare.

"It's a long story," he answered, gazing intently at her lips. "You really want to hear it? 'Cause I can think of some better uses of our time . . ."

Mali batted her lashes seductively.

"I could tell the Teresa story. She's this woman from Puerto

Rico, my town actually," Alex started, but he stopped mid-sentence when my brother cupped Mali's face and kissed her.

It was a nauseating sight. When his upper body pushed toward her, I cringed and jumped to my feet.

"Okay, I realize that Mom and Dad went to bed, but that doesn't make this a peep show," I groaned. "I'm going to bed."

Lilly instantly stood. "Me too."

Alex rose behind me and wrapped his arms around my waist, his chin pressing into the crook of my neck. I wiggled quickly, but he didn't let go. He pressed his hot lips against the back of my ear. Chills ran up my flesh, but I abruptly shook him off and pulled his hands from me.

"I'm going to bed," I said sternly. "See you tomorrow."

His brow creased with confusion.

"Come on, Alex. The night's over," Lilly stated as we walked toward the stairs.

Alex slowly trudged after us (thank God—I was worried he'd stay to watch). I shuddered at the thought.

Chapter 18

Monday's lunch was awkwardly silent. I sat at the table, eating tomato soup and grilled cheese, and avoiding eye contact with my friends. Alex was off visiting the University of Delaware, which was a relief because it meant he was no longer trailing after Mali. He spent most of Sunday, while I was at ballet, flipping through photos of her gymnastic triumphs. He seemed more proud of her accomplishments than Vince did. Funny, since he never asked to see pictures of my dance routines.

But right now he wasn't the worst of my problems. Emily and I hadn't spoken since Suburban Square, not even a "hello" during practice yesterday. And I wasn't about to be the one to break the silent treatment.

"Okay, why aren't you guys talking?" Madison snipped as she sipped her bottled water. Her lunch was a grand total of six celery sticks and six cherry tomatoes. If Evan didn't acknowledge her existence soon, I was worried she wouldn't even eat that.

"Who said we're not talking?" Emily asked, swishing her spoon in her soup.

"Uh, since when do we sit at lunch like a bunch of mutes? Clearly, there's something going on," Madison pointed out.

Emily and I stared at each other.

"All right, change of subject," Madison offered. "Where's Alex?"

"Visiting another college," I muttered. "Or possibly up Mali's butt. Either or."

"Eck, I don't like that girl," Madison hissed.

"You barely know her," Emily offered.

"So? I don't need the hoochie's life story to know that she's a slut."

"Madison!" I shrieked.

"What? Like you don't think it's true."

Actually, I did. But I still wouldn't have phrased it that way.

"I think Alex has a thing for her," I said under my breath.

"I knew it! She's working her freaky Asian magic on him . . ."

"Why do you say that?" Emily asked, speaking to me for the first time.

I peered at her, half tempted to not answer just because she had asked the question. Normally I would have been that stubborn, but my desire to talk about my uncomfortable romantic situation was outweighing my willful streak.

"It's just the way he acts around her. It's the same way he looks at and talks to me."

"That's doesn't mean anything."

"No, it's something," I muttered.

Just then, Evan strolled past our table. He nodded, but I couldn't tell if his greeting was aimed at Madison or Emily. Clearly, Madison didn't have the same confusion.

"Did you see that?" She smiled, her face glowing.

"Yeah, I did," I answered, carefully, looking toward Emily.

"He said he might go to the film festival," Madison continued as she leaned across the table and grabbed the crust of my sandwich. "You gonna eat this?"

I shook my head as my friend bit into more calories than she'd eaten in the past week. I continued to stare at Emily, but she never met my gaze and never glanced at Madison.

I finished copying the notes from the screen. Mr. Berk had just completed a forty-minute Power Point presentation on radioactivity to correspond with our problem set on alpha and beta decay equations. I was halfway through the alpha decay equation for the first nuclide, but I could already see that Bobby had a different answer.

"I don't think you have number one right," I said quietly as the pairs around us discussed their work.

"I don't think I have any of them right. I fell asleep midway through that snooze fest." Bobby yawned.

"I know. It was godawful." I examined his work.

"As soon as he showed the mushroom cloud with the smiley face, I tuned out. I mean, how could you have a happy nuclear explosion?"

"Must the end of the world always be dreary?"

"If it ends with a giant bomb crashing into your backyard, then yes."

"So there are no smiley faces in heaven?"

"Not from clip art." He chuckled.

Bobby copied my work onto his paper. He didn't even ask me to explain. He just trusted me to be right. It was rather nice to have that sort of absolution.

"Man, I can't believe the film festival is in a couple days. It's crazy." He sighed. "Did you hear how many tickets we've sold?"

"Almost a hundred. The children of Ireland will soon be rolling in it thanks to you."

"And Bono thinks he's a philanthropist. Please, let's see if he can match my five-dollar ticket sales."

"Charities everywhere will be hunting you down." I smirked.

"You know it." Bobby suddenly stared at his paper, his mood changing. "So, did your friend get his photos mounted?"

"His name's Alex and yes, my mom got them mounted at the museum. It pays to have connections. I think they're archival quality now."

"Impressive." Bobby nodded sincerely, his blond curls swishing. "I haven't seen him around lately."

"He's been visiting colleges."

"Oh." He nodded. "So is Vince home yet?"

"Yup. Got back this weekend with his tropical princess," I scoffed.

I tried to focus my eyes on the next set of chemistry problems, but I was suddenly feeling very distracted. I didn't like discussing Mali.

"What are you talking about?"

"He has this girlfriend from Malaysia who makes Lucy Liu look like the elephant woman."

"Wow, I hope he brings her to the festival."

"Shut up," I said teasingly, punching his biceps.

"Hey, let's not resort to physical violence. The festival is about peace."

"Yeah, well, you're a *piece* of work," I teased with a grin.

"Oh, I think you just want a piece of me." Bobby did a half-body wave as his long hands slid down his torso.

I giggled and when our gazes met, I didn't look away. My eyes kept smiling even after the moment I knew it wasn't just friendly.

Chapter 19

The next day, Vince orchestrated a trip to the Italian Market to purchase sausage for the Thanksgiving stuffing. My mother thought it would be a cute activity for Vince and his new girlfriend, and it would have been if Vince didn't use the opportunity to show Mali how popular he was by including a half dozen of his closest friends.

We strolled below the green metal awnings in South Philly that protected the sidewalk vendors selling fruits and vegetables. There were rows of weathered town homes above family run shops that had probably been passed down through generations. The fragrant smell of seasoned meats and sauces wafted through the cool air, mixing with the fresh scent of pizza in my hands.

I bit into the white cheese and broccoli slice, grease covering my lips. It made every fast food pizza joint seem like it was selling an entirely different food.

"The pizza's not this good in Puerto Rico," Alex stated as he strolled beside me, devouring his meat-covered slice.

"Pizza's not this good in Spring Mills," I told him.

Vince and Mali walked ahead, engulfed by Vince's boys. (Each one had already made a not-so-subtle comment complimenting Vince's big "score.") Lilly was nestled between them, basking in the attention of Vince's friend Kyle. He was the only one not home for Thanksgiving break, only because he never really went away. He was a freshman at Swarthmore College, and though the commute from Spring Mills to his campus was less than twenty minutes, he chose to room in the dorms—not that I blamed him.

"I love outdoor shopping," I said, my breath freezing in the air. "I know malls are more practical because of the weather and all, but there's something about shopping outside that makes it more fun."

"I agree," Alex added as he shivered, pulling his coat tight.

My mom used to take us to the markets in Philadelphia all the time. We'd go to the Polish market for kielbasa and perogies, the Italian market for meats and cheeses, and the Asian market for fish and produce. Usually, the week before Christmas, the lines in front of the stores looked like they were selling concert tickets rather than ingredients.

Vince turned into a butcher shop. About a dozen twenty-something guys stood behind the meat counters, taking orders at rapid fire.

"Wow, there's a lot of meat here," Lilly said, gazing around the shop. "Sometimes doesn't the concept of chewing flesh from a living creature gross you out?"

"Oh, don't go all vegetarian on me," I moaned.

"What's the matter, Lilly? A little ground cow make you queasy? Moooo!" Kyle teased, nudging her shoulder.

"Ew, stop. I'm trying to block out the meat's animal form."

"Yeah, well, then don't look at the baby pig with the apple in its mouth."

Lilly followed his gaze. "Ew, gross!"

The tiny pink mammal looked like it could get up and trot out. My stomach recoiled.

"You know, I'm taking this class on microbiology and you should see the bacteria—"

"Stop!" Lilly ordered, cutting him off mid-sentence. "I don't wanna hear it."

"Have you ever seen a slaughterhouse? 'Cause the E. coli in most ground beef . . ."

"Nahaahahaha." Lilly plugged her fingers in her ears.

Finally Vince's order was called and he grabbed his bag of sausage and rejoined the group.

"You ready?" he asked. *"Vamonos, muchachos."*

"You know, I've been friends with Vince since, like, middle school and I didn't even know your family was Hispanic," Kyle stated, glancing at Lilly, Alex, and me as we headed for the door.

"Yeah, we get that a lot," I answered.

"I had to break her in when she was in Puerto Rico," Lilly teased. "She's my contribution to the Latino society."

"Well, with a Puerto Rican dad, a Polish mom, and a Malaysian girlfriend, Vince is turning into a regular old United Nations," Kyle joked.

"Oh, these Americans just can't resist an accent," Lilly cooed, batting her thickly coated lashes.

"You got that right." Kyle reached over and clasped her hand.

The smile on Lilly's face was uncomplicatedly happy. Maybe Emily's mom would soon no longer be our only reason to visit Swarthmore College.

It was two days until the big Thanksgiving dinner, and my mom was making calligraphy place cards for the dining room table as if she were hosting a group of dignitaries rather than our immediate family and a couple of stragglers. At last count, she had four different desserts ordered—apple pie, pumpkin pie, sweet potato pie, and death by chocolate (just in case someone didn't like pie). She was making the rest of the meal herself, from scratch.

When we returned home from the Italian Market, she had a stir-fry dinner waiting for us, though she didn't touch a bite. She simply snatched the sausage from Vince and returned to her holiday preparations. Our dad heated up the food and we all gulped it down in virtual silence, afraid of setting off my mom on another cooking-related tirade. And just like old times, my dad ordered Vince and I to wash the dishes. Lilly, Alex, and Mali relaxed in the living room, flicking through the TV channels.

"So things seem better between you and Alex," Vince noted as he put yet another unrinsed plate in the dishwasher.

"I guess. You know I shouldn't have called you that night," I said regretfully.

"Why? It worked. He swore to stay outta your pants. . . ."

"When did you have a conversation about my pants?" I gasped.

"When you were at ballet. Please, I'm your brother *and* a guy. I know what's up." He shook his head dismissively, his black hair flopping.

"Just forget it ever happened," I groaned.

"Why? So Chester the Molester can get his freak on?"

I laughed in spite of myself. "Like you do with Mali?"

"Ah, you've got that backward. Mali's the freak."

"That doesn't surprise me." I smirked as I dried another pot and hung it on the rack above the island. "She seems rather . . . friendly."

"Trust me, she is." Vince giggled mischievously.

"I meant she's a flirt."

"No more than Lilly."

"Worse than Lilly," I said in an ominous tone.

"Dude, I think Kyle was totally into Lil."

"Too bad he's, like, eighty years older than her." I hung up my dish rag.

"He's seventeen. He skipped a grade. The guy's crazy-smart." Vince slammed the dishwasher closed and started the cycle. "He's younger than Alex."

He was right. Alex was already eighteen, but he wasn't in college.

"I wonder if Kyle knows Emily's mom."

"I don't think the dude takes poetry classes . . . but speaking of which." Vince shuffled his feet.

"What?"

"Remember I told you about that English paper?" Vince winced, his shoulders pushed high.

"How bad is it?" I asked cautiously.

"If I don't ace this paper I could, kinda, well, maybe, fail the semester."

"What?" I screeched. "You mean fail, like a 'C' or fail like an 'F'?"

"Like an F. Like I won't be able to play baseball, like Mom and Dad might legally disown me."

"Vince, I can't believe you!" I shook my head with disapproval.

"I know," he whined with puppy dog eyes. "But I helped you with Alex!"

"Like that's the same thing."

He already knew that I wouldn't let him fail. When he got his first C in sophomore geometry, my father grounded him for two months and snapped into a heated lecture that sounded more like Vince was guilty of a federal offense rather than poor study habits. My dad still brought up "that semester" every time Vince so much as mentioned a difficult class.

We trudged out of the kitchen and Vince veered toward the TV room.

"Oh, don't even think about it." I snatched his arm. "You have five days to write a paper that will determine whether you stay in college."

Vince groaned and obediently followed me up the stairs.

Four hours later, I was still in his room speed-reading *Macbeth*, while he scoured the Internet for every intellectual musing ever written on the play.

"Well, it's obvious that a major theme is whether Macbeth's ambition defines his entire character," I stated, looking up from the text.

"Well, duh. Even I know that," Vince grunted. "You don't get it. This professor is, like, thirty. He's not some old wrinkled, Shakespearean scholar. He harps about us being 'critical thinkers' and using our creativity to shape new meaning to the text. I can't go in there rehashing Cliff's Notes."

"Well, Vince, I'm not a college student. I've never read Shakespeare outside of *Romeo and Juliet*. How am I supposed to help you?" I groaned.

"Mariana, you're smarter than me . . . as much as it kills me to admit it," he grumbled. "I need to come up with a way to frame this essay so it's the most creative piece of crap ever written."

"Ah, so eloquent. I think that should be your thesis."

I stared back down at the prose, hoping the answer would be lying there.

"All right, so Macbeth is the villain. He's the bad guy," I noted. "And the more he craves power, the more evil he gets. Like a politician who'd do anything to win the election . . ."

"Like a president," Vince said, popping his head up from his laptop.

I quickly flicked my eyes toward him. "Like a president who would start a war just to create his own legacy."

"He kills in order to gain more power." Vince stated, his eyes brightening. "Macbeth is Bush."

"Whoa, don't go crazy. Your professor could be a republican," I warned. "Just say that Macbeth is like any modern-day politician. I'm sure there are plenty out there who would do anything to stay in charge."

"Nope, he's Bush," Vince insisted as he started typing. "Trust me, this guy's a flaming liberal. He's got all these eco-bumper stickers glued to his desk and tons of anti-war posters."

As soon as I saw Vince in a writing groove, I headed to my bedroom. It was almost midnight and the hallway was dark. I padded past Alex's room and paused to listen to him sleep. Not a single noise squeaked out. He must have been out cold. I continued to my bedroom and gently closed the door behind me.

The glow of my laptop shone as I plopped down at my desk. I had two new e-mails: one from Teresa and one from Bobby. I opened Teresa's first. It was sent to Lilly and me.

¡Hola, chicas! I took my gown to the dry cleaners today, you're not going to believe how much they charged! It's more than the dress! *Dios mio.* But Carlos has been wonderful. I'm so excited for Manny to come. I miss him and I can't wait for you to see him at Thanksgiving—he's so big! Almost three years old!

I started looking at bridesmaid dresses on the Internet and here are a few links to some I think you might like. We'll go shopping after the holiday. See you on Thanksgiving!

Love,
Teresa

She included three links in her e-mail. The first was to a fire engine–red dress with flutter cap sleeves and a ruffled skirt that was shorter in the front than in the back—it screamed eighties prom dress. I flinched. The second dress was at least a more respectable shade of red but it had a high empire waist that made even the size zero model look pregnant. I couldn't imagine what Lilly's double-D boobs would look like in it. The last dress was a deep shade of burgundy, only the shiny satin fabric clung to the model until it belled out like a mermaid tail at the knees. I shook my head at the designs. Lilly and I would need to stage a serious intervention. I didn't care *whose* day it was.

Finally, I clicked open Bobby's e-mail. It was only a few lines long.

> Hey Mariana,
> I was just thinking that in a few days the entire school is going to see my documentary. That's pretty damn cool and I have you to thank. Maybe someday I can pay you back. You rock!
> —Bobby

I smiled, and I read his message three more times.

Then I slid into my bed, and I flicked off the light. My mind drifted to stillness just as I heard the sounds of footsteps padding down the hall. Then a door carefully opened and closed. My eyes flew open. It sounded like Alex's room.

Chapter 20

When I got up the next morning, I could hear Vince typing. I yanked on my robe and moved through the hall.

"Have you been writing all night?" I asked as I spied him at his desk.

His dark hair was sweaty, his eyes were bloodshot, and his fingers were flying over the keys with pure concentration. I hadn't see him work that hard in the eighteen years he spent in Spring Mills.

"No, I dozed off for about an hour. Sometime after Alex went to bed," he muttered, not looking away from his laptop.

My lungs seized. It wasn't a dream. I had heard Alex return to his room late last night.

"Wait? You heard Alex go to bed?" I scratched at my matted hair.

"Yeah, after midnight. I think he was keeping Mali entertained, which is fine because I totally blew her off."

At this point, I was fairly certain my brother wasn't thinking clearly. Why in the world would Alex stay up after midnight with my brother's girlfriend? It wasn't like they were long-lost friends losing track of time. What could they possibly have to talk about for hours, alone?

"Why were they up so late?" I asked, my face crumbling as I envisioned Alex whispering soft Spanish nothings into her tan ear.

"I don't know. They were probably watching TV." Vince flicked his eyes toward me. "You freak out too much."

I grunted and spun toward Lilly's room. My soul quietly prayed that Lilly was their chaperone and that they all had watched *Mary Poppins* together.

I knocked on my cousin's door. She immediately flung it open as if she were expecting me.

"I still think it's so weird that you guys knock first," she said as she walked toward her mahogany full-length mirror, clutching a couple of outfits. "Anyway, Alex was all up on Mali last night."

My jaw dropped as I stared at her reflection.

"I heard you talking to Vince. That's why you're here, *verdad?*" she asked as if what she had just said was utterly unimportant.

"Lil? What do you mean? Huh?" I gasped, rubbing my temples.

"I went to bed around eleven, actually Kyle called me. It was so sweet. He's coming to the festival, by the way. But that's another story. Anyway, when I left, the two of them barely noticed. They were all whispering and giggling on the couch."

She held a pink sweater to her reflection as if not noticing the horror on my face.

"Hello? And you just did nothing? You didn't think to get my back here?" I asked, shaking my head in disbelief.

"I don't think it would've mattered."

I blinked rapidly.

"Wait, I mean, are you saying . . . that they hooked up?"

My empty stomach roared, and it wasn't out of hunger. I couldn't believe I was having this conversation. This guy leaves his home country and flies all the way to the States to be near me, and then goes and hits on the first girl he sees—my brother's girlfriend, no less. It was way too Jerry Springer for me to comprehend at six o'clock in the morning on a school day.

"I wouldn't go that far. But there was definitely more flying between those two than friendly conversation. I actually saw her whisper in his ear. It was like they didn't even see me in the room."

"Oh. My. God." I sunk onto Lilly's unmade bed. She slept on my old floral sheets from middle school. Back then the only things I worried about were pimples and braces, not secret affairs and scandalous divorces.

"So, let me tell you about Kyle. We totally talked for, like, an hour about everything—"

"Lilly!" I yelped, flopping onto her pillow. "My boyfriend may have just gotten it on with my brother's girlfriend *in my parents' house*! Can we stay focused here?"

I felt the room close in on me.

"Since when is he your boyfriend? You're the one who freaked out over those pictures . . ."

"That's just it! A couple of days ago I thought he was stalking me with devotion, and now I think he's lost interest! How is that possible?"

My breathing accelerated as I closed my eyes. The image of Mali and Alex kissing on my parents' couch, the couch I watched TV on, the couch my dog slept on, was causing a headache to form behind my eyes.

"Okay, we don't know if anything happened. I can't imagine the girl could be that tacky. All I'm saying is that there was a definite 'something' going on. But they may not have acted on it."

"So if they're attracted to each other, if they *want* each other, if they flirt with each other and don't act on it, then that's okay?"

"Technically, yes. Am I wrong?"

My lips parted as I looked at Lilly, stunned. I wished I could be that blasé about it, but in my world, I wanted my boyfriend to think of me and only me. If he's fantasizing about someone else while he's holding my hand, that's not okay.

"Mariana, the boy lives down the hall. You can just ask him what happened."

"You think he'll tell me the truth?"

"No, but I also don't think you like him as much as you say you do."

"What?" I coughed, sitting upright.

"Mariana, you liked him in Puerto Rico. I know you did. You were borderline obsessed. But since he's gotten here . . . maybe it was the photos or maybe . . . something else. I don't know. But it's been different."

Lilly looked away as she said this. She never avoided confrontation, and the action made me pause. It made me remember what she was like in Puerto Rico. How she tried to keep Alex and I apart so she would get more of my attention. Suddenly I began to wonder if any of what she was saying was true (while the other half of me secretly worried that it was *all* true).

"I don't know what to say," I said simply, examining her face for clues.

"Well, good. Because you don't have to say it to me. You have to say it to him."

She pointed down the hall toward Alex's room. This was not the way I wanted to spend my last morning before Thanksgiving break.

A half hour later, after a long shower, I got dressed and wandered to the kitchen. Madison was probably on her way, and I knew it was time to face my quasi-cheating, sort-of boyfriend. As expected, he was seated at the table with my father, sipping coffee. The sight of him made my teeth grind.

"Um, *hola,* Mariana," he said, not looking up from his collegiate brochure.

I nodded and headed to the refrigerator, saying nothing.

"Am I going senile or was that your brother up this morning typing?" my father asked from behind his newspaper. "Please tell me that you're finally rubbing off on him."

"I don't know what you're talking about," I lied with a smirk.

"Sure." My father hummed.

"You guys were pretty busy last night," Alex stated.

"Mmhmm," I said, sipping my orange juice.

"Did you get a lot done?" he asked casually.

I sighed and plucked a banana muffin from the fresh bread basket on the counter. Alex stood up, the metal legs of his chair screeching across the floor. His heavy footsteps stopped behind me, but I didn't turn around.

"You okay?" he asked.

"*Sí, estoy bien,*" I responded in my cockiest tone.

"*Bien,*" he said, leaning back.

I could smell his coffee breath, and it was making me even more nauseated with him than I already was.

"What's wrong?" he asked.

"Hey, where's Mali?" I snipped, my eyes wide.

My father grunted, then left the room as if he could sense an argument brewing. Clearly, this wasn't how he wanted to start his morning either.

"Why would I care about Mali?" Alex asked softly, turning away from me.

"Because you obviously cared a lot about her last night."

"You were busy."

"Yeah, and I heard you guys got along just *great,*" I growled.

"Yeah, well I wanted to hang out with *you.*"

"Really? Well, I guess it's good that Mali was there as a substitute."

"Yeah, it was. At least she made time for me."

"She's here on vacation! What, did she take time out of her busy schedule of doing nothing for you? Gee, how nice of her."

"Why are you being like this?"

"Like what? This is *my* house. I can 'be' any way that I want."

"*Claro.* I've noticed."

Just then Lilly bounded down the steps, dressed in an outfit I got for Christmas last year. "You guys ready? I think I just saw Madison pull up."

"Yeah, I'm ready. Let's get out of here," I hissed, charging toward the front door.

The only one who spoke on the drive to school was Madison. She was gushing over the fact that Evan finally called her cell phone last night rather than texting it. Her brief conversation with a live boy was enough to fill our entire drive.

We all slammed our car doors shut and headed into the building.

"So Evan is totally going to the film festival. And he said that he loved the posters I made," Madison chirped as we headed to our lockers.

Alex was still following us even though he had no locker to go to and he could have gone straight to his advisor's office. The fact that he was still in my presence made my body hot with tension, though I didn't think anyone (aside from Lilly) noticed.

"He loved the pink posters with glittered hearts that you made to advertise Ireland?" I asked, an eyebrow raised.

"What? Like all the signs had to be doom and gloom because of the holy war thing? Pink is a more eye-catching color," she defended. "At least, Evan thought so."

"This coming from a wrestling jock."

"So his opinion doesn't count?"

"I didn't know jocks had opinions," I snapped, hoping to spread my bad mood onto everyone.

"What's up your butt?" Madison hissed as we trudged through the crowded hall.

"Nothing, that's the problem," Lilly joked.

I smacked her arm.

"Mariana," Alex said carefully. "I want to talk to you. . . ."

"Yeah, well, I want a lot of things, starting with not seeing you right now."

I shot Alex an icy look and caught Madison's face twist with shock. Alex stopped in his tracks, his dark eyes faded. Lilly reached out, but he shook her off.

"*Está bien,*" he whispered, before turning in the opposite direction.

I watched him march off and said nothing.

"What the heck was that?" Madison asked, glaring at me sideways.

"Nothing."

Emily was waiting in front of Madison's locker. Her corporate driver was always freakishly punctual.

"Clearly, there's something going on," Madison said, as she nodded to Emily and moved toward her locker.

"What? What'd I miss?" Emily asked, surveying our faces.

"You might as well tell 'em." Lilly gestured toward my friends. She barely paused a second before continuing. "Alex was being all 'Latin lover' with Mali last night."

"What?" Madison shrieked.

"He hooked up with your brother's girlfriend?" Emily gasped.

A random student at a locker nearby swung his head toward us. I guess it was hard not to eavesdrop on a conversation so worthy of a daytime soap. I met the boy's stare, and he quickly turned back to his locker.

"Nothing, it's nothing. Lilly caught him flirting with Mali." I shrugged.

"But they didn't hook up?" Madison clarified.

"I don't know. I don't think so," I said softly.

Madison peered at me, her pale blue eyes sincere. "If he touches one hair on that diva's head, I will ship him back to Puerto Rico in the taco he came in on."

Her tone was so serious and her face so stern that I couldn't help but crack up.

"Watch it!" Lilly yelped, obviously offended as she swatted at me for laughing.

"I'm sorry," I choked, still giggling.

"We don't even eat tacos," she said. "That's an entirely different country . . ."

"Yeah, well, I wouldn't start," Madison grumbled.

Lilly rolled her eyes muttering something about "racial crap" as Emily stood silently beside her. Madison might not have been the most politically correct person, but she sure knew how to break the tension.

By lunch, I had calmed down. A ninety-minute lecture on the horrors of World War II can put your life into perspective (seriously, like I can claim I have problems while listening to that). I strutted into the cafeteria prepared to see Alex. Only I wasn't as prepared to find my friends grilling him like FBI interrogators.

"So do you have feelings for this *Mali*?" Madison asked.

"It's the Asian thing isn't it?" Emily added. "She's sooo exotic."

"Or are you just some perv who gets off on banging strangers in your girlfriend's home?" Madison continued.

"I did not 'bang' anyone," Alex insisted, staring at his hands.

"Ah, did you hear his sweet Latin accent? I almost believe him," Madison mocked, looking at Emily.

"Whoa, whoa, whoa." I stepped up behind the girls.

Alex's black eyes immediately darted toward me, repentant.

"Mariana, I don't know what you've been thinking. *Pero mi amor . . .*"

"Alex, stop," I said, tossing my hands in the air. "I don't want to hear it. I don't want to think about it. Let's just let it go."

"What?" Madison slammed her hands on the cafeteria table. Heads swiveled all around us. "We almost had him. He was ready to break."

I glanced at Alex. He looked exhausted and regretful. I wanted to believe that he wasn't interested in Mali, and I wanted to believe that my brother and I hadn't found people so horrible that they would actually hook up in our parents' home.

"Let's just move on everybody," I said, sitting down.

I slid my chair a few inches away from him. I didn't want to risk brushing against his foot. I wasn't in the mood. "We have other things to worry about."

"Like what?" Emily asked.

I pulled a container of sweet potato puff out of my bagged lunch. My mom was testing out her Thanksgiving dishes on us and had insisted on packing meals for Lilly, Alex, and me. In addition to the maple-covered potato dish, I also had a salad with green apple slices and walnuts, and a thermos of spiced cider. I noticed Alex wasn't eating.

"Not hungry?" I asked, an eyebrow perked.

"I already ate." He nodded humbly.

I didn't know if I believed him. Suddenly, I distrusted everything he said. Maybe I made a huge mistake by inviting him here. Maybe I really didn't know him at all.

"So any news on the film festival?" Madison asked, snapping me back to the conversation.

"They need people to hand out programs and work the lights," I told her.

"So? Can't the AV geeks do that?" Madison scoffed.

"They also want someone to introduce Bobby. *And* . . . his parents are insisting that the dean mention the money is going to one of 'their charities.'"

"What, are Bobby's parents acting like they're still this happily married couple?" Emily's forehead scrunched.

"Well, they are still married."

"Yeah, that's because they're cowards who can't face the truth. God, if I hear a single person congratulate my mother's bed buddy . . ."

"Em, if it wasn't him—"

"Madison!" I cut her off, my face full of warning.

The last thing Emily needed was to hear that her mother was a tramp. I didn't care how much she and her mom were fighting, she was still her mother and Emily was our friend. You just don't say stuff like that no matter how true it might be.

Emily's eyes hardened and her nostrils flared.

"Hey, forget him," I stated. "You probably won't even see the guy."

"And who cares if you do? Focus on the wife," Madison reasoned. "Hit him where it hurts. I'm sure she can make his life a whole lot more miserable than we can."

"Wow, you guys are tough," Alex whispered.

"Yeah, don't forget it," Madison shot back—all ninety pounds of her.

I couldn't imagine anyone would take a threat from her seriously, but Alex looked genuinely concerned, which made me smile.

Chapter 21

By the end of the day, the whole school was talking about Bobby's impending documentary debut. The auditorium was sold out, and according to Dean Pruitt, we had already raised more than $4,000 for poor, starving children in Ireland (who said Africa was the only trendy place to donate to?).

Bobby was excused from last period to work on last-minute details, so I was stuck at my lab table alone, drumming my nails and watching the clock tick—only a few more minutes. I yawned, covering my mouth.

Suddenly, I felt my purse vibrate. I stealthily slid my hand into my bag and clutched my cell phone. Mr. Berk had his back to the class, his hand flying across the chalkboard. I quietly flipped open my phone and peeked at the screen. It was a photo message from Vince. Mali was seated on his lap on the Spring Mills football field's fifty-yard line. Below it, the text read:

I always wanted to do that!

I immediately cringed and shoved the phone back into my bag. It meant only one thing. Our school had a long-standing rumor that any guy who got a girl to give it up on the football field would have his name listed in some hidden book in the library. I had never seen such evidence, but students talked about the "Fifty-Yard Line Club" like the members were rock stars.

I clenched my eyes shut, trying to block the vision of my brother and his girlfriend. If she was willing to get naked in broad daylight during a school day, then was it really too hard to believe that she'd also cheat on my brother? In his own house? Clearly, she was lacking in the modest morality department (not that my brother was innocent).

My mind drifted to the way Alex had gazed at her. He and Mali had hardly spoken a word since their controversial late-night conversation. While this should have made me feel better, for some reason it only made me more suspicious. Every time I envisioned his eyes twinkling at her, my stomach turned. He hadn't looked at me that way all week. Not that I gave him much of an opportunity. Between the film festival and ballet, I was hardly home. Part of me wondered if he even noticed, while the other part was grateful that I didn't have to pretend that everything was okay.

Finally, the bell rang. I sprang from my stool and headed to the door. The hallway was crowded as usual, and I pushed my way through the masses until I spied Evan standing at Emily's locker. They were in the middle of a conversation, joking casually. I tightly gripped my purse.

"Hey, guys!" I greeted in my sweetest voice as I marched over.

Emily straightened her shoulders. "Um, hey. I was just about to head down to Madison's."

"Good, me too." I looked at Evan. "Didn't realize you were helping with the festival."

"Oh, I'm not." He coughed slightly. "I mean, I'm going. But I'm just not helping. Or whatever."

I cocked my head, suspicious.

"Um, uh, I better go." Evan ran off before I could even say "bye."

"All right, let's go," Emily said nonchalantly as if nothing had happened.

"You wanna tell me what that was about?" I asked.

"He wanted to know what time the festival started. So I told him. Is that a crime?"

I snorted and shook my head. I didn't know who I could believe anymore.

I divided the golden programs into four stacks, one for each of the volunteers, and mentally practiced my introduction for Bobby. He plugged me as the "festival manager" in the program—an official title I didn't ask for or deserve, but which now required me to give a public speech before the show.

"Hey, manager, where do we hang your friend's pictures?" asked Jay Mackey as he held up two of Alex's mounted shots of the Puerto Rican rain forest.

He really was a talented photographer. The glistening water droplets he captured on the emerald leaves were so crisp you could almost touch them. It was hard to believe that I had actually wandered through something so beautiful, and that the same camera was used to snap hidden-camera pictures of me (I tried to block that out).

"We're hanging them in the lobby," I answered.

Jay grabbed Alex's prints and headed out of the auditorium doors.

"Hey, manager, where are we putting these reserved signs?" Lilly asked, holding up a handful of sheets.

"Stop calling me that." I cringed.

"Okay, *la presidenta,* where do these go?"

"Very funny," I said. "In the first row. They're for Bobby's family."

"Should I draw a little skull and crossbones on the one for his dad?"

"Don't start. I don't want her to hear you." I glanced to where Emily was currently hanging posters of the Irish countryside. She hadn't mentioned Bobby's dad since the preparations began, and I was hoping to keep it that way.

I followed Lilly to the first row and held down the black cushioned seat as she taped a "Reserved" sign to the back.

"So is Kyle still coming tonight?" I asked with a crooked grin.

"Yup. He's coming with Vince . . . and Alex. Maybe we could all hang out after?" Lilly peered at me curiously as she pressed a sign against a chair, smoothing out the wrinkles.

Even though Lilly was my cousin, I knew she had known Alex for a lot longer than she'd known me. If he and I were fighting, I couldn't be certain she'd take my side.

"Lil, I don't know what's going on with Alex."

I pushed another seat down.

"Mali leaves in a few days. Maybe things'll go back to normal after that."

"Why? Because my competition's gone?"

"I don't think it's like that. Besides, you never even called him your boyfriend."

"So? Do I really need to spell out that it's not cool to hook up with my brother's girlfriend? Kinda thought that was implied."

"He said he didn't, and *you said* you believed him. So why are you still giving him crap?"

"Who says that I am?"

Ever since Alex and I first kissed, Lilly had been tight-lipped with information about him. I didn't know if she was trying to divide her loyalties, or if she truly didn't want us together. But if Alex was really her friend, she should be able to pry the truth out of him. I would do it for her if she asked.

Before she could respond, Bobby called from center stage.

"Mariana, where's my mike? Do you know where my mike is?" He was pacing the stage, frantically.

I looked around and spied a microphone in the orchestra pit. I trotted down to grab it, but its cord was tangled in a web of thick black wires.

"There's one down here," I said, tugging at the cords.

Bobby hopped into the pit to assist with the knotted mess.

"There's just so much to do. I don't know how I'm gonna get it all done." He aggressively yanked the plugged cords from their sockets. "My opening remarks are all wrong. Jay hasn't finished hanging the pictures. In the program, I forgot to thank Dean Pruitt. This mike isn't where it's supposed to be. My parents haven't called me back . . ."

"Bobby, it's gonna be fine."

"What if we can't get the movie to work? Or what if no one claps at the end? What if they all hate it?"

"Bobby, it's gonna be fine," I repeated, slower this time.

He finished untangling the cords, freed the mike, and plopped onto the dusty wood floor.

"This is sooo freaky," he said, hanging his head.

I dropped beside him, pulling my knees to my chest.

"You know, I get so nervous before every ballet performance that I almost pee in my tights. I'm not kidding. It's a verified state of emergency."

"Amber alert?"

"No, red." I chuckled.

"Wait, wouldn't it be yellow?" He laughed.

Lights flickered on the projection screen above. The opening of his film began to play, the audio blaring from the speakers, confirming all technical tests.

"You did that." I smiled with pride.

"Is it too late to take it back?" He ran his chewed nails through his dirty-blond hair.

"A bit. Yes."

"Promise me that this won't suck."

"Okay, I promise."

He sighed. "I believe you."

Chapter 22

The auditorium was bursting with the sounds of muffled conversations. Students scurried into their well-worn seats alongside parents and teachers. I walked up the carpeted aisle with a fresh stack of programs. Bobby was currently hiding backstage, breathing into a paper bag. His mom was at his side, and I was guessing he didn't want an audience for his freak out. Plus, it was very possible that his mother knew who I was and knew that I was at Cornell for the infamous confrontation that ruined her marriage. I thought it safer to keep my distance.

"So, how we doing?" I asked Madison as I added to her wad of programs.

"Evan's here."

"Well, thank God. The show can begin now."

"Shut up," she said, swatting at me. "He made sure to come through my door so I could give him his program."

"Ah, true love."

She sneered. "I asked what he was doing after the show. We might get together."

"Was he with his friends?" The boy had yet to acknowledge his "friendship" with her to anyone aside from us.

"Well, yeah. I mean, sort of. They were in the lobby."

"Uh-huh." I nodded.

I walked over to Emily's door and handed her more programs.

"So did Evan say 'hi' to you too?" I quipped.

"Very funny."

"I wasn't kidding."

She rolled her eyes with boredom. "It's not what you think."

"Well, how would I know what to think if you don't tell me?"

Just then, Emily's mom appeared in the lobby. Her long graying hair was tied in a tight bun and her white peasant blouse was buttoned all the way to the top. She wore a long blue skirt with Birkenstocks and pale blue socks. How the woman attracted so many men, I couldn't imagine.

"Oh, look. It's my daughter," her mother said as she stopped in front of us. "I'd almost forgotten what you look like." Her lip curled up.

Emily looked away, shaking her head in irritation. "Ah, Mom, I thought you forgot about me long ago."

Her mother sighed loudly. "Glad you're so happy to see me."

"Surprised is more like it."

"You didn't think I'd show? Why, is your father here?"

"No, he's working," Emily mumbled.

"Figures."

Mrs. Montgomery snatched a program from her daughter's hand. "Nice to see you, Mariana."

"Uh-huh." I nodded as she walked away.

"Sometimes I hate her so much I can taste it," Emily hissed.

"Don't say that. She's your mother."

"Don't remind me."

Emily turned back to the guests waiting for their programs and I stepped away. This obviously wasn't the best time to discuss her feelings.

I trotted over to Lilly.

"Was that Emily's mom I just saw walk in?" she asked as she snatched a stack of programs from my hand.

"Yup."

"Does she know that Bobby's parents are seated right backstage?"

"Probably. The woman's a college professor. She's not an idiot."

"Maybe she came here to see him."

"At this point, I wouldn't put it past her."

My family suddenly walked through the large glass doors to the school's lobby, pulling my attention. My parents were dressed as if they were headed to church, my dad in a dark gray suit and my mom in an ivory dress with pearls. Alex and Kyle were behind them with Vince and Mali bringing up the rear. Mali's black dress was so short that I was certain people would consider it a shirt with some fringe on the bottom. Male eyes were flickering all around her.

"Figures," I mumbled.

Lilly twisted her neck and eyeballed Mali. "Oh."

"Well, hey, your boyfriend's here." I gestured toward Kyle.

"Yours too."

Alex gazed through the crowd and met my eyes. He smiled, his dimples lifting the tiny hairs on my arms. I was happy to see him. From this distance, it was like nothing had happened.

My parents popped through the arched doorway to the auditorium.

"Our two favorite girls," my mother cooed.

She held out her French manicured hand and clutched a program.

"So, how long is this thing?" my dad asked, glancing at his PDA.

"Ninety minutes. So get comfortable," I answered.

"Aw, Mariana, you're the festival manager!" my mom cheered as she scanned the program. "That's very official!"

My father grunted. "It'll look good on a transcript."

"You're already thinking about her admission forms?" Vince asked, sounding annoyed. He was tightly clasping Mali's hand. Her stormy gray eyes didn't look my way, but they clearly noticed the nearby stares. Strangers couldn't stop gawking at her beauty.

"Actually, I don't have to remind Mariana about what's important. Not like you," my father pointed out.

"I know. I'm such a disappointment, aren't I?" Vince asked, his lips tight.

"All right, come on. We're in a public place," I groaned.

"*Hola,* Mariana," Alex greeted.

"Hey." Kyle smiled at Lilly.

For the first time since we'd met, I actually saw Lilly blush.

I handed Alex a program and his finger brushed the back of my hand. He didn't pull away.

"Your pictures look great. Don't they?" I congratulated Alex before turning to my parents.

"I know!" my mother cheered.

"Yeah, nice." My dad sighed.

I didn't know what else to say to him, and thankfully I didn't have to. The glowing amber lights in the auditorium flickered, signaling the start of the show.

"I gotta go."

I smiled at everyone and darted up the aisle.

When I found Bobby backstage, he was breathing in quick puffs. A couple of his friends were at his side, but his parents were gone.

"You ready?" I asked as I strolled over.

His friend Jay shot me a panicked look. Clearly, Bobby wasn't okay.

"I don't know why I'm doing this. Why am I doing this?" Bobby pleaded.

"Everything is going to be okay. Just keep repeating that."

"I can't. Because it's not. How can it be?" His eyes were wild and his shoulders were choking his neck.

"Just two more hours and it'll all be over," I reasoned.

"Two hours!" He clutched his stomach.

"Bobby, breathe."

"I'm spazzing aren't I? I know it. I'm spazzing." He rubbed his abdomen.

"A little, yes. But that's okay. You're the star. A little diva behavior is expected."

"I am *not* a diva!" he hissed, smiling for the first time all evening.

Just then I heard Dean Pruitt take the stage. I was on right after him, so I grinned at Bobby and rushed toward the edge of the hunter-green curtain. The dean quickly thanked everyone for their donations, including Bobby's parents, and gestured to me.

"Ladies and gentlemen, our festival manager, Mariana Ruíz."

He held out his arm toward me. I took a deep breath and walked onto the scuffed wooden stage. The spotlights from the balcony blinded me with a star of white. I gripped the metal mike stand as I looked into the abyss. I couldn't see a single face. I tried to pretend that they couldn't see me either, but my heart thumped in my throat. If all I had to do was introduce Bobby and I was this nervous, then I couldn't imagine how he felt.

I pulled a white note card from the pocket of my tailored black slacks.

"Hello, everyone. Thank you for coming," I said. A few

people applauded. "We're here tonight not just to celebrate the amazing film you're about to see, but also to inspire more students to get involved in the arts. Thank you all for giving us a place to express our talents."

Everyone clapped politely. I heard Madison "Whoo hoo!" in the background.

"Now, I'm lucky enough to have already seen the film you're about to enjoy. I know how brilliant it is, and I am *certain* that everyone will love it as much as I do. It was put together by one of our school's most gifted students. Remember his name because this won't be the last time he walks onto a stage to promote one of his films. Ladies and gentlemen . . . Bobby McNabb."

Bobby strutted out and hugged me politely. In that brief moment, I couldn't have been more proud than if I had made the movie myself. My body tingled with excitement and when he let go and walked to the mike, I saw a confident look in his eyes. It was as if his brief panic attack had never happened.

I hovered behind the heavy curtain as he addressed the audience.

"Thank you, Mariana, for that undeserving introduction. And hello, everyone."

The crowd ripped into applause and Bobby stepped back, cleverly looking behind him.

"Okay, just making sure Oprah wasn't standing behind me," he joked as the audience cheered louder. "You get a car! You get a car!"

He pointed into the seats and everyone laughed until he put up his hands to quiet them down.

"No, really. Thank you all for coming to see my little flick. You know, movies are very subjective. And when I started making this film, I never thought anyone would see it. I don't know whether you're gonna like it . . . *or* hate it for that matter"—[the crowd giggled]—"but I know for me it was worth it to just tell the story of these two teens. Now, I don't want to spoil it for you, but Ireland's got some religious troubles [the crowd chuckled at the understatement]. And I hope that when you leave here tonight, the film's got you all talking. If that happens, then I've done my job."

He nodded to the audience, and everyone applauded once more. I could hear Madison whistling in the back.

"Please enjoy, *God Save Ireland!*"

I clapped as Bobby walked off stage and the lights in the auditorium dimmed.

"You were awesome," I whispered, grabbing his arm.

"I think I'm gonna throw up."

"Okay. Bathroom's over there." I pointed.

He tore off for the hall as I watched the opening titles hit the screen.

Chapter 23

I sat backstage by Bobby's side during the entire film. He didn't look at the screen once. His eyes were focused on the crowd, his leg jittering uncontrollably as he tried to read their expressions. But when the lights went up, it was to a standing ovation.

"I told you that you were brilliant," I stated as the stage lights rose.

The crowd continued hooting and stomping on the floor.

"Do you hear that?" I asked.

Bobby exhaled, his eyes closed.

"You're a hit," I reiterated.

He peered at me. "Thank you."

Then, unexpectedly, he grabbed my shoulders and hugged me tight. His lanky body squished mine as I rested my head on his chest. For a moment, it reminded me of my birthday party, dancing in his arms. I closed my eyes, inhaling the soapy smell of his skin. His embrace felt nice.

"Thank you," he whispered again, his breath warming my ear.

A shiver sped down my spine.

"Mariana! Mariana! It was great!" Madison squealed as she darted backstage, Emily and Lilly right behind her.

Bobby released his grip and I stepped back, my face hot. Emily's eyes darted between us.

"Bobby, they loved it. Absolutely loved it!" Madison bounced on her toes.

"You should hear people talking," Lilly added. "They're all saying it's as good as any Michael Moore documentary ever made."

"God, I still can't believe it," he muttered.

"How cool are you?" Madison punched his arm.

"Seriously, it was even better the second time around," Emily added.

Bobby smiled at her, but stopped when his parents suddenly pulled back the stage curtain. They walked right behind her.

Emily immediately caught the change in his expression and spun around. I held my breath. I knew it was the first time she'd seen his father since Cornell. I glanced at Madison, but by now everyone was panickly staring at his parents.

"Bobby, we're so proud of you." His mom brushed past Emily completely oblivious.

Bobby's dad, however, was frozen. He smiled awkwardly, saying nothing, but apparently that was enough to catch his wife's attention. Her eyes immediately darted toward Emily. In that silent moment, she knew. Emily was his mistress's daughter.

"Are these your friends?" she asked softly, her voice shaking.

"Yeah," Bobby murmured, all the elation lost in his voice.

"Nice to meet you," she said hollowly.

The tension was so strong I could hardly breathe. "Why don't we meet you out front? Maybe we can all hit up Rosie's Diner to celebrate?"

"Yeah, I'd like that," Bobby answered, shuffling his feet.

I grabbed Emily's arm and steered her away. I could hear

Madison and Lilly following our lead. I flung back the curtain and suddenly stopped short. I nearly collided with Emily's mother.

"Omigod," I blurted. "I mean, sorry."

"Um, I wanted to see you before I left," Mrs. Montgomery explained calmly. "To say 'bye.' "

"Okay, bye," Emily said in a quick burst.

Her mom's eyes tightened. "The film was good. I enjoyed it."

Emily grunted with annoyance and, for a moment, I thought that was the end of the conversation. I thought her mother was going to leave peacefully. But she knew Bobby's father was nearby, and I could tell she was determined that he notice her. And she got her wish.

Mr. McNabb stepped out from behind the curtain, his wife and son at his side. Mrs. Montgomery's gaze instantly shot to her former lover, and even I could see the longing in her face.

"Jim," she greeted.

Bobby's dad quickly turned to his wife, only it was too late. Anger was exploding from her face.

"I can't believe this," she hissed, dropping her son's hand and rushing backstage.

"Vivian!" he called, but she disappeared and he didn't chase after her. Instead he turned back toward Mrs. Montgomery. "I should go. It was . . . good . . . seeing you."

"You too." She nodded with a desperate smile.

They stared at each other for another moment, and then Mr. McNabb disappeared behind the curtain. Bobby was left standing beside us to watch Emily's mom, his father's mistress, stroll away. She might as well have ripped his soul out and carried it with her, because I could see his chest deflate at the sight of her. He no longer looked like the confident filmmaker. He looked like a little kid.

Chapter 24

We sat huddled in red vinyl booths at Rosie's Diner. Half the school was there, enjoying the post film–festival wrap party—we filled nearly every chrome table. It was the start of Thanksgiving break, which was enough cause for most students to celebrate.

I scanned the laminated eight-page menu loaded with chicken fingers, mozzarella sticks, pizza fries, and plenty of things laced with bacon.

"They don't offer low-fat salad dressing," Madison noted.

"It's Thanksgiving. Who cares? Eat up!" I suggested happily.

"I'm sure Madam Colbert would love to have a bunch of plus-size ballerinas in her performance."

"Hey, when is that dance of yours?" Bobby asked.

He was seated across from me, alongside Lilly and Kyle. Madison, Emily, Alex, and I were shoved on one side of the booth, and I could see my brother across the diner with Mali and a pack of his high-school buds.

"Right before Christmas," I noted.

"Mariana's the star," Lilly cheered, fluttering her eyelashes.

I looked at Emily, who quickly stared down at her menu.

"We all have good roles," I said.

"Speak for yourself," Madison whined. "I'm Puss 'n Boots."

"Puss 'n Boots? What does that have to do with Sleeping Beauty?" Bobby asked, one eyebrow pushed high.

"Hey, it's a good part. She has a solo," I defended.

"I have to wear a furry cat head and dress like a guy," Madison whined.

"So? My part is usually danced by a guy," Emily pointed out, grabbing a sip of water. "Mariana's got the good role."

"She plays a princess." Lilly smiled at me. "How fitting."

I grabbed a sugar packet and tossed it at her.

"Mariana *is* a princess," Alex purred, rubbing my thigh under the table.

"Mariana?" Bobby choked. "She's the last person I would call a princess. And I don't mean that in a bad way."

"No, I know. Thank you." I smiled at the backwards compliment.

Alex squeezed my knee firmer. I squirmed to brush him off but he didn't get the hint. Thankfully, the waitress arrived.

"So I'm surprised Vince isn't out getting wasted right now," Madison said after we all placed our orders.

"He did point out that the day before Thanksgiving is 'the biggest drinking night of the year,' " I groaned. "But he's not at Cornell anymore. His access to beer is limited."

"He should come back to Puerto Rico," Lilly suggested.

"Please, your family runs on alcohol," I teased. "I don't think they're aware of other liquids."

"This is true." Lilly nodded.

"You guys just take things too seriously here," Alex added.

I cocked my head. "What, 'cause we're not a bunch of lushes?"

"Tsst." Alex shrugged. "Alcohol is bad. Cigarettes are bad. Sex is bad . . ."

"I don't think anyone's saying sex is bad," Kyle commented with a smug grin, nudging Lilly. "Let's not get crazy."

"No, but you think too much." Alex released his grip on my leg.

It was starting to sound as if his opinions were not a general view on society, but more of a personal attack on me. My shoulder blades clamped together at the implied insult.

"Well, maybe there's something to be said for taking things slow and considering the consequences," I huffed.

The table grew quiet, and I could see everyone stealthily peering at each other.

"I'm just saying, not everything has to be a big deal." Alex gulped a sip of water.

I opened my mouth to say something, but Lilly cut me off.

"I wish I thought about things more before I acted. Heck, I wish I thought first before opening my mouth." She laughed awkwardly.

I tried to laugh with her, but I was still feeling offended.

"Hey, I'm not one to talk. You should've seen me freaking out backstage before the show," Bobby added, changing the topic. "I threw up right after my speech."

"No, you didn't!" Madison yelped.

He smiled with pride. "Yes, I did. Mariana saw me run off."

"But, I wasn't gonna sell you out." I chuckled.

"It's not like you witnessed the chunks."

"Though I would've held your hair back if you asked me to."

"Hey, my hair's not that long!"

"Not for a girl," I teased.

He grabbed the sugar packet I'd thrown at Lilly and chucked it back at me. I swatted it, laughing, and when I placed my hand back on the table, I noticed everyone staring at us with overt suspicion.

"What?" I asked.

Lilly quickly shook her head. "Nothing," she answered, though her tone implied more—as if she thought Bobby and I were flirting.

Clearly Alex shared her view, because he quickly stretched his arm around my shoulder. It was heavy and stifling, but I smiled politely until the waitress popped over with an over-flowing tray of food. I took the opportunity to loosen Alex's hold on me. Madison grabbed her dry salad.

"Mmm, looks good, Mad. Plain iceberg lettuce." I grimaced as I ate my potato skins.

"Please, if I ate what you're eating, I'd be five hundred pounds by tomorrow." She pushed a leaf around her plate.

Her eyes kept moving toward the diner door. I knew she was waiting for Evan. She had invited him to come with us, but he said he already had plans with "his boys." Before he took off, he offered the slight hope that he might "stop by." I knew she was clinging to that tiny possibility, and I hated him for making her so needy.

"So, Em, you going back to the city tonight?" I asked as she chomped on her chili dog.

"Mmm hmm," she gurgled.

"You need me to drop you off?" Madison asked.

"No, I have a ride."

"Just you and your driver?" I asked.

She looked down at her food saying nothing.

"So what are you doing for Thanksgiving?" Madison asked her, concern in her voice. "You know you can come to my house."

"We don't want you eating turkey sandwiches," I added.

"No, it's cool. My dad made reservations at some Chinese place. We're having an anti-Thanksgiving."

"An anti-family moment with your dad, seems fitting," Madison snipped.

"Well, it's better than dinner with my mom and one of her skank boyfriends."

Bobby coughed on his burger, nearly spitting the ground beef. I glared at Emily.

"What?" she mouthed.

"I know you didn't mean his dad," I said sternly.

"No, it's okay." Bobby nodded. "Let's not go there. I've had enough tonight."

Before I could respond, a wad of wet paper towel flew toward our table and plopped with a thud directly on Alex's ham sandwich.

"Bombs away!" Vince cheered from across the room, laughing hysterically.

"Oh, no he didn't." I grabbed the soaked wad of paper and chucked it back at his table, nearly smacking Mali in the face (which I secretly would have loved).

"Please. You're battling with a future major leaguer. You can't out-throw me!" Vince grabbed his leftover hamburger, wadded it in his hands and launched it, accidentally smacking one of the cheerleaders in a nearby booth.

That's all it took. The cheerleader's date snatched a roll from his plate, dipped it in his water glass and chucked it at Vince. A full-fledged food fight was breaking out. Our waitress ran out from the back, screeching, but not before Alex got hit with a piece of bread doused in ketchup. I burst into giggles. Clearly, he didn't find the red glob sliding down his face nearly as funny as I did. He grabbed a tomato from my sandwich to toss back, but Vince nailed him again with a wad of lunchmeat and salad dressing.

I slid down the vinyl seat, slumping low as I covered my

face with my hands, cracking up. Bobby also ducked, hoping to fly below the radar, as Lilly and Kyle mounted an attack. They tossed everything from my sour-cream-covered potato skins to chili-covered buns. When the owner came out from the back, turned off the diner lights and hollered that he was calling the police, the fight ended. I managed to escape unscathed, but Alex was covered with stains.

My brother didn't have a single spot.

Chapter 25

I was still on the first page of his essay. It was almost noon, and I had spent nearly an hour editing the introduction to Vince's grand Shakespearean thesis while the rest of the family staged the house for the "most perfect Thanksgiving meal ever"—or so my mother hoped. One thing was for sure, the meal would be a lot better than this paper.

How could he be eighteen years old and attend an Ivy League school, yet still not know how to punctuate a sentence? Not to mention his constant use of slang words and clichés— he actually started his paper with the phrase, "In life as in literature . . ." It was a practice sentence taught to all Spring Mills' eighth graders learning to write their first five-paragraph essays. Students who still used that phrase in high school are chastised, and he was trying to pass it off at the collegiate level.

After much research, I managed to find a classic Bush misquote to launch his politically charged paper. It was a trick I'd perfected last year. Any paper I started with a quote was guaranteed to get an *"Excellent Intro!"* scribble from my teacher, and the more creative the quote, the more enthusiastic the note. I once launched a paper on anorexia in America with a line from an MTV *Real Worlder*. My teacher ate it up. So I put my skills to use for Vince:

"If we don't succeed, we run the risk of failure," George W. Bush, Jr.
A thirst to succeed at all costs has led many great men to commit
heinous acts. Shakespeare knew it in the 1600s and America knows it
today. . . .

It wasn't my best writing, but given that I hadn't spent a
single minute in Vince's class nor had I spent any real time an-
alyzing the famous play by one of the world's greatest writers,
I thought it wasn't half-bad. But if I continued at the pace of
one page per hour, I wouldn't be making it to dinner at four
o'clock.

Vince popped his head through the bedroom doorway.

"Awesome, isn't it?" he said and flung himself onto his bed.

I swiveled in the desk chair, my forehead tight with wrinkles.

"Did you ever learn the difference between a sentence
fragment and an actual sentence?" I shook my red hair, bewildered.

"What? Is there something wrong with it?"

"Vince, you go from having six-word sentences with no
verbs to having a sixty-word sentence with no commas!"

"Is that bad?" His eyes were blank.

"Yes! Yes, it's bad. How did you graduate from high school?"

"With honors, actually."

"You know, that kinda scares me."

I turned my face back to the laptop. "I've rewritten the entire first page."

He darted over and scanned the screen. "You know, I didn't
say you had to rewrite it. I think my version is pretty good."

"Vince, this would fail my high school English class. Hell, I
don't think it would fly in middle school."

"Oh, it's not *that* bad," he huffed as he flopped onto his bed
and checked his phone messages.

I turned my eyes to the screen and read:

"Macbeth is an evil character. Bush is an evil guy. They're alike in that way. Macbeth kills the king Bush starts wars but both are bad because both result in death and horrible consequences for innocent people."

"In case you couldn't tell," I added, "there was no punctuation in that entire last sentence."

"Okay, so that wasn't the best paragraph," Vince muttered.

"It sounds like a retarded person wrote it."

"Well, that's why I'm going to be a physical therapist. I'd rather work on sports injuries than diagram sentences."

Then he glanced at his phone and erupted in laughter.

"My frat buddy in Florida went to the zoo this week with his sister and her kid, and listen to what he wrote. *'I love the zoo. Nephew looks at animals, I look at bombs!'* "

Vince cracked up as he spat out the words. "That guy is freakin' hysterical!" He wiped at the tears in his eyes.

"Vince, I realize that you're probably one of the most popular kids in the history of Cornell, but you're also about to have one of their shortest academic careers if you don't fix this essay."

He sat in his antique wood bed and peered at me.

"Loosen up, woman! It's Thanksgiving! Let's go gorge on food and forget this crap."

"Oh, trust me, I will. Once Uncle Diego gets in the same room as our lovely *tía* Teresa, it's safe to say your collegiate career might not be the only thing killed."

"I can't wait!"

"I think you'll be singing a different tune when Mali sees your family turn into a WWE Smackdown."

"Love it!"

I shook my head. The sad thing was, if anyone could find laughter in the chaos that was our extended family, it was Vince.

Chapter 26

I anxiously popped a cube of sharp cheddar into my mouth and bit a cracker. Then I grabbed another and another. Watching my family and friends attempt to make small talk (or not) was enough to drive the hors d'oeuvres through my lips as fast as my hands could shove them. And the worst had yet to happen. Teresa had yet to arrive.

My leg shook nervously. I didn't know how long I'd been bopping it (and our love seat), but finally Alex reached over and grabbed my knee. I stopped and felt a sudden stillness I hadn't realized I was missing.

"So Mali, do you miss home?" asked my aunt Joan as she chewed on a cracker stacked with crab dip.

"Sometimes. It's easier when I'm at school 'cause I'm so busy. But days like today . . ." She ran her hand through her spiky black hair and glanced around the bustling living room. "It's harder."

My aunt nodded knowingly.

"Are you Catholic?" My uncle Diego blurted as he leaned back on our sofa.

"Uncle Diego!" I scolded, glaring at him and Vince.

My brother simply laughed. Mali wasn't even my friend,

and I still felt more of an urge to defend her than my brother did.

"No, it's okay." Mali looked at me. "My family's Buddhist."

"Oh, so you pray to, what, a golden statue?" My uncle chomped into a carrot stick.

"And you pray to, what, a wooden cross?" She smiled smugly.

"I wouldn't say it's the same."

"Of course not," she replied curtly.

"I always found other religions fascinating." Alex sat beside me (though his eyes were not pointing in my direction).

"Me too," Mali replied.

"Well, apparently so do the Ruízes," my uncle Diego said as he shot my brother a stern look.

It was interesting that my father and both his brothers had married women who were not Latina, who could not speak Spanish, and whose families were not overly enthusiastic about their relationships—yet they all thought marrying outside of our religion was a cardinal sin. I could come home with an ax-murderer on my arm, but if he were Catholic, no one would object (well, at least not until the ax-murderer thing came out).

"I'm making my confirmation this spring," my cousin Claire said in a small voice.

My twelve-year-old cousin was almost as frail as her mother. Her bony arms and knobby knees looked as though she hardly ate a morsel, which, given my aunt Stacey's anorexic example, I could almost understand. But that wasn't the worst part of her sickly appearance. Her hair was so limp and blond, it was as if she were wearing a bad white wig; and her skin was so fair I could count the blue veins pumping through her sunken cheeks. She was a dead ringer for her mother, my aunt Stacey, who at forty probably weighed under one hundred pounds. They were both hard to look at, and if I ever needed a visual as to where Madison was headed if she didn't start consuming calories, they were it.

"That's in April, right? When my David made his confirmation, he chose his father's name." My aunt Joan smiled lovingly at her son, who rolled his eyes.

The accomplished saxophone player, whom my aunt had praised for fifteen years straight, now seemed to be moving down a different path. Since school had started in September, he had dyed his hair jet-black and had taken to wearing thrift store T shirts and black nail polish. I was secretly hoping he would turn into some indie rocker who would quit school to perform at underground clubs, all the while driving my aunt and uncle crazy.

"Like I had a choice," David muttered.

"What?" his mother squeaked.

"In making my confirmation. Like I had a choice," he grunted.

"Of course you had a choice." My aunt laughed awkwardly. "Confirmation is a rite of passage."

"No, it's a mandatory exercise enforced by parents who toss their kids into Sunday school against their will."

The room grew quiet.

"So," I interrupted, rising to my feet. "I'm gonna go see if Mom needs help in the kitchen."

"Me too," Lilly offered, running after me.

The kitchen, where my mother and a staff of helpers were busy tending to six gas burners and two wall ovens, was hotter than most tropical countries. Even with the hood fan blowing, the air was so thick and humid it reminded me of Utuado.

"Man, your family's nuts," Lilly gasped.

"What, you just caught that?" I slid past a kitchen helper carrying a refreshed tray of cheese and crackers.

"Yeah, but your uncle goes after everyone. Poor Mali."

"Oh, that girl gets no sympathy from me. Besides, he likes *you*."

"Well, what's not to like?" Lilly waved at her curvaceous figure.

I chuckled.

My mother was at the kitchen table arranging a mass of salads on tiny crystal plates. The way she artfully spaced the sliced green apples and candied walnuts made the first course look like a study in still life.

"Oh, thank God you girls are here." She sighed, rushing toward us and clutching our arms. "I need six walnuts on each salad. Space them out evenly over the lettuce. And please leave two without. Mali's allergic and you know your aunt Stacey won't eat anything with calories."

My mother raced off toward the wine fridge.

"You'd think you guys were hosting the president," Lilly muttered as she carefully counted the walnuts.

"You kidding? She was like this when she had to make cupcakes for my school bake sales. She thinks people are always judging her."

"Well, I can see why," Lilly whispered. "Your aunts always are."

Just then, the doorbell rang and a high-pitched cry squeaked through the solid front door. My head snapped toward Lilly's.

"Sounds like Teresa and Manny are here," I said.

"And you thought turkey was the main course." She smirked.

Around four o'clock we all finally sat down in the dining room, minus the hyperactive two-year-old, Manny, who was sprinting laps around my family home screeching like a wild monkey. My head was pounding.

Vince nudged my side. "Does this remind you of Puerto Rico, or what?"

His eyes shot toward Manny, who was swinging two drumsticks over his head in a rare break from pounding on my parents' furniture. How a grown adult could let her child bang someone else's possessions with wooden sticks was beyond me.

"It's like we're right back at the *Quinceañera*," I mumbled as I watched Manny scream. "Think we should call him a demon again like we did at the church?"

"What about my *Quinceañera*?" Lilly asked from across the table.

I gestured to Manny with my eyes.

"Oh," she muttered.

"Manny, *mijo*, please sit down. *Por favor*," Teresa begged, grabbing for his arm as he darted past. She missed.

I didn't know if it was because Manny wasn't Carlos's biological son, or because Carlos was the king of patience, but he barely flinched as the two-year-old shot past.

"Sorry for all the commotion," Teresa apologized, glancing around the table at the annoyed faces. "He can get jumpy in new surroundings."

"Well, that happens when they're not taught manners," my aunt Joan hissed under her breath.

My uncle Diego grunted, briefly catching Carlos's eye. The look exchanged wasn't exactly holiday-friendly.

"So, Carlos, how's work?" my mother asked politely.

Clearly she was hoping to ease the tension.

"Been getting a lot of overtime, which is good." He gestured toward Teresa. "Wedding money."

"Oh, how are the plans going?" asked my aunt Stacey as she picked the apple slices from her salad.

My mom gawked as her guest nibbled on a plate of plain lettuce beside her frail twelve-year-old daughter, who mimicked her mother's every move.

"*Bueno.* We found a location," Teresa answered, taking a sip of water from her crystal glass.

"What church are you having it at?" Aunt Joan smiled maliciously as she bit into a walnut.

"Uh, we're not having a church service. We're getting married at the hotel," Teresa mumbled.

My uncle Diego coughed indiscreetly and dropped his dinner roll. "There's a surprise."

"I haven't exactly been here long enough to join a church . . ."

"Don't you go to mass?" My uncle stared at Carlos.

"Not since I was ten."

"You can still have a priest perform the service," my aunt Joan told her.

Teresa looked at Carlos. "We're more comfortable with a justice of the peace."

"Hey, I guess you're right. This way, if you end it, you won't have to worry about getting an annulment. The church won't even recognize the marriage." My uncle chuckled darkly.

"Dad!" I glared at my father. I was growing increasingly more embarrassed by my family, and it bothered me that my dad took no responsibility for his brother's actions.

"Why don't we all enjoy our meal." My father sat diplomatically in his seat at the head of the table.

"Would anyone like some more salad?" My mom rose from her cherry wood chair and gestured to one of the helpers from the kitchen. A forty-something brunette immediately rushed in and began removing the empty salad plates.

"So where will the wedding be held?" my aunt Joan asked, continuing her line of questioning.

"At a hotel in the city," Teresa answered.

"Really! Where? I've done a lot of modeling gigs downtown," said my cousin Jackie.

As far as I knew, in Jackie's thirteen years on this planet, she had done one real "modeling gig" and it was for a JCPenney ad in the local paper (not exactly *Teen People*).

I smiled at my cousin. "It's near City Hall."

"How do *you* know?" My aunt raised a dramatically plucked eyebrow in suspicion.

Lilly and I looked toward my father. Alex grabbed my hand under the table. It was as if we all knew the truth was about to erupt.

My dad coughed slightly. "I think we're ready for the main course, right?" His change in subject was not exactly subtle, but my mom quickly followed his lead.

She waved to one of the kitchen helpers and trays of food began to appear. The table was filled with sweet potato puff, corn, string beans, stuffing with sausage, fresh cranberry sauce, pumpkin bread, butternut squash soup and, of course, a massive golden turkey. The smell of Thanksgiving was enough to trigger every memory I ever had of the holiday—most of which included my grandparents sitting across from me. Carlos and Teresa now sat in their chairs.

"Everything looks lovely," my aunt Joan said.

"Yes, really, it does," my aunt Stacey added (as if she were going to eat it).

My father rose and lifted the electric carving knife. It was almost comical to see my father cutting meat. The man didn't make his own sandwiches, yet he was going to pretend to be the big chef of the household.

About thirty minutes later, after all of our plates were clean and the leftover food was cleared, I thought I could write the holiday off as a success. Aside from a few rude comments, my family behaved itself (a miraculous feat). Even little Manny sat down and ate a slice of turkey, which thankfully made him sleepy. He was currently napping on the living room sofa.

My aunt Joan, however, got a nasty second wind.

"So, Mali, how was your first Thanksgiving?" she asked.

"Wonderful, thank you."

"Must be a far cry from what you eat in the third world."

Mali sighed, her face twisted.

"Actually, Mali's family's quite wealthy," Vince defended.

"Vince," his girlfriend snapped.

"What? It's true."

"I know. But it shouldn't matter," Mali replied, her eyes narrowed as she glared at my brother.

"I didn't say you were poor," my aunt stated. "I'm sure you live quite well . . . over there."

Mali bit her lip so hard I thought her teeth might poke through.

"Hey, well, you all know my family's poor," Lilly stated. "They live right down the street from where all the Ruízes grew up."

Lilly smiled wide at my aunt.

"Yeah, I think you can say our parents' houses don't look like this place," Alex added.

"Well, I'd like to see *your* parents' place," Vince said as he leaned in and pecked Mali briefly on the lips.

I could almost feel my entire family cringe simultaneously. The Ruízes were not big on public displays of affection, and Uncle Roberto quickly stood from the table.

"Claire, why don't you help your aunt Irina with dessert?"

It looked as though he thought my cousin witnessing a spontaneous romantic gesture might corrupt her in some way. (It also said a lot about his marriage to my sickly looking aunt.)

"So, Teresa," my aunt Joan interjected, moving the topic back to her favorite target. "Did you get your dress yet?"

Teresa looked hesitantly at Carlos. "Yes, actually, I did."

"She won't tell me anything about it. She's superstitious like that. But the girls say it's *perfecto.*"

As soon as the sentence passed his lips, he drew a quick breath. My aunt's pointy face darted toward me.

"You were there when she got her dress?" she growled.

"Um, yeah. It's really nice." I glanced awkwardly at Lilly.

"Why would you take my niece and her cousin to try on bridal gowns?" Her tone was clearly disapproving.

Teresa dropped her head toward her lap and balled her cloth napkin in her hands. No one said anything—until my brother spoke up.

"Well, you know they're bridesmaids, right?"

My aunt gasped and dropped her coffee spoon. I didn't have to look at my brother to know he was smiling from ear to ear. He was waiting all day to stir up trouble.

"You're joking, right?" she barked.

"Why would it be funny to have my niece as a bridesmaid?" Teresa sat up.

"Your *niece*?" my aunt croaked.

"Well, she is my brother's daughter."

"Oh, for the love of God . . ."

"What? I'm her biological aunt. Can you say the same?" Teresa cocked her head.

My aunt Joan immediately jumped to her feet, her husband at her side.

"My wife was there when those children were born. The fact that you would even begin to compare your relationship to ours is offensive. But I shouldn't expect any better from you," my uncle Diego snarled at her. "And by the way, don't call yourself my sister. You're nothing to me."

If I had been eating, I would have needed the Heimlich maneuver. I knew my uncle was tough. I even knew that he could be cruel, but I never expected to hear him be so deliberately heartless.

Chapter 27

Dessert wasn't exactly sweet. The food was fine, but the company lacked the holiday spirit. My mother convinced everyone to stay and politely finish their meal. This, however, was an impossible request given that Carlos was shooting spears from his eyes every time my uncle so much as coughed; Teresa refused to make eye contact with anyone; and the rest of my family barely spoke for fear of worsening the situation. After nearly twenty minutes of silent chewing, Alex grabbed my hand.

"What are we doing?" he whispered in my ear.

"What do you mean?"

"I mean, why do I have to whisper?"

"Because we're all avoiding the situation," I answered honestly.

"Well, I don't think that's helping."

He pumped his eyebrows at me, a gesture Lilly saw from across the table.

"What?" she mouthed.

"Nothing." I shrugged.

Lilly flicked her eyes around the room. *"What's going on?"*

I gestured to Teresa with my eyes and then at my uncle, who was picking at his pumpkin pie. Lilly followed my gaze, then uncomfortably looked down at her plate, which was licked clean of fresh apple pie and handmade ice cream.

"Can I get up?" she mouthed.

Finally, Vince chimed in. Clearly he was watching our muted interaction.

"All right," he said loudly, breaking the silence. "We're gonna get up now and sit in the living room where it's not so . . . weird."

"Vince," my father warned, his mustache twitching.

"What? I can't say this is weird? Because there are a lot of other adjectives I could use instead."

My brother pushed out his antique chair. Mali followed his lead.

"Vince, it's Thanksgiving. Don't start." My father's tone was harsh.

"Me start! Are you kidding? I think the ball of tension is already rolling here, and it has nothing to do with me."

My brother started to walk away, but I stayed firm in my seat. I knew an argument was about to break out. I wondered if everyone else did too.

"Must you make a scene?" My father rose from his chair.

"I didn't realize leaving the room would cause such a problem."

"You haven't changed one bit, have you? I thought you'd finally grow up in college."

"Yeah, I know, I've been gone three months. Looks like your hopes for my personality transplant might take a little longer." My brother lifted his cheek and scrunched his nose. It was a bratty look I knew all too well.

Mali grabbed his arm as if to soften his rapidly hardening exterior, but I knew it was too late. My father and Vince loved to push each other's buttons, and since my father wasn't about to argue with the person he was really angry with (my uncle Diego), he decided to take out his frustration on his son. The annoying thing was that my brother was too stubborn to avoid the trap.

"Vincent, you have such a talent for making every situation worse."

"Gee, I wonder where I get that from?" Vince stared at my father, then my uncle.

Simultaneously, my mom and I popped to our feet. She placed her palm on my father's chest as I stepped in front of Vince, blocking his view of our dad.

"What?" Vince huffed, his frown tightening.

"Let's see if *A Christmas Story* is on TV somewhere," I suggested. "You know we can't get through Thanksgiving without at least one inappropriate Christmas movie."

I heard my mother whisper to my father, and already the pressure in the room eased. I looked at Alex and Lilly, then dragged my brother out of the dining room.

I decided to hide in front of the laptop. Lilly, Alex, Vince, and Mali were downstairs laughing as they counted the amount of Christmas ads on television. I, however, was sitting alone in Vince's room, finally able to focus on something within my control—a homework assignment (even if it wasn't mine).

Shortly after we stormed out of the dining room, my uncles and their families bolted out the front door. Teresa briefly said good-bye before scooping her son onto her hip and sprinting from the house with her fiancé. It amazed me how much abuse she could take from my uncle Diego. I had been a member of this family since birth, and I could honestly say that I didn't think we were worth this much trouble. I couldn't see why she didn't just cut her losses and form her own family.

Just then, I heard Mali giggle from the living room. Even her laugh sounded seductive. I imagined her smile twinkling at my brother (or worse, at Alex) while her gray eyes absorbed the lust in the room. She and Vince were scheduled to hit the road Saturday morning, and I was counting the remaining minutes.

I stared at the screen. I had rewritten nearly ten pages of Vince's essay. He had explored some incredibly original ideas, but his use of language was so clunky that it was often hard to muscle through the pages. I worked to maintain the integrity of his theories while changing virtually every word, and ultimately accomplishing what I thought would be a grade-saving essay.

Suddenly, an instant message popped onto my screen. I clicked the window open, expecting to find Madison. Only I was wrong.

FILMGEEK21: Happy Turkey Day! How was the chow?

I stared at the text. It was from Bobby. He hardly ever IMed me unless it was chemistry related. But knowing what I did about his family situation, I was guessing that Thanksgiving wasn't anymore joyful for him than it was for me.

MARIRUIZ: Good as can be expected. Yours?

FILMGEEK21: My dad sliced turkey while my mom criticized every cut he made. Then he told her the meal was dry, and she started crying.

MARIRUIZ: Wow, sounds like a blast. My uncle told my *tía* Teresa that she'll never be a real member of this family.

FILMGEEK21: I just love precious family moments.

MARIRUIZ: Got any other plans for the weekend?

FILMGEEK21: Aside from talking to you?

I smiled as I read that.

MARIRUIZ: Well, obviously this conversation is the highlight of your weekend. I was just wondering if you planned to venture away from the computer.

FILMGEEK21: That depends. I have a busy schedule of online porn planned.

MARIRUIZ: Excellent visual. Thanks for sharing.

FILMGEEK21: LOL

MARIRUIZ: Well, anything to take your mind off things, I guess.

FILMGEEK21: You're all the distraction I need.

I reread his last sentence. I couldn't tell if it was a compliment or just a bit of sarcasm. I debated what to write next, but he beat me to it.

FILMGEEK21: Sometimes I think you're the only person who gets it. You know, with my family.

Clearly the tone had changed.

MARIRUIZ: Well, you only need one person to really get you, right?

FILMGEEK21: Then I'm glad it's you.

Before I could write back, Alex appeared in the doorway and I swiftly minimized the screen. My entire body jolted with guilty surprise.

"Did I startle you?" he asked as he stepped closer.

"I guess. I was wrapped up in the essay," I said, shaking my head.

Alex placed his hands on my shoulders and lightly started to massage. "Enough work. Come hang out."

I smiled up at him, my pulse racing. I didn't know why I was so nervous. Bobby was my friend. It was natural that we'd IM each other.

"I'll be down in a minute," I promised.

"I'll hold you to that. You've got sixty seconds," he said as he ceased kneading my muscles and turned for the door.

"Time me."

I quickly spun back to the laptop and saw the IM light blinking once more. I flicked it open.

FILMGEEK21: I should get back to the porn, I mean fam. Enjoy the rest of your weekend, *chica*. See you Monday!

FILMGEEK21 has just signed off, read a timestamp.

I clicked off the laptop and headed downstairs. I could hear Alex counting backward from ten as I bounded down the steps.

"You just made it," he teased.

I laughed and plopped down by his side.

Chapter 28

For the first time since she stepped foot off the plane from Utuado, Lilly managed to organize plans with my friends for an entire afternoon. Rather than just tagging along as Madison drug us from one shopping complex to another (it was Black Friday, after all), we were headed to Swarthmore College. Kyle and his friends offered to show us around campus while it was empty—most students were home on break. They couldn't have picked a better day for a tour, either. The temperature was freakishly twenty degrees higher than normal. We weren't even wearing coats.

"So you think we'll see your mom?" Madison asked Emily.

Her "driver" had dropped her off at Madison's unusually early. She claimed that her Thanksgiving with her father was fine and "not worth talking about." Then she changed the subject. I was guessing her mother didn't bother to call.

"Well, school's not in session so I doubt it. But who knows?" Emily answered as she watched the campus pull into view.

A commuter train rumbled on the bridge ahead, pulling into the tiny station, which was flanked by the campus's vacant athletic fields. An elderly couple strolled on the sidewalk, window-shopping in the English-Tudor-style boutiques selling stuffed animals, Guatemalan clothing, and used books.

The town called itself a "village," which fit with the vibe resonating from its old stone homes, mature trees, and well-educated residents. The college only added about one thousand students to the population, and previously when we'd driven by (there was a mall a few blocks away that Madison, of course, frequented), we hardly ever saw any students. I wasn't sure if that was because they rarely ventured beyond the campus limits or if it was because they all congregated at some secret place that drivers couldn't see from the road. Either way, visiting during the campus's off-hours wasn't going to help us find out.

"So we're meeting Kyle at that coffeehouse." Lilly pointed.

Madison pulled into a parking space, and we piled out of the car.

"Why isn't Alex here?" Madison asked as she pulled at her leather bag (it probably cost more than most students spent on books in a semester).

"He said he had some paper to write for his school in Utuado. It's due on Monday," I noted.

"You left him home with Mali?" Madison raised an eyebrow.

"Dude, it's his grade."

"Besides, not all guys cheat," Lilly defended.

"No, just *most* of them," Emily muttered as she pushed open the door to the shop.

A heavenly coffee-filled breeze immediately enveloped us. There was no sign of Kyle, so we all packed into a booth. We hadn't even sat down before I heard the phone buzz in Madison's purse. She quickly dug it out.

"It's Evan." She smiled. "He says he's hanging out with his bro and wants to meet up later!"

"I didn't know Evan had a brother," I said.

"It's a half brother. He's, like, way older," Emily replied absentmindedly.

Madison's eyes shrunk to tiny slits. "How did you know that?"

"Everyone knows that," Emily said quickly, chewing the inside of her cheek.

"He just told me about him last week. He's visiting from California."

"I guess I heard you mention it."

I couldn't tell if Madison was buying her story, but I wasn't. And from the way Lilly jabbed my side, I was guessing she agreed with me.

Just then Kyle pushed open the shop's door, his eyes scanning the room. He was dressed in a tan polo shirt and shorts, and the friend at his side was similarly dressed with a racquet slung over his shoulder.

"Good, you guys are here!" Kyle approached the table.

I eyeballed his athletic wear. We were all dressed in jeans and fancy boots.

"I forgot I told my buddy that we'd play tennis today. He's stuck here over break 'cause his parents didn't want to fly him back to Wisconsin for four days. I swear we have the shortest break of any school," Kyle griped, speaking rapidly and smiling at Lilly. "But I know you're a big tennis player . . ."

Madison dropped her phone onto the table. "I'm sorry, what?"

"I figured we could all play a few matches. It's, like, summer outside." He nodded.

I swallowed a laugh. It sounded like Lilly, while talking up her tennis team membership to Kyle, may have forgotten to mention that she almost broke a girl's nose in her first match and that her coach refrained from putting her in any more competitive meets. As of now, Lilly was benched until she learned to control her follow through. So far, she couldn't keep her balls on the court.

"Are you nuts?" Madison shrieked. "I'm wearing heels!"

"She doesn't like to sweat," Lilly whispered, rising to her feet.

"Yeah, like ballet doesn't make you sweat," Madison hissed.

"I just don't like to ruin my outfits . . ."

"Wait," I said. I smiled sympathetically at Kyle. "We have our ballet clothes in your car, Mad."

"You want me to wear a tutu on a tennis court?" Madison quipped.

"You don't have a tutu in your car!" I squeaked.

I looked at Lilly, whose eyes were desperate to please Kyle. "We'll figure it out."

"Great, 'cause I've got extra racquets," his friend offered, pumping his eyebrow ring. "I'm Derek, by the way."

"Oh, hi." Lilly extended her hand. "This is Mariana, Madison, and Emily."

"Wait, do I know you?" Derek pointed to Emily as he squinted his blue eyes.

"Her mom teaches here," I said. "Professor Montgomery."

"She's a poetry professor," Emily added, staring at a napkin.

"No, I'm a poli-sci major." Derek ran his hand through his moppy brown hair. His stubbly beard made him look a lot older than Kyle. "I guess you just have one of those faces. . . ."

"I guess," Emily said, sliding out of the booth.

Madison eventually fought her way out of participating in any tennis-related activities, offering to sit on the sidelines and "judge" (which was code for "stare obsessively at her cell phone"). Luckily, my ballet bag had enough wardrobe changes to dress both me and Lilly in reasonable-looking tennis outfits. I was wearing a pair of black knit cropped pants, a black tank top, and wrap shirt, while Lilly was in a pair of maroon leg warmers, black leggings, and a thin black, long-sleeved sweater. Emily was set in a pink terry track suit. We were all going to play in black dance sneakers.

"You look ridiculous," Madison pointed out as we strolled toward the campus's courts. She was the only one still in her jeans and high-heeled boots.

"Thanks for the confidence boost," I muttered.

"I think I look cute in leg warmers. You guys should wear these more often," Lilly stated, tugging at her leggings (her curves filled my clothes in a way that my body never did).

"It's a good look for you," I noted.

"Oh, look at my little ballerinas," Kyle cheered as we approached the court he and Derek were already playing on. "Your racquets are on the bench over there."

We trudged over and each grabbed a well-worn men's racquet. The silver tape on my handle was sticky from years of use. Not that the quality of the equipment mattered much, I knew I wouldn't be able to hit the fuzzy green ball even if I were using the racquet straight out of Venus Williams's hand.

Madison plopped on the wooden bench and peeked at her cell phone. She was checking it at a rate of about once per minute. There were no new messages.

"Mad, you'll hear from him." I sighed as I stared at her frowning eyes. "I mean, at least he's trying to make plans with you."

"I know. He'll call," Madison repeated, trying to convince herself.

We left her on the benches and jogged onto the tennis courts. Dried, rust-colored leaves kicked up in the warm breeze, reminding us of how dramatically the temperature had changed. The guys stopped their match as we arrived, hands pressed to their foreheads to shield them from the sun. Clearly, we didn't have even numbers for a tennis match; there were five of us, and I knew I wasn't about to go one-on-one with the boys.

"Hey." Kyle's eyes moved to Lilly's butt. "You look cute."

Her cheeks filled with pink.

"I was thinking maybe Lilly and I could play a match, and you two could play Derek." Kyle nodded to his friend.

"You're that good?" I yelled over as he approached the net.

"I'm nationally ranked." Derek smirked. I could see his tongue was pierced as well.

"Then why are you playing with this fool?" I swatted at Kyle.

"'Cause he's my roommate and 'cause he promised to let me whoop his ass before it got too cold to play."

"Well, did you succeed? Or do you guys need a few more minutes?"

"Please, the match was over in about five seconds. The boy couldn't return a single serve."

"Well, that's promising." I stretched my eyes at Emily.

She barely had an ear in our conversation. Her eyes were gazing into the distance, toward the campus buildings. I wondered if she was looking for signs of her mom.

"Don't worry. I'll take it easy on you guys." Derek bounced a tennis ball on his racquet, flipping his wrist in an awesome display of control as he walked toward the next court. The ball never dropped.

"Well, this is gonna suck," I grumbled to Emily, who finally shook herself out of her daze.

"We're on the same team?" she asked, her eyebrows forming a crease above her nose.

"Yeah, where you been? Space out much?"

We walked to our side of the net, and I took my place on the right side of the court. I always played on the right in doubles—that way I would never have to use my backhand. All balls shot close to the middle were left to my partner (the strategy worked through two years of private tennis lessons until my coach put me in a singles match and I was forced to quit. Perfecting my backhand just wasn't worth the effort.).

"You guys serve first!" Kyle batted the ball lightly toward me.

I awkwardly snatched it with my left hand.

"You better help me out here," I said to Emily. "You know I suck at tennis."

"I'm not much better." She twisted her short chocolate hair in a fresh ponytail.

"At least you play with your mom." I paused. "I mean, you *used to* play with your mom."

Emily grunted. "Well, don't get your hopes up. She didn't teach me much."

I bounced the ball on the court and looked toward Lilly. Kyle was about to hit his first serve. My jaw tightened as I watched him lightly tap it to her. Lilly swiftly rushed toward the ball and swung like Barry Bonds reaching for a homer. The tiny green ball landed with a smack on her racquet and soared over Kyle's head, crashing into the chain link fence behind him. I flinched. It was going to be a long afternoon.

"All right, you ready?" I asked as I bounced the ball on the court one more time.

I tossed the green target in the air and gently swung, directing it straight toward the correct serving box. I didn't have much power (or technique), but at least I could keep it on the court. Derek casually jogged toward it and swung like a guy volleying to his grandma. The ball gently glided over the net. I lunged and swung, sending it back as hard as I could. Derek jogged over and easily volleyed it back, this time aiming for Emily. I waited for her to move, but she never did. Her eyes stayed squinted toward the trees in the distance, and the ball blew right by her.

"Em!" I shrieked.

"Oh, sorry." She shook her head.

"Dude, I can't hit 'em any slower!" Derek whined.

"What, did you see your mom?" I followed Emily's gaze but could only see a group of students clustered near some evergreens smoking—they were the first students we saw all day.

"No," she said, absentmindedly still staring.

"Well, then, pay attention."

I looked over to Lilly's court just as Kyle ducked out of the way of another speeding bullet.

"My God, woman!" he hollered, throwing his hands up in self-defense. "I thought you were on the tennis team!"

"Did I forget to mention that I broke a girl's nose?" Lilly shouted, giggling.

"Remind me never to take you boxing!"

He ran toward the fence and grabbed the ball—it was wedged into one of the diamond-shaped openings. It took a lot of force to slam a tennis ball into one of those holes.

"I'm scared to serve it back!" Kyle joked as he trotted to the line. "I feel like I need a helmet and football pads."

"Whoever said tennis wasn't a contact sport obviously never played with me!"

"Hey! Are we gonna play or what?" Derek yelled.

I swiftly grabbed the tennis ball from where it had landed by the fence and gently patted it back to Derek.

He connected, sending a line drive straight toward me. The sad thing was I knew he was going easy on us, and his return was still the fastest I'd ever played against. I swung at the ball, popping it high into the air. I knew Derek could have rushed the net and smashed it in my face, but mercifully he didn't. He waited for it to bounce, and then lightly tapped it toward

Emily. Only she was standing on the court like a statue staring into the fields. The ball whizzed by her once more.

"Em, what's your deal? Do you wanna play or not?" I squeaked, annoyed at her behavior.

"Sorry, sorry." She shook her head.

"Take that! Ahahahahah!" Kyle yelled from the next court, swinging at the ball with all his might in a clear attempt to give Lilly a taste of her own medicine. It backfired.

I watched as she wildly made contact, flinging the ball straight toward his head. Kyle dropped to the ground just in time and stayed on his belly, laughing in spasms. "You're a nut!"

"I'm *aggressive*," Lilly corrected, rushing toward him.

"John McEnroe was aggressive. You're a train wreck!" Kyle rolled on the ground, wiping at the tears in his eyes as Lilly sat on his gut. "Agh!"

"I'm a train wreck, huh!" she hollered, thrusting her face down to his.

"You're lethal," he grunted, grabbing her hands.

In one swift move, he yanked her toward him and kissed her right there on the court. I watched, smiling. Clearly, Madison didn't find the embrace as cute as I did. She stomped right past them, crushing the moment as she waved her cell phone in the air.

"He texted me! Evan texted me!" she cheered, running toward our court. "He wants to hang out. Like, tonight! Do you think it's a date? Like a real one?"

I sighed and glanced at Emily, but she was still in her own world.

"It sounds like a date," I answered.

"What happened?" Lilly asked as she jogged over, sounding annoyed at the interruption. Kyle was holding her hand.

"Evan texted me! He wants to hang out. I wonder if it'll be just me and him . . ."

"If it ever happens, then I'm sure it will be," Lilly huffed. "It's not like his friends even know about you."

"What's that supposed to mean?" Madison jerked her head toward my cousin.

"I didn't realize I was being obtuse."

"All right, stop it." I smiled kindly at Madison. "I'm glad you heard from him. That's awesome."

"So, are we even playing tennis today?" Derek asked as he jogged toward us.

I swung my head to apologize and saw Emily slowly moving toward the back fence. She was still staring toward the trees at the group of students. I glanced at Madison, who was too absorbed in her own drama to notice, and then gradually followed our friend. When I approached the fence, I finally realized what had caught Emily's eye.

A blond guy was sitting crossed-legged on the grass, sucking a cigarette between his thumb and forefinger. A skinny blond girl leaned toward him as he offered her a light. The glow from his Zippo illuminated his face. It was Emily's date from the restaurant, and the girl sharing his lighter was the same date he'd had with him at the coffeehouse.

"Em," I muttered, staring in horror.

She spun toward me, her lower lip trembling. I could see the tears building behind her eyes.

Then I heard the shuffle of feet behind me.

"Hey, Em, isn't that your mom's research assistant? Eric something?" Madison asked, pointing to the co-eds in the field.

My entire upper body contracted as my hand shot to my chest. I knew he had looked familiar. I couldn't believe I hadn't placed him sooner. I must have met him a half dozen times at Emily's house, helping her mom edit her poetry anthology and organizing her background research. He was one of her students.

"*Oh. My. God,*" I muttered.

Emily's bleached eyes snapped toward me. "What?"

"Um, nothing." I shook my head, trying to erase my stunned reaction.

All the color seemed to have drained from Emily's face. I could see tiny tears clinging to the corners of her eyes. She spun around to stare at her secret date once more.

"That's why you look familiar! I've seen you around campus, with Eric," Derek noted, the realization suddenly hitting him.

When Emily looked back, her pupils were huge. "I told you my mom works here. He's her assistant."

Derek sized up Emily. I could tell that he didn't believe her, but he merely shrugged her off. "Whatever," he grumbled.

"Why don't you say 'hi,' " Madison suggested innocently, not knowing the gravity of the situation.

"He looks busy. I don't wanna bother him." She paused, staring. "We should go."

I could only see the back of her head, but the pain was swimming off of her.

"She's right. Sorry, Kyle, but I think tennis was a bust," I stated, patting his back and hoping to quickly get us as far away from this scene as possible.

"Well, I had fun," Lilly glinted.

"Yeah, fun trying to kill me!" Kyle joked.

The two of them stared happily into each other's eyes. Then he kissed her and we all pretended not to notice. At least someone was happy.

Chapter 29

By the time we left the campus, Emily had completely stopped talking. Madison filled the air with a relentless discussion about her impending date, while Emily's faded emerald eyes stared idly into the distance. I wanted to hug her and tell her that everything would be okay, that the guy wasn't worth being upset over, that he was a pig for dating his boss's daughter in the first place—but I couldn't. How could I talk to her about a situation that she refused to acknowledge?

Madison dropped Lilly and me at home. I pushed open the door to the house and walked lazily into the foyer. I hung up my pea coat and stopped suddenly when I heard the sound of hurried rustling. I peered at Lilly, then tiptoed toward the living room. As soon as I reached the doorway, I saw Mali and Alex's heads pop up from the couch.

"Oh, hey," Mali said, smoothing her black hair.

"*Hola*," Alex said quickly. "We were just playing some video games."

I glanced at the flat-screen TV. The game was paused.

"Oh, we stopped it when we heard you come in," Mali explained as she sat up straighter.

"Where's Vince?" I asked, scanning the room.

"He's still working on that essay," Alex puffed as he hopped off the couch, adjusting the lines of his button-down shirt.

"Upstairs?" My eyes narrowed.

"Yeah, he wants to have it done before we head out. Apparently his frat is having a big 'back from Thanksgiving party' tomorrow night." Mali grinned, her cheeks unusually rosy.

"Of course they are." I abruptly turned toward the steps.

"He asked me to keep Mali busy," Alex called after me.

"I'm sure he did," I grumbled as I stormed up the stairs.

Lilly chased after me as I darted up the steps two at a time. I didn't know what I'd walked in on, but I could feel guilt vibrating off them. My stomach sloshed.

"Mariana, wait," Lilly insisted, but I kept moving. "I'm sure it's not what you think."

"How would you know what I'm thinking if you weren't thinking the same thing?" I snapped.

I flung open Vince's door.

"I'm done!" he sang, gesturing to the pages pouring out of his printer.

"You got that right." I shifted my weight to one hip.

"What's with you?"

"What's with *me*? What's with you leaving your slutty girlfriend downstairs all day with Alex?"

"What are you talking about?" He wrinkled his slender nose.

"I'm talking about me walking through the door and interrupting the two of them!" I waved my hands in the air, aggravated.

"The two of them doing what?"

"God only knows. But they sure as hell weren't playing video games."

Lilly jumped in front of me. "You don't know that."

"Oh, so their rumpled clothes and matted hair and flushed cheeks, that was all because of video games?" I peered at Lilly.

"Yes, that's what I think," she said.

Vince stared at me, his brow furrowed.

"Wait? Are you saying that you think they were hooking up? Right now. Downstairs? While I was *here*?"

"Yes," I said bluntly.

"Come on, Mali wouldn't do that." He gathered the papers from the printer, brushing me off.

"Mali had sex with you on the football field in the middle of a school day. I can't say I'd put much past her." I tilted my head.

"We didn't have sex," he muttered. "We just messed around."

I hesitated. At least she wasn't as loose as I thought, but that still didn't alleviate the twitching in my gut.

"Vince, I could *feel* that something was up. I just know it."

My brother paused. I knew he had the same ability to sense tension from a mile away. It was a Ruíz family trait.

"If it's true, then your boyfriend is just as guilty."

"If it's true, then he's not my boyfriend . . . if he ever was."

Lilly plopped onto my brother's rumpled comforter.

"I can't believe you guys are even thinking this," she said, disgusted.

"Let's see, I trusted Emily and she lied to us. I trusted my dad and he shipped me off to Puerto Rico. I trusted you and you kept me from Alex half the summer." I shot my head toward her. "I think it's safe to say I have some reasons not to blindly trust people."

Lilly stared awkwardly at the area rug. There wasn't much she could say. The ones who should be doing the talking weren't in the room.

* * *

For Vince and Mali's last night in Spring Mills, we went bowling. When we had planned it, we had thought it would be a fun couples activity—Alex and I, Vince and Mali, Lilly and Kyle. Only at the moment, Kyle and Lilly were the only ones speaking to each other in non-abusive tones.

"Ouch, another gutter ball. You really aren't good at this, are you?" I smirked as Alex trudged, crestfallen, back to the plastic seats.

He said nothing as he sunk beside me. I wiggled to create more space between us.

"Nice try," Lilly offered, patting his leg.

Vince stood up next, grabbed his heavy cobalt ball from the return track and took three careful steps toward the line. He swung his right leg behind his left and flung the ball at full force. It curved expertly as it spun down the lane, crashing into ten pins with a decisive clatter—a perfect strike.

"Yes! In your face!" Vince screamed, pointing at Alex. "Take that! Ahhhahhahah!"

He growled at him, his face pulled tight. Alex attempted to laugh and pass the display off as a friendly competitive gesture, but I think we all knew that it wasn't.

Vince slammed down on his orange seat, shaking the row of chairs bolted alongside it.

"Yeah, you're going down! Suck on that!" he hollered again, pointing at Alex.

Mali tentatively stood up, glancing cautiously at my brother. Her eyes were frightened, and I couldn't say I blamed her.

"Don't blow it, sweetie," my brother barked. "*Blow it*. Huh."

He looked at me to see if I caught his double entendre. I was certain everyone did.

Mali slowly walked to the ball return, lifting the lightest, pinkest ball available (it could have serviced a kindergarten's bumper ball birthday party). She walked unevenly toward the line (she had never been bowling before), and stood there like a statue. Then she swung her arm back and tossed it as hard as she could. For a nationally ranked gymnast, I expected the girl to have a bit more natural ability. But so far, we were in the fourth frame and her balls were lucky if they stayed out of the gutter; and when they did, they moved at the speed of a slug. This one was no exception.

"Wow, dropped the ball again," Vince hollered. "Get it? Dropped the ball."

He laughed in her face.

She waited patiently for her ball at the return, not looking at any of us. As soon as it popped up, she charged down the lane and flung it with all her might. It soared in an arch about three feet in the air before crashing down and landing in the gutter.

"A big zero again! It's like you can't even *see* the pins!" Vince snorted.

Mali closed her eyes and sat beside him, slumping low in her seat, her arms folded.

"I didn't realize you guys were so competitive," Kyle said uncomfortably, standing up.

"Yeah, neither did I." Lilly looked at me wide-eyed.

"Well, my dad used to take us bowling when we were little. He's really good, and he taught us to *respect* the game. You know what that's like, respect?" I stared at Alex.

"Of course." He nodded with false innocence.

Vince and I had confronted Mali and Alex earlier. They both vehemently denied that anything sexual had happened between them. Alex claimed he spent most of the day working on his Utuado assignment and that he and Mali had just turned on the video game moments before I had arrived. But the two of them hadn't looked at each other once since we got to the bowling alley, and the Ruíz bullshit antennae were up in full force.

Kyle tossed his ball down the lane with athletic force. It clanked loudly as it slammed into eight pins. Given his record, I knew he'd manage to catch the other two.

"Good job, Kyle! Keep it up," Lilly cheered.

My cousin had currently knocked down a total of nine pins, which was pathetic. But given that Mali had a whopping score of three and Alex had a grand total of fourteen, it was safe to say that the Spring Mills natives were cleaning the floor with our guests. Only Vince and I seemed to be enjoying that fact.

Kyle struck down the final two pins. "Spare!" he chanted, pumping his arm.

"Nice!" Lilly jumped to her feet and hugged him tight.

They both smiled easily. I envied them. When I scanned the area, it looked like Mali, Vince, and Alex's grim faces had the same sense of longing.

Kyle bounced into his seat and clapped his hands.

"All right, Lil! You can do it! Just aim straight!" he coached.

Lilly strutted up to the line, her hips swaying. She cradled a lime-green ball, paused to adjust the heel of her red, black, and green bowling shoe, then tossed it ahead. It turned slowly as it waddled down the lane in an almost perfectly straight line. We watched for what felt like hours until it lightly collided with the pins. Four wobbled down (if she had thrown it harder, it probably would've been a strike).

"Whoo hoo!" she yelped, jumping up. "Four pins!"

Kyle applauded wildly at her meager accomplishment. "Just six more! You can do it."

I rolled my eyes at his enthusiasm, while my brother sighed.

Lilly once again swaggered to the line, chucking the ball with the force of a toddler. It rolled leisurely down the lane and tapped two more pins off balance.

"Yeah! That's six, *verdad*?" Lilly bopped on her toes.

"Yup, six! You're on a roll!" Kyle cheered, high-fiving her.

They were so happy it was disgusting.

Finally, I stood up to take my turn. I marched right past my blissfully happy cousin and snatched my black ball from the return.

Alex tapped his hands together warily and droned, "Go, Mariana."

He wasn't exactly bubbling with support.

I took three quick steps toward the line, flung my leg behind me and lunged. The ball flew down the lane and smacked thunderously into the pins. I hit nine.

"Nice one!" Vince chanted. "That's how you do it!"

He smirked at his girlfriend, who was gnawing her cheeks, refusing to look at him. Alex continued to applaud weakly. *"Bueno."*

I grabbed my black ball once more, charged toward the line and flung it at full force. It hit the last pin dead on.

"Yes!" I stretched my arms overhead.

Alex jumped up to hug me, but reflexively I stepped back. Everyone noticed. I didn't know how else to react. If the boy had in fact stuck his tongue into my brother's girlfriend's mouth, while sitting on my parents' couch, I was never touching him again. Ever.

Chapter 30

I left the next morning for ballet practice without saying good-bye to Mali. I knew it was the last time I'd see her and frankly, I hoped it stayed that way. I did, however, quickly poke my head into my brother's room and tap his shoulder. He opened one eye, grunted his rank morning breath, and rolled over.

Madison picked me up not long after. Since she was no longer driving Emily to practice (her corporate driver still carted her around), I always got shotgun on the way to practice. I rushed to the car—the air had returned to its normal brisk chill—and relaxed into the heated leather seat.

"So how was last night? Did you hear from Evan?" I asked cautiously as the familiar sights of the Main Line blew past.

"Yes!" I could hear the smile in her voice. "He stopped by!"

"Omigod! Seriously?" I shouted.

"And he kissed me." Her face was gleaming with bliss.

"Omigod!"

"I know!" She lifted her hands from the steering wheel briefly to clap for herself. "It was soooo awesome."

"Tell me everything," I insisted, turning down the radio to give her my full attention.

"Well, he texted me around eight o'clock saying that his brother was going to visit some friend near me and that he was going to stop by. So around nine, his brother dropped him off . . ."

"Did you meet his brother?"

"No, he just pulled into the driveway."

"Okay, continue," I ordered.

"So he came in and met my parents. They *loved* him! You know my mom, she kept telling him what a 'handsome young man' he was. And my dad talked to him about golf. Did you know Evan played golf?"

"No, why would I know that?"

"Anyway, we went down to the basement to watch a movie . . ."

"Your parents let you go down alone?"

"Yup, we even closed the door."

"This is awesome!" I said, smiling so wide my lips cracked.

"Anyway, we had watched, like, twenty minutes of this horror flick when he put his hand on my thigh. Like, *on* my thigh." Madison pointed to her upper leg to show exactly what area he had touched. "Of course, I was freaking out. And I kinda turned my head to see what he was doing and we made eye contact. That was it. He kissed me."

"How long did you kiss?"

"It felt like forever. It was amazing."

"Did he try anything?" I asked in a serious tone.

"Not a thing. He was a perfect gentleman."

I could see the excitement ready to burst from her face.

"That's awesome, Mad. Really. So how'd you leave it?"

"He said he'd call me later today."

"Do you think you guys are, like, together now?" I asked, optimistically.

"God, I hope so."

Madison pulled into the ballet studio's parking lot and stopped the car. Then she paused without opening her door.

"But something weird did happen," she said slowly, staring at the wheel as she pulled her key from the ignition. "He asked me if I was gonna tell Emily."

I stiffened at the sign of trouble. "Emily? Do you think he was just asking if you were gonna tell your friends?"

The last thing I wanted was to be the messenger who told Madison that her best friend may be having a secret relationship with her new boyfriend. (Why am I always the messenger? Can't someone else be the bad guy for once?)

"I don't know," Madison admitted. "He didn't mention you, and he knows I'm just as good of friends with you as Emily. It was strange."

"So what'd you say?" I asked nervously.

"I said that I probably was, and I asked him if he had a problem with that. He kinda got quiet and then said it was fine."

"So are you gonna tell her?"

"Yeah, I mean I have to. But I might not get into the whole story, you know?"

"Okay, whatever you want."

I opened my car door, ending the conversation. I was feeling uncontrollably compelled to fess up, and the last thing I wanted to do was to burst Madison's bubble.

I tossed my gym bag on the floor and hung my thick winter coat on a metal hook. Emily was already at the barre stretching when we arrived. She barely looked our way. I immediately charged over and flung my leg beside her while Madison headed to the bathroom.

"Hey," I said, pressing my chest to my thigh and grabbing my foot.

"Hey," she murmured, not looking over.

I stretched silently, lowering my head to my knee. I knew Madison would be back soon. If I was going to confront Emily, now was the time.

"You know Madison's got some big news," I blurted.

Emily half turned toward me.

"She hooked up with Evan," I told her.

Emily closed her eyes, placed her pink nails on her forehead and exhaled.

"Wow, you seem really happy for her." My sarcasm was biting.

She turned to me, her eyes red and the skin around them pink and puffy. I could tell she must have been crying, hard, for quite a while.

"Whoa," I whispered. "What happened?"

She swiftly turned away. "Nothing."

"Em, you've obviously been crying." I paused and considered the situation. "Please, tell me this isn't about Evan."

"This isn't about Evan." Her voice was taut.

I didn't say anything, but the look on my face must have conveyed my doubt.

Emily sighed. "This has nothing to do with him, really."

She dropped her leg from the barre and started to walk away.

"You know, he brought you up to Madison."

She spun back around. I could see her pale skin was blotchy, and it looked like her short ponytail was already sweaty though we hadn't yet begun practice.

"He asked her if she was going to tell you about them getting together."

"Is that all he said?"

"Gee, I didn't ask for a direct transcript. But apparently, that was enough to make her suspicious. I think you need to tell her what's going on between the two of you . . . whatever it is."

"There's nothing to tell." She shook her head.

I swung my leg off the barre and thrust my face within inches of hers.

"Em, you have been acting weird for so long, I don't know if I can believe a word you say anymore."

She grunted and licked her lips as if she had a reason to be annoyed with me.

"This is your chance to come clean. If you don't, and I find out that there's *anything* going on between you and Evan, that's it. We're through. I will never speak to you again."

Emily stared me dead in the eye. "I guess I know where I stand then."

Just then, I saw Madison enter the studio. I stepped away from Emily and calmly rejoined my fellow ballerinas.

Chapter 31

W hen I got back from ballet, Alex was in the kitchen helping my mother prepare dinner. A white apron, decorated with
black poodles in chefs' hats, was tied around him as he sliced
tomatoes. My mom was grilling salmon as she offered him her
detailed opinions on every college in the tri-state area.

"You can't beat Penn's reputation," my mom explained as
she sprinkled salt on the fish. "Sure, it's not in Cambridge, but
Philadelphia's really cleaned up recently."

"I agree, I'm just not sure I'll get in."

"Sure you will. You have to think positively." My mom
looked up when I strolled in, her blond hair sticking to her
face as heat sprayed from the indoor grill. "How was practice?"

"Grueling," I answered. I collapsed on a stool across from
where Alex was chopping.

"Getting excited for the performance?"

"Not really. I'm too tired to be excited."

"Ah, it's good for you." She returned her attention to the
sizzling fish.

"Where's Lilly?" I asked.

"At Betsy's," Alex replied as he cut the tomatoes into perfect triangular slices. "She's eating over there."

The house was quiet. Aside from the sounds of the indoor grill and Alex's chopping, not a peep could be heard. It was refreshing after the hectic holiday. I could feel my shoulders sink away from my neck.

"I guess Vince and Mali left."

"Yup, around lunchtime," my mom answered.

"I'm sure they'll be missed." I looked at Alex as I said this, though he didn't glance up. He just grabbed a bag of lettuce and began filling a giant wooden salad bowl.

He handed me a cucumber. "Wanna help?"

What I wanted to do was take a shower, steam my muscles, and relax. But with my guest acting like the happy little kitchen helper, it was hard to excuse myself. I reluctantly grabbed the vegetable and began hacking at it with a peeler.

"You should be a bit gentler," Alex said as he watched me shave cucumber skin.

"What are you, the cucumber police?"

"No, I just thought you'd want some pointers." He emptied the sliced tomato into the bowl of lettuce.

"I can figure it out on my own, thank you."

I was hacking thick chunks of skin when Alex walked around the island and grabbed my hands. He took the peeler and the cucumber and began shredding in long, thin layers.

"See?" he pointed out.

I rolled my eyes. "My way is just as good."

"Mariana, he's just trying to show you how to do it properly," my mom butted in.

"Well, excuse me if I don't defer to his views on what's 'proper.' "

Alex peered at me. "You're different than you were in Puerto Rico," he mumbled.

"Sorry to disappoint you."

"Things don't have to be like this."

I snatched the cucumber from his hand. "You're right. I shouldn't need instructions on how to 'properly' make a salad."

Alex sighed and walked back to the other side of the counter. He opened a package of feta cheese and crumbled it into the salad.

An hour later, after a nearly silent dinner, I started to head upstairs. I only made it a few steps before Alex grabbed my arm.

"I was hoping you could help me with an application essay. A lot of colleges list sample questions, but I don't know which one I should use . . ."

I was still angry with him, but I wasn't sure why. Ever since he'd shown up in Spring Mills, my life had grown increasingly more complicated. He brought a level of tension into our home that wasn't there before (not even with the addition of Lilly). Half of me wanted him to leave so my life could return to normal, and the other half wanted to find the guy who made my head spin in Puerto Rico.

"Fine, whatever." I sighed.

He smiled tentatively and led me to my father's den. The desktop computer was already logged onto a website offering tips on how to write the "perfect essay." I grabbed one of the extra chairs and plopped down beside Alex.

"I don't know what to write about. I'm only eighteen. It's not as if I've had some huge earth-shattering experience," Alex explained.

I eyeballed the list. Topics asked prospective students to explain a hobby, an important life experience, the influence of a living role model, the inspiration derived from a fictional character, and an opinion held on a controversial topic, among others.

"Well, does anything jump out at you?" I asked.

"I know not to write about my dead grandmother."

I offered a short laugh. "Well, you could write about Puerto Rico."

"I'm worried that'll just stereotype me."

"But you *are* Puerto Rican."

"Still, I don't want to get in just to fill some quota . . ."

"Do you know how hard it is to get into college?" I raised an eyebrow. "Most kids would kill to be able to check that minority box on an application. Trust me, Vince did so with pride."

"It's funny. You guys are happily trying to include yourself in a minority group to be accepted, while I'm trying to prove I don't need to use my minority status to be accepted."

"Well, maybe that's your essay."

He looked at me as he ran his palm on the back of his neck. "I don't know."

"Okay, then. You could write about how tutoring changed your life. Or how your dog Fido taught you responsibility. Or how Ghandi is your role model. Those are much safer topics that I'm sure the admissions' boards haven't heard before." I smiled condescendingly.

"What? Tootsie isn't your greatest life lesson?"

Alex looked into the kitchen to where my curly black dog was lapping at his water bowl.

"Yeah, poodles are collegiate gold." I nodded.

"I could write about how your father's influenced me," Alex suggested with a straight face.

"Oh, God. Please don't." I groaned. "You write something like that and it might give him ideas. The last thing I need is pressure to write about how he's affected *me*. I don't think 'raising my voice' and 'being argumentative' are traits colleges want to see idolized."

Alex shook his head and grew quiet.

"You could write about the differences between Utuado and Spring Mills."

"I don't think I have enough paper." He chuckled.

"How about how Ricki Martin put Puerto Rico on the map?" I joked.

"I think the island would disown me."

"What, you can't take pride in one of your own?" I smirked.

He scrunched his nose at me. "Or I could write about how *Rocky* is an accurate, historical portrayal of Philadelphia."

"Hey, don't knock Balboa. We don't shun our cultural icons."

He laughed and leaned his shoulder into me. It was nice speaking to him (in a civil tone). I smiled as I turned back to the computer and continued to help.

Chapter 32

The first day back at school after a holiday break is always miserable. When my alarm sounded this morning, I felt nothing but annoyance at having to resume academic activities. I had spent half the night talking to Alex about colleges. He had tons of inside information about the schools I was hoping to visit next year. He knew what the dorms looked like at Princeton, what the course loads were like at Villanova, and who the famous professors were at Penn. I couldn't wait to be the one filling out those applications. College had to be much more interesting than high school.

I slammed the car door shut and followed Lilly, Madison, and Alex into school. Students trudged around us like zombies. Backpacks were slung over their shoulders, visibly empty from the lack of books they'd brought home over the holiday. We all wore a look of dread, knowing that our teachers would cram as much work as possible into the space before Christmas. I already had four tests scheduled.

"So do you think I should go up to Evan at his locker?" Madison asked as we weaved through the hallway crowds.

"Why don't you let him come to you?" I urged.

I was still waiting for Evan to willingly acknowledge Madison's existence in a public space. Now that they had groped one another, the time had come.

"I'm so glad Kyle's in college, and I don't have to worry about this stuff," Lilly pointed out.

"No, you just have to worry about him hooking up with slutty college girls in the dorms," Madison mocked.

Lilly pulled her lips tight. From the shocked expression in her eyes, it looked as though the thought had never occurred to her.

"Don't you think it's weird that a college guy is going out with a high school freshman?" Madison continued.

"He's younger than Alex!" Lilly pushed Alex's shoulder. "Kyle skipped a grade."

"So doesn't that just make him more mature? Wouldn't he want someone his own age?" Madison was clearly fueling Lilly's insecurity.

"Who says I'm not mature?"

Madison glanced at Lilly's chest as it stretched my black cardigan sweater. "We weren't talking about physical maturity."

"Oh, shut up!" She swung at Madison. "At least I have boobs."

"And at least I know where my boyfriend is Monday through Friday!"

I cringed. The fact that Madison was openly calling Evan her boyfriend while I knew Emily was secretly hanging out with him was starting to turn my stomach into an ulcer-fest. I couldn't look at either of my best friends without feeling guilty.

"Well, I have an essay assignment to turn in," Alex said as he leaned in for a kiss.

I let his lips brush my cheek.

"See you later."

He walked away, and then I absentmindedly brushed at my face.

"Wiping off his kiss. Very romantic," Madison offered.

"Don't rush me. I'm still getting over the whole Mali thing."

"You don't even know if there was a Mali thing," Lilly defended.

I paused as I watched Madison scan the hallway. I knew she was looking for Evan and frankly, at this point, so was I.

"I don't see him," I told her as I spied his empty locker.

"Who said I was looking?" Madison asked unconvincingly.

She veered to her locker as Lilly and I continued forward. I could see Bobby already filling his bag with textbooks.

"*Hasta luego,*" Lilly offered as she sped toward the freshmen hallway.

"*Adios.*" I waved.

"Ah, still working on that Spanish," Bobby teased as I approached my locker.

"Got to keep up appearances, you know. I *am* responsible for the school's Latino population."

"Yes, all three of you."

I turned to say something, only my gaze caught on Evan. He had just turned the corner. I closed my eyes and said a silent prayer that he would buzz straight to Madison's locker. Only before I could finish, another familiar face emerged. Emily was walking a few strides behind him. Just seeing them together in such close proximity made cold sweat erupt on my neck.

Only as Evan blew past, Emily halted and steered directly toward me.

"Hey," she said.

I barely looked at her. I was concentrated on Evan's path. I craned my neck, but Emily stepped in my line of sight.

"So are we still friends? Or are you gonna threaten me some more?" she asked unapologetically.

"Why does everything around you have to be so freakin' complicated?" I moaned.

"Because not all of us are lucky enough to have perfect existences where everything is simple and always goes right."

"Yeah, because that's how I'd describe *my* life."

Emily looked at Bobby, but he had intentionally buried his head in his locker. I knew he was listening.

"Somehow my family goes to shit, and I end up the bad guy." She sighed.

"No one's blaming you for your family problems. Your problems with Madison, however, *are* your doing." I slammed my locker shut and tried to see around Emily—no luck.

"Well, right now I don't have problems with Madison, and I'd like to keep it that way."

"Then I suggest you stop being 'friends' with Evan. Don't you have other guys to worry about?" I cocked my head.

She took an involuntary step back, and then stood up straighter.

"I don't know what you're talking about. I'm not the one stringing guys along." She stared at the back of Bobby's head, then marched away.

Somehow a girl I'd known since childhood had become a "frenemy," and I never saw it coming. I glared down the hallway, only when I caught sight of Madison, she was standing alone at her locker. Evan was nowhere in sight. And Emily breezed right by her without saying hello.

"What's with her?" Bobby asked as he smashed his locker door closed.

"I have no idea."

"Well, whatever it is, it's her problem."

"Because I do no wrong?" I asked dryly.

"Exactly. You're the Spring Mills Mother Teresa."

"Considering she's dead, I'm not sure if that's a compliment."

"Fine. I take it back. You're the Spring Mills Lindsay Lohan."

"Gee, thanks." I chuckled half-heartedly.

It almost worked. I almost felt better.

Chapter 33

By Friday, Evan still had yet to acknowledge Madison's existence in front of witnesses. Sure, he'd stop at her locker occasionally if none of his friends were present, or he'd send her a text during lunch, or he'd stay up half the night typing her IMs. But he never held her hand, or kissed her cheek, or introduced her to a single one of his wrestling buds. Madison never admitted this though. With Evan promising to stop by this weekend for what I was certain would be another covert booty call, she was floating in the heavens.

"Another Friday night at ballet," Madison noted as she drove us to practice. "I swear, if we keep practicing like this we're never going to have lives."

"Like we ever did," I huffed from the backseat as I listened to Top 40 radio.

"Speak for yourself. *I've* got a boyfriend." She smiled into the rearview mirror.

Emily was staring out the passenger window, ignoring our conversation. Clearly, she was angry at me for thinking whatever I was thinking about her and Evan (though not angry enough to clear up any doubts), and I was guessing she was still upset that the research assistant she was seeing behind her mother's back was seeing another girl behind *her* back. But she refused to discuss any of it. She was so shut down that I was beginning to be disgusted by her moping.

"Well, do you think your boyfriend would be willing to take you to the movies tomorrow night?" I asked, peering at her sideways.

"Are you going with Alex?" Madison asked incredulously.

"Yup, we're seeing a romantic comedy. Kinda ironic."

"I don't know if Reese Witherspoon is really Evan's 'thing.' "

"We didn't know that ballet was his thing before we saw him with his *nana*," I teased.

"Yeah, make fun of his grandma," Emily huffed, her voice sounding irritated.

"Who said I was making fun?"

"Oh, I'm sorry. Do you just use that snarky tone all the time?"

"Maybe I do. How would you know?"

Emily reached over and turned up the stereo volume. A British folk singer was crooning about how he'd lost the love of his life on a subway. The song could send a circus clown into a fit of depression.

"Em, uh, we were having a conversation," Madison pointed out as she turned the volume back down.

"Oh, of course, talk. That's all we ever do," she droned.

"Well if I don't obsess about my life, who will?" Madison stared at her friend like she had horns sprouting from her ponytail.

Emily sighed and turned her focus back to the car window.

Madam Colbert had me perform my array of solos so many times that I was having out-of-body experiences. My tired legs leapt and spun as fresh blisters formed on my toes, yet all the while my mind felt like it was floating around the room watching my performance as a spectator. When the music stopped, I almost had to be reminded that it was me dancing. I couldn't remember a single step, which was worrisome given that the performance was only two weeks away.

"All right everyone, up!" our instructor insisted, clapping her hands. "We're going to rehearse the finale."

I chugged from my water bottle, my eyes barely open.

"You're doing really well," Madison whispered.

"Shoot me now," I grumbled.

Emily sauntered to center stage. She hadn't said a word since practice had begun, not that I had actually expected her to offer me encouragement. She took her position on the opposite side of the floor from me and stretched her arms overhead, waiting for the music.

I grabbed my partner's hand to practice our "wedding dance." When the music began, my body flowed into autopilot. The room swirled as ballerinas danced their congratulatory solos. Finally, I pirouetted in rapid succession across the floor. I spotted my eyes on the brick studio wall, focused on nothing else—until I felt a foot jut out and collide with mine. I instantly rocked off pointe and tumbled onto the floor.

"Ow!" I screeched as my butt landed hard on the wood planks.

I looked up and saw Emily standing beside me. She swiftly drew her leg in.

"Did you trip me?" I yelped, my eyes furious.

Emily shot me an uneasy look as her eyes darted between the gawking faces. "Mariana, you fell. Big deal."

"No, it is a big deal if someone intentionally trips me."

"What, is it impossible for you to make a mistake? Does it have to be someone else's fault?" Emily's full lips curled to the side, unrepentant.

Madam Colbert stopped the music and rushed over. "Are you all right?" she asked, panicked.

"I'm fine." I rubbed my sore rear end.

"Mariana, I don't think Emily would intentionally try to hurt you," Madison said as she helped me to my feet. "I'm sure it was an accident."

"I never touched her," Emily barked.

"Someone did."

"Or *someone* was so exhausted that she couldn't keep her balance, God forbid." Emily waggled her eyebrows at me.

"Ms. Montgomery, I don't know what went on just here. But if I find out anyone intentionally tried to hurt a fellow dancer, I will immediately cut her from the company. I will not tolerate that type of disrespect." Madam Colbert stared at Emily through her tiny wire-frame glasses.

Emily grunted and rolled her eyes.

"I'm glad you're okay. Why don't you sit the rest of the rehearsal out. You've worked hard enough," Madam Colbert offered.

"Oh, please," Emily muttered under her breath.

Half the dancers caught it. I couldn't imagine that our friendship had deteriorated to a point where she might try to permanently injure me. Madison caught my eye, her brow wrinkled with confusion. I shrugged as if to brush off what had happened, but it continued to eat at my soul. I watched my fellow ballerinas dance without me. Emily even got to practice as the understudy for my role.

Chapter 34

I didn't have ballet on Saturday. It was Madam Colbert's birthday, which meant our company blissfully had the day off. I could actually take my time getting ready for my date with Alex. Though I never really understood why couples went to the movies to deepen a romantic connection—two people sitting silently focused on a giant screen for two hours didn't really create much quality time. But given our rocky relationship, a good dose of forced silence was exactly what Alex and I needed.

We sat in the theater, a jumbo tub of popcorn between us. Only about a third of the theater was occupied, so we had the entire row to ourselves. We were about fifteen minutes early with plenty of time to whisper in the dimly lit theater, only both of our gazes were uncomfortably locked on the screen ahead.

"Do they always show commercials before the movie?" Alex asked as a classified ad for a local business flashed.

"They'll sell ads anywhere these days. I heard couples are now selling space on their wedding programs to bands and florists." I shoved a handful of buttered popcorn into my mouth.

"Seriously?"

"Yup. Madison's dad saw a special on the news. He thought

it was brilliant," I said with a hint of condescension. "He's in marketing."

"Oh," Alex nodded. "Teresa's not doing that, is she?"

"God, no."

A lull fell over the conversation. I chewed another mouthful of popcorn and studied an ad for a local drycleaner. Alex coughed and took a sip of soda. A Century 21 ad flicked next. I read every line of text down to the real estate agent's phone number. Then I waited anxiously for the next one.

Finally the lights dimmed and a warning appeared threatening cell phone users with a penalty of death. I clicked off my phone, then Alex reached over and grabbed my hand. His fingers were greasy. I wanted another mouthful of popcorn, but I couldn't exactly reach across myself with my free hand to dig into the tub in his lap. I also wasn't sure about the etiquette of breaking our hand-holding session.

I watched a preview for an upcoming action flick, then peeked at the popcorn. I could smell the butter. Alex reached his own free hand into the tub and engulfed the kernels. That had to be a sign. If he could eat popcorn, he couldn't expect me not to eat it just because he wanted to act all couple-like.

I tugged my hand away from his, smiled sheepishly, and dug into the warm, salty mess. I chewed, returning my arm tight to my side, out of his reach.

After the movie, we strolled down Main Street. Usually when a movie was over, Madison, Emily, and I would head home, but I knew other couples hit the pastry shop next door. It was an obvious post-film couple-zone, only I had never been invited to join in.

We walked past the bustling storefront; colorful cupcakes

and desserts filled the window. The scent of butter cream icing wafted from inside.

"Wanna get something?" Alex asked as he eyeballed the hordes of teens seated two-by-two at the wrought-iron café tables.

A spiky-haired guy dangled a pink cupcake out for his girlfriend. She grinned seductively and bit into the chocolate treat as her boyfriend oh-so-originally rubbed icing on her nose. Then the giddy pony-tailed girl laughed as her boyfriend reached over to wipe the frosting from her face with a flick of his tongue. They kissed.

That scene was repeating itself in an endless circuit throughout the shop.

"Um, I guess," I muttered as I gawked at the forbidden zone.

Alex clutched my hand and led me into the shop. We stopped in front of the glass pastry counter. Everything from vanilla cupcakes and caramel mousse to chocolate-chip cannolis and peanut butter cheesecake was offered. My stomach roared with delight.

"What'll you have?" asked the pimple-faced boy behind the counter.

"I'll have a mascarpone cannoli." I pointed to the hollow pastry. They filled the crust with creamy cheese on demand.

"I'll have the cookie dough cheesecake." Alex pulled out his wallet.

"Oh, I'll pay," I offered, reaching for my purse.

"No, let me."

I would have paid if he let me, though I would have secretly thought he was a tactless jerk. I didn't care how far the women's movement had come, there is still such a thing as common courtesy.

The scrawny acne-faced teenager handed us our desserts, and we made our way to a vacant table right in front of the shop's picture window. Alex pulled out my chair.

"So how did you like the movie?" I asked as I dug my fork into my cannoli, breaking its shell.

"It was sweet," he answered.

I savored the creamy dessert in my mouth, barely listening to his answer as I focused on the perfect blend of sugar and salt. I could eat an entire truckload of these desserts if left unattended.

"You like it?"

"The cannoli? It's awesome." I grinned.

"No, the movie."

"Oh, yeah. It was cute."

"This is really good," Alex mumbled as he swallowed a bite of cheesecake.

He held out a bite for me. I knew what I was supposed to do. I just never thought I would have to perform the infamous, date cliché that Madison, Emily, and I had often ridiculed. However, in this moment, sitting across from Alex's dimples, the scene didn't seem so embarrassing.

I leaned across the table. He pushed his fork to my lips, and I slid my mouth over the thick, heavy bite. When he pulled his fork away, he brushed my nose. I could feel the icing on my skin. Then he reached over, perfectly scripted, to lick the residue. As he moved to kiss me, I caught a glimpse of our reflection in the mirror. We looked like a happy couple.

His lips pressed against mine for a short, sweet moment and as I opened my eyes, I smiled. That is, before I saw Bobby.

Standing on the sidewalk, outside of the shop, was my locker buddy and a group of his friends. His eyes were locked on mine, but they quickly dulled, his lips turning down. I went to stand up, but it was too late. Bobby's friend grabbed his arm and yanked him away. I watched his silhouette until it was no longer in view.

"What? What is it?" Alex asked.

"Nothing," I muttered, a dull ache filling my chest. "It was no one."

Chapter 35

I spent the next morning engaged in four straight hours of ballet, not like I needed the exercise. After our date ended at the pastry shop, Alex again parked along the curb rather than pulling into my driveway. We kissed for nearly twenty minutes, which meant twenty minutes of me swatting his hands from where they were not welcomed. I was exhausted, both mentally and physically, and now I had the ballet sweat to go along with it.

But of course I was not permitted to relax. The minute rehearsal was complete, Lilly and Teresa appeared in the parking lot ready to shop for bridesmaid dresses. I could barely move my legs, only that didn't faze them. I was dragged along by them and by my destined-to-be-a-wedding-coordinator best friend, Madison.

"Tell me again why Madison's here?" Lilly huffed as she struggled to zip a satin halter gown over her hefty boobs.

My dress had room to spare.

"She's here because (a) she actually likes this stuff and (b) she has good taste," I answered as I clamped the dress to my torso. With so much extra fabric, my hands were the only things keeping it up.

"*I* have good taste." Lilly frowned.

"You saw the dresses Teresa picked out!" I shrieked. "No one looks good with a bow-butt and flamenco sleeves. At least Madison can offer an objective opinion."

Lilly grunted, then gave up on the zipper and stared at the flesh swelling from the gown.

"I look like Shamu."

"No, I look like a beanpole."

"Beanpole is code for 'skinny,' so don't rub it in."

"Yes, having the anatomy of a twelve-year-old boy is what every teenage girl dreams of." I clutched the dress to my body with one hand and carefully turned the doorknob with the other.

For being a fitting room in a low-end boutique, it was remarkably spacious. Lilly and I both fit rather comfortably. Given that Teresa's wedding was only weeks away, we didn't have time to order high-end gowns. We were buying off the rack (a fact that made Madison throw up a little in her mouth).

The door flung open and Madison immediately pulled me to the tattered, carpet-covered pedestal. Six angled mirrors were positioned in front of me.

"Well, obviously, the fit is horrible," Madison stated. "But we can get that altered. What do you think?"

She looked at Teresa, who was sitting on a fraying white sofa shoving her rejected magazine clippings back into her bridal book. Every single dress she had selected was shot down. And while I did feel slightly guilty for not supporting the bride's vision, I was much more grateful to Madison for talking some sense (and taste) into my *tía*.

Teresa shrugged. "I guess it's okay. A little bare."

She pointed to my exposed back and shoulders. The dress was the definition of sexy. All it needed was to shift colors from blue to fire-engine red to make it any more sensual. Just then, Lilly stepped out of the dressing room still fighting with her dress.

"Who said you were a size six?" Madison scoffed.

"I *am* a six. It's just. . ." She stared at her bulging chest. "I'm not a six all around."

"Clearly," Madison huffed. "We'll get you tens from now on."

Lilly frowned as we stared at our reflections in the mirror. Our hair was almost an identical shade of auburn; our freckles had nearly the same patterns; our eyes formed strikingly similar shapes; and our skin glowed the same snowy color, yet our bodies couldn't have been more different. She was short where I was long and I was flat where she was round.

"I don't think there is a dress in the world that is going to look good on both of us." I sighed in defeat.

"Oh, trust me. There is. And I'll find it," Madison said as she darted toward the racks of gowns.

Thirty minutes later, our dressing room was filled with a new collection. Some gowns were long, others short, some were form-fitting, others poofy; but all were in an identical shade of "Tiffany blue," Madison's chosen color scheme. How she managed to talk my *tía* out of her lipstick-red hues, I didn't know.

I pulled up a tea-length strapless gown. It zipped quite snuggly compared to the other dresses I had tried. Lilly wiggled the same gown past her hips.

"Want me to get the zipper?" I asked, strolling over.

"Whatever," she moaned, dejected.

I tugged, and surprisingly, her zipper slid up with ease.

"Hey, it fits!" I cheered.

Lilly spun around to stare at her reflection. Then she turned to the side to glimpse her back zipper to ensure I wasn't lying.

"Whoa!" she muttered in wonderment.

I rushed to the white wooden door and swung it open.

"We have a winner!" I announced triumphantly.

★　★　★

Lilly and I stumbled into my foyer with our purchases. My mom practically knocked us over to see the gowns.

"Ohhh, I love the color," she cooed. "Teresa picked this out?"

"Of course not. Madison did." I snickered.

"She has wonderful taste," my mom complimented as she stared at the simple satin gown.

"Let's just say Teresa had her heart set on a different *look*." I pumped my eyebrows to emphasize the understatement.

Just then, Alex bounded down the stairs, his dimples catching my eye even through the dimly lit stairway.

"You're home." He smiled, then shifted his gaze to the plastic garment bags. "Is it bad luck to see the dress?"

"No, why would I care? It's not like we're getting married," I grunted.

Everyone paused awkwardly at my tone before Alex stepped toward me and took the dress from my hand. He carefully hung it on the railing of the stairway, without peeking, and kissed my cheek.

"I missed you," he whispered before turning to Lilly. "Kyle called."

"Yay!" she cheered, clapping. "I'm gonna ask him to be my date to the wedding."

"Date? We haven't even gotten our invites yet," I noted.

"Teresa said they'd be here this week. Plus, your date is already on the invite list." She nodded to Alex.

Of course, Alex didn't know that a few more friends had also made the cut. In addition to Madison and Emily (who were of course invited with "plus ones"), Teresa had also invited Bobby. She remembered him from my birthday party as "that nice *chico* who danced with me," and she felt compelled to include him given that he witnessed her horrific ordeal with my uncle Diego and he didn't run screaming. I didn't fight her on the suggestion. Part of me was glad he'd be there.

"So how was rehearsal?" my mother asked as she walked toward the kitchen.

I could smell the sausage and peppers cooking. I loved that my house always smelled of home-cooked food.

"Draining. I'm gonna take a shower." I looked at Alex and grinned. "I'm gross."

"I think you smell nice."

He leaned in and nuzzled his lips against the dry sweat on my neck. I brushed him off.

"Trust me, I disgust myself right now. I felt guilty trying on dresses with such funk."

I headed up the steps and to my room. As soon as I closed my bedroom door, I saw the screen saver on my computer flashing. I sunk into my desk chair and checked my messages.

No word from Bobby.

Last night when he saw Alex and I kissing, I felt like I had betrayed him somehow. Bobby knew we were just friends, but if it weren't for his father's affair, who knew where we'd be right now? I still thought about him often, and even if we couldn't be together, I didn't want him to have to see me being romantic with someone else.

My eye caught an e-mail from Vince.

> Hey,
> I need talk to you. I tried calling, but your phone is off.

I dug into my purse and plucked out my phone. I had never turned it back on after the movie.

> Mali and I broke up. I'm so not bringing her to Teresa's wedding. Dude, she's a skank. I may be a male slut, but she's a skank. I can't believe

I ever liked her. But, I hooked up with this 22-year-old blond last night who has a chest bigger than a Playmate. And they're real. Too bad I was so drunk I don't remember her name.

Anyway, did Mom or Dad say anything about a fire alarm? I was playing floor hockey in the dorms the other night and accidentally hit a slap shot into a sensor. Broke the glass and every-thing—it was classic. But the lame R.A. said he was gonna write me up. Whatever. They got the sprinklers off eventually.

Oh, by the way, I aced that Shakespeare essay. Pulled my grade up to a C! The 'rents will be pissed, but at least I'm not failing. So, I guess I should thank you. Too bad I won't!

—Vince

I rolled my eyes—so Vince.

Then I heard my phone beep from my lap. In addition to Vince's missed call, I also had a text from Madison sent only a few minutes ago. I clicked it open.

Just saw Em on Main St. Honked but she didnt c me. Was w/moms asst. WTH???

I swiftly called her back. She answered on the first ring.

"She was walking with that Eric guy," Madison started in mid conversation. "I know it was him. We just saw him at Swarthmore."

I closed my eyes and breathed hard. "Was she 'with' with him?"

"*Chica*, he was holding her hand! What the freak is wrong with that girl? Is she dating her mom's research assistant? Oh, my God!"

I took a deep breath. "I think it's been going on for a while."
A hush fell over the line. It was time to confess.

After ten minutes of me relaying every detail I knew about
the first time I saw Emily with him at the restaurant, about her
constant lies, and about seeing Eric out with another woman,
Madison finally let me take a breath.

"So lemme get this straight. You've known about this for
what, a month? And you never told me! Did you not think this
would interest me? She's *my* best friend too!" She was shrieking
so loud into the phone, her voice was vibrating my earpiece.

"At first, I didn't want to get on her case. She's been so
weird lately. And I thought maybe I had read too much into it.
Maybe it wasn't a date. But then . . . you know, I just got pissed
at her. I'm sick of all her crap." The words were flowing out of
me at a speed too rapid to stop. "I know she's got issues with
her mom and all, but seriously, why is that our fault? Why is
she lying to *us*? I mean, why do I need to run around spilling
her business *for* her?"

"So, wait, she doesn't know that you know?" Madison gasped.
"Nope."
Another long pause.
"Well, we have to tell her," Madison insisted.
"Why?" I shot back.
"Because she's our friend. You two might feel like it's okay
to lie to each other. But I'm not gonna keep my mouth shut.
I'm asking her about this dude."

I clenched my eyes shut. I felt like I was being warned that
a drive-by shooting was about to happen and I was helpless to
stop it. I knew that Madison felt that she was doing the right
thing, but I also knew she had no idea how much Emily was
keeping from us.

Chapter 36

Emily was late getting to school on Monday. I knew she was commuting from the city and forced to fight rush hour traffic each day, but at the same time I couldn't help but wonder if she was purposely late. If Madison honked the horn of her red Audi, Emily had to have seen her. She was avoiding us, just like she had refused to answer our phone calls yesterday. Now I was trudging toward the cafeteria with no idea what to expect.

At least Alex wouldn't be around to witness the scene. He was busy taking an exam for his school back in Puerto Rico. It was as if the universe were setting up this perfect confrontation. I half expected to stroll in at high noon and find the cafeteria transformed into a Wild West saloon with Madison and Emily at opposite ends, their pistols drawn.

I stepped into the bustling lunchroom, and my eyes quickly shot to our table. No one was there. I scanned the lunch line. I didn't see them. I walked further into the room, my eyes sliding frantically from table to table—no one.

Finally, I heard Evan laugh from across the room. Without a thought in my head, I marched over.

"Do you know where Madison is?" I hollered.

His eyelids dropped as he surveyed the looks on his friends' faces.

"Madison who?" he grunted.

"Don't give me that crap. Have you seen Madison in here? I can't find her."

Evan stood up so rapidly, his chair almost tumbled to the ground. He strutted over to within inches of my face.

"Why do you gotta be like this?"

"Evan, just answer the question and I'll leave you alone," I snapped in a hushed tone.

"I saw her go into the bathroom." He exhaled loudly as if annoyed.

"Thank you." I turned to leave, but stopped myself. I spun back around, my face pressing within inches of his. "If you don't like her, then leave her alone. Stop jerking her around. Otherwise, man up and admit it. Because she's not gonna put up with this crap forever. You're not worth it."

With that, I stormed off.

The silence was eerie. As I pushed open the door to the girls' bathroom, I expected to hear shouting but instead I saw Emily and Madison glaring at each other. I could almost hear Madison's teeth grind.

"Hey," I said softly as I placed myself in between the two of them.

"I can't believe you didn't tell me," Madison spat in angry bursts. Her eyes pierced through me.

"Come on, Mad. What was I supposed to do? Emily swore there was nothing going on. And Betsy told Lilly that she and Evan are 'just friends,' " I defended, my eyes desperate. "I mean, I told her to stop talking to him."

My head swung to Emily's. Her pupils had swelled to the point that I could hardly see a hint of green.

"Evan!" Madison hissed. "What the hell?"

I glanced back at Madison; tears had sprung to her eyes. Her jaw was hanging down. I closed my eyes. She didn't know.

"Thanks, Mariana! Just make things worse!" Emily shouted. "Wanna drag my mom in here to grill her about her sex life? I mean, really. Why not just go there?"

"Don't you dare try to turn this around! This has nothing to do with your mother." Madison pointed a finger sharply at me. "What is Mariana talking about? What's this about 'you and Evan'?"

"There is no me and Evan!" Emily shrieked.

Madison locked eyes with me. She didn't have to say a word. I couldn't lie any longer.

"Lilly saw Evan and Emily show up at a party together," I confessed as calmly as I could. "She asked Betsy about it, and Betsy said they were friends and acted like they had been for a while."

I stared awkwardly at the floor as I spoke. The grout between the tiles had long since blackened. It looked like the floor was set in mud. No amount of washing could fix it.

"When the hell was this?" Madison yelped.

"A few weeks ago."

Emily sighed loudly and stepped back on her heel. "Just great," she muttered.

"Oh. My. God!" Madison screamed, her manicured nails making fists in her pale blond hair. "You've both been lying to me for weeks!"

"No, not really," I pleaded, reaching out for her. She shoved my hand away. "Mad, it wasn't for me to tell. I tried to convince Em to come clean . . ."

"Oh, great. Just sell me out more," Emily grunted.

"What? I did!" My face twisted with frustration. "I practically begged you to tell her."

"There's nothing to tell!" she shrieked again, shaking her short brown locks. "Some of us have *real* problems to deal with. I can't spend my life worrying about Madison and Evan."

"Oh, don't even try to play the victim here," Madison scoffed. She took a deep breath, and then stared fiercely in Emily's eyes. "I want to hear everything. Everything! Since when have you been talking to Evan?"

"Ask *him!*"

"Don't pull this crap again!" I shouted, tossing my hands in the air. "It's *your* responsibility to tell her. *You're* her best friend. Not Evan."

Just then, a girl from my honors English class pushed open the creaky bathroom door. I took one look at her, fury filling my eyes, and she quickly turned around and slammed the door shut.

"What the hell is wrong with you, Em?" Madison choked in disgust. "Since when are you such a liar?"

"I'm not lying," Emily murmured in a tone that sounded irritated more than apologetic. "Evan and I are not together. We're not in a relationship. We have no romantic interest in each other. None, whatsoever. In fact, we almost always talk about *you!*"

Emily dropped her head back and glared at the fluorescent lights. A fly was circling a flickering bulb, ramming into it again and again. It hadn't yet realized that the pulsing light wasn't the way out.

"Since when do you and Evan even talk!"

"Since I moved into the city. I ran into him. That was it. No big secret meeting. I just bumped into him. And we started talking . . ."

"And you never told me!"

"He asked me not to."

"Why?"

"That's what you need to ask him."

Madison threw her arms up. I could feel the exasperated energy steaming off her. I didn't know if she was going to wail like a lunatic or burst into tears. Instead, she clutched her purse tighter onto her shoulder and pushed past me, almost knocking Emily down in the process.

When she flung open the bathroom door, I could see my English classmate still standing outside. So were about a dozen other girls. All waiting to enter, all listening to our conversation.

Chapter 37

Madison and Emily didn't speak for nearly two weeks. I tried to play Switzerland and mediate a truce, but in less than a day Emily had stopped speaking to me too. She had completely retreated within herself. She lurched down the halls with a vapid look in her eyes, her hair pulled into a wet ponytail and her clothes sagging from her body. At ballet, she practiced without saying a word—to anyone. Even Madam Colbert confronted her about her undereye circles and constant silence, but Emily refused to open up. She merely drifted through the motions of her performance, and her life.

Madison stopped taking Evan's calls. She refused to IM him or to respond to his text messages. She felt like a fool for falling so hard while he was seducing her best friend (or whatever they were doing). Now Christmas was almost here. The first night of our performance was tomorrow, Teresa's wedding was in a week, and my friends hated each other. Thank God I had Lilly. Teaching someone how to shovel snow was refreshingly simple given my current situation.

"*Ay Dios mio,* I've never been this cold in my life," Lilly complained, her newly purchased mittens pressed to her lips.

My mom and I had taken her shopping for a proper winter coat and accessories the minute we smelled snow in the air. But even with a wool hat and down insulation, she was still shivering.

"At least it's not windy. Trust me, it could be worse." I dug our old-fashioned shovel into the snow, the metal scraping a path on the porch.

We got a fresh three inches today—enough to cause a mess, but not enough to cancel school.

"It is kinda pretty," Lilly conceded as she awkwardly pushed snow off our front step with her red plastic shovel. She nearly impaled herself in the gut.

"I love the way it looks in the yard and on the trees. But you should see it in the city, yuck," I gagged. "It's all black and slushy."

"Well, I guess I'll see it soon. I can't believe the wedding's almost here." Lilly patted her mittens together, shaking off the excess snow.

"I can't believe it's almost Christmas." I tossed a mound of snow from the porch into the yard, then paused, staring at it. My pile had disturbed the perfect, unbroken layer of white on the grass. It was ruined now. "I miss Vince. This is usually his job."

"Well, he'll be here tomorrow," Lilly grunted as she slid another mound off the step. "We should save him some."

"Seriously." I brushed off the snow on the banister. "At least he's coming alone this time."

"He ever tell you why he dumped Mali?"

"Nope. He just said she was a skank and that was it."

I stared into the black sky, my eyes landing on Orion's belt. It was one of the few constellations I could pick out. Finding it always felt comforting, like some things never changed.

"All right, I'm officially freezing. Are we done yet?" Lilly asked as she finished clearing the last step.

I grabbed the heavy bag of salt by the door and hastily tossed the granules around the porch and steps. It was amazing—I was freezing and sweating at the same time. I had spent three hours at a dress rehearsal for tomorrow's production. You would think my parents would have given me the night off to rest, but no. They put me to work.

Just then, the front door of the house pushed open.

Alex's eyes widened. "Why didn't you tell me you were shoveling? I would have helped!"

He immediately grabbed the bag of salt from my hands, but it was too late. The job was done.

"You were in the shower," I stated simply.

"You could've come in and told me . . . or joined me." He winked, and I forced a smile on my chapped lips.

I moved to the door, pounding my snow-covered boots on the frozen welcome mat. The heat radiating from inside felt heavenly. Alex placed his hand on my back (though I could hardly feel it through my puffy coat) and guided me inside. I quickly slid my feet out of the wool-lined boots.

"You ready for your two big shows?" he asked.

"Yeah, I guess," I answered, yanking my coat and ski gloves off.

Alex quickly wrapped his warm hands around mine; the difference in temperatures made me shiver.

"Hey, you know I invited Kyle?" Lilly asked, as we all walked into the living room.

I wrapped a thick quilt around myself as I plopped on the couch. Lilly instantly nuzzled beside me, burying herself under my blanket. Alex sat on the outskirts.

"Yeah, it's cool. I think my parents bought at least twenty tickets. There will be a whole Ruíz family section."

"I can't wait to see you dance," Alex purred.

"It'll be fun," I said flatly as I cuddled closer to Lilly.

Chapter 38

I sat in Chemistry the next day with my leg bouncing so uncontrollably that I was shaking our lab table. The first day of *Sleeping Beauty* was tonight, which was also the first night of winter break. Most kids were anxiously awaiting the final bell so they could jet out, enjoy the rest of their Thursday, and kick off the holidays. I, however, was gnawing at the inside of my mouth.

"So, you freaking out?" Bobby whispered, peering at me.

"How'd you know?"

"I threw up before and after the film festival." He stifled a laugh. "I can detect the signs of panic."

I patted a rapid rhythm against my thighs. "I've never been this nervous before. The production isn't for hours, and I'm already developing the bladder of a small child."

Bobby giggled. "Once you get on that stage, it'll be easier. You'll switch to autopilot, trust me."

He nudged my shoulder with his. It was a small gesture, but I found it oddly comforting. My jaw relaxed.

"I think the whole thing's gonna be a disaster. My friends hate each other. How can we dance together if we can't stand each other?"

Bobby lowered his gaze to the table. "I heard about the fight . . . in the bathroom."

He wasn't the only one. In the past two weeks, enough rumors spread about Madison and Emily's lunchroom showdown that I was starting to wonder if *Entertainment Tonight* would be reporting the details. A girl in my Geometry class actually asked me if Madison was pregnant with Evan Casey's baby (what is this, a Lifetime movie?). Another girl asked if Emily and Evan were living together in a hotel in Center City, planning to elope on their eighteenth birthdays. It was ridiculous.

"So lemme guess, you heard Madison was inseminated with an alien's offspring? Or that Emily was selling herself as a mail-order bride?" I pumped my eyebrows.

"Actually, I heard they were lesbians trapped in a lovers' quarrel."

"Oooo, that's a new one."

I placed my palms on my forehead and rubbed. Somewhere in the background I could hear Mr. Berk reading off news headlines focusing on chemistry-related themes. It was our standard pre-Christmas filler-class. No teacher could start a new lesson or give an exam before the holiday, so we all sat around daydreaming. I half expected them to hand out crayons and coloring books.

"Well, I'll be at the performance tonight. So if you need anyone to talk you off a ledge, feel free to give me a call."

"Don't give me any ideas." I pulled my hands from my face.

"You're gonna be awesome. And remember, no one in the audience knows your routine, so even if you mess up we won't know."

A small smile slipped across my face.

"See, that's the spirit. Just picture us in our underwear."

"Hey, would you actually show up in your underwear? Because that might help."

"Miss Ruíz, are you suggesting that you'd like to see me naked?" He grinned mischievously.

"Oh, I would never."

A lull fell between us. I stared at my notebook.

"So," he said abruptly. "I got the invite to your aunt's wedding."

"My '*tía*,'" I corrected.

"I was kinda surprised . . ."

"Well, she invited all of my friends. She doesn't really know anyone here, and since she actually met you at my party, that made you a genuine acquaintance."

"Oh, should I be honored?" he asked, smirking.

"Of course. It's a Ruíz family get-together. You know it'll be action-packed."

"Well, in that case, how can I refuse?"

"Good, at least I know I'll have one friend there. Who knows if Emily'll show?"

Bobby bit his lip. "Do you ever wonder what would've happened if my dad and Emily's mom never—"

"Sometimes," I admitted, cutting him off.

"Me too," he mumbled. "Maybe . . . I dunno. Maybe one day it won't matter as much."

"Maybe."

Our eyes lingered on each other's just before the bell rang.

Only five more hours until curtain call. I could feel the vomit rising in my throat.

I sat at a vanity in the backstage dressing room. Nearly twenty ballerinas were crammed into a space intended for half as many. The two boys in our production shared an entire dressing room all their own—the same size as ours.

I coated my lips in a layer of red "lady danger" lipstick. My reflection looked foreign. Even after years of performing, the stark stage makeup of a ballerina still felt uncomfortable. I spritzed the hair by my ears, hoping to lock back any loose strands. My bun was so tightly knotted that my eyes pulled back at the corners.

I spied Emily rising from her makeup stool, adjusting her heavy black costume. Her makeup was as dark as death, very fitting with her mood. She yanked at her dense, layered skirt, re-centering the waistline. I smiled through the mirror, catching her eye.

"You look good," I stated.

"I look like the grim reaper," she hissed, pushing at her teased brown hair.

For a girl whose locks were silky-straight for fifteen years, then barely washed for the past two weeks, it was odd seeing her hair frozen like a bad Tina Turner wig. The crazy frizz combined with her black-and-white Goth makeup really created an evil fairy vibe.

"You look awesome. Just like Carabosse." I twisted my neck to kindly look at her directly. "Can you believe this is it?"

She snorted, saying nothing.

I had hoped her brief remark was a sign of an olive branch about to be extended, but from the way she now intentionally avoided my gaze, I was guessing that our conversation represented more of a lack of better judgment on her part.

Just then, Madison popped out of the girls' bathroom dressed in her standard "chorus" tutu. She would spend the majority of the performance dancing in the background or waving a white ribbon, until the final act where she got to dress in a giant white cat head to dance her only solo.

"Okay, there is officially no liquid left in my body. I've peed, like, seventeen times," Madison joked, adjusting her tights.

"Tell me about it. If I'm not peeing, then I'm meditating to keep the puke from creeping up from my stomach," I moaned.

I glanced at Emily, but she immediately retreated to the opposite side of the dressing room. Madison watched her departure and smirked, satisfied.

"My parents are sitting next to your parents," she said. "I already peeked."

"What about . . . ?" I nodded toward Emily.

"I haven't seen her mother yet, but I'm sure she's here. Wonder which bachelor she's brought with her," Madison whispered.

I felt guilty talking about Emily, especially when she was only a few feet away. She was our best friend (at least she had been for more than a decade), and I wasn't ready to give up on her entirely.

"Did you see anyone else in the audience?" I asked as I blotted more powder on my forehead.

"Alex is here. And your brother. And . . . Bobby."

"You saw Bobby?" I asked, a bit too excited.

"Yup, he's here with Jay from the photography club. Don't ask me how he dragged that boy to a ballet."

I sucked in my lips to keep them from spreading across my face.

"Is that smile for Alex? Or Bobby?"

I coughed slightly and stared awkwardly at the makeup littering the battered wooden vanity. "Is Evan here?"

"Didn't see him. Not that I care. Even if he did come, it would probably be for *Emily.*"

She snatched the aerosol can from the vanity and aggressively spewed another coat of hairspray onto her already frozen locks.

"Hey, you never know. Maybe he'll show. You told him when it was . . ."

"Let's face it. The boy didn't care enough to acknowledge my existence even when we were talking, I highly doubt he'd do it now."

My head jutted back. It was the first time that Madison had admitted she'd noticed Evan's lack of commitment. Maybe she wasn't as blinded by lust as I thought.

At that moment, Madam Colbert swung open the dressing room doors. Her hair was tied high, similar to the rest of us ballerinas, and her sharp black pantsuit was so freshly ironed that I could still see the creases in the seams. She frantically looked up from her clipboard, surveying the room.

"Okay, girls. This is it!" she cheered.

Her eyes flicked to each of us, wild and nervous. "Amy, more foundation. I can see my reflection in your nose. Jen, you better make sure that hair stays back. I will *not* have a ballerina fussing on stage!"

She walked closer to me, examining my face. "More eyeliner." She turned to Madison. "You help her. I want her eyes to look like yours. They're perfect."

Madison's face lit up from the compliment. It may have been the first time our instructor had praised Madison in years. It didn't matter that it wasn't about her dancing.

Madison peered at me with sparkling azure eyes. "Okay, let's do you up."

She clutched the jet-black liquid liner, the apples of her cheeks full. I looked away as she moved toward me with the wand. For a brief instant, I caught a glimpse of Emily across the room. She was smiling and something inside me prayed that she was happy for Madison's compliment. Because if she was, then maybe I did still know her, after all.

Chapter 39

I stood motionless behind the curtain. Hot blood roared in my ears.

I had never danced in this theater before. Madam Colbert had always conducted our performances in our studio or in an ailing performance theater. I was used to the audience being seated in folding chairs and an unchangeable set due to the lack of a stage curtain. Now we were dancing on a real stage at a respected community theater. I saw *A Christmas Carol* performed here last year by semi-professional actors (okay, my old babysitter was Mrs. Cratchit).

This stage was authentic and spacious and constructed of polished wood. Lights hung from the ceiling, illuminating our every move. A sound system was linked throughout the theater, and a heavy velour curtain hid the dancers from view. It was real.

I closed my eyes and gripped a pleat in the curtain. The music was about to start. The theater was dark. I could hear the stillness in the air. My bladder pulsed for my attention, but I knew it was just my body's way of acknowledging my nerves.

"You're gonna be great," Madison whispered.

I forced a smile.

Emily stood a few feet away. She was the first to dance on stage. When our eyes met, she nodded.

"Break a leg," she whispered.

"And bad luck to you too," I replied.

It was our standard pre-production ritual. We hadn't danced a show in more than ten years where those lines hadn't first been uttered. A warm calm filled my body.

The curtain pulled open, and the sounds of Tchaikovsky rang.

I paused to catch my breath, looking for glimpses of Emily, then I heard my cue. I stepped on stage, and all the terror in my body washed out of my toes. A dark abyss sat before me. I couldn't see a single face. My body moved gracefully, remembering steps that my mind consciously didn't recall. I floated outside of myself in a dancing blur.

Exhausted and sweaty, I exited the stage and Madam immediately yanked the tutu from my waist. Members of the chorus threw me into my next outfit as Madison dabbed the sweat from my forehead.

"You were awesome. You're doing great," she whispered, but her voice sounded as though it were traveling through water.

Before a clear thought entered my mind, I felt my instructor thrust me back on the stage. I popped to my toes and twirled around my fellow ballerinas. Applause rang out. I soared into a jump so high that the elevation surprised even me. The crowd rang out once more, but I kept on dancing, lost in the movement.

The show continued like this for more than an hour. Occasional breaks in performing would be met with frantic wardrobe changes. I hardly got a sip of water, and my body never rested. Before I knew it, intermission had arrived. The curtain closed.

"Holy shit," I muttered, the blood finally rushing to my brain as lights in the theater pumped higher.

"You were on fire," remarked Gabriel, my male counterpart, as he patted my back.

"Coming from Prince Charming, I should be flattered."

"Florimund, I'm Prince Florimund," Gabriel corrected.

Madison rushed to my side. "Did you hear how people were cheering for you?"

She hugged my side.

"Barely. I think I'm only semi-conscious."

"People are still applauding," Madison gleaned as she rushed toward the seam in the curtain.

Ballerinas were not supposed to peek. It was considered "bad taste," according to our instructor. Madison stopped listening to those reprimands when she was seven. She always looked, all the time.

She pulled back the heavy velour and twisted an eye into the opening.

"I can see your mom. Oh, wait, I can see *my* mom," she cooed. "Your mom looks so happy."

"Lemme see, lemme see." I nudged her out of the way. "Are my uncles here? Is Teresa?"

I shoved my face into the gap in the curtain. My eyes slid from face to face in the audience.

"What section are they in?"

"The front right."

I craned my neck further and finally caught a glimpse of Lilly holding a conversation with my mom. Vince and Kyle were stifling laughs behind her as my brother licked his finger and moved toward my father's ear. Even from here, I could see that my father was sleeping. I sighed, rolling my eyes.

"Yeah, I know. Your dad's out cold." Madison laughed.

"Thanks for warning me."

"Like you're surprised."

Next to my mother sat my aunts and uncles, but Teresa was nowhere in sight. I couldn't really blame her. Her wedding was in a week, and without a coordinator and with such short notice, she had a list of things to do that would make the president of the United States look lazy. Finally, I spied Alex seated on the far end of my family's section, next to my aunt Stacey. My eyebrows squished together. Why wasn't he sitting next to Lilly? Or my brother?

"You know, you're hogging the curtain," Madison griped.

"Hold on, hold on. Give me a minute."

My eyes moved across the auditorium. People were standing in the aisles stretching their legs. We didn't serve any refreshments during intermission, so hardly anyone left the theater (the whole production was shorter than most Hollywood blockbusters). Finally, my eyes landed on their desired target. Bobby was seated next to his friend Jay, chatting and smiling. I strained to read their lips, but couldn't make out the conversation. At least he looked happy.

"All right, enough. Lemme have another peek," Madison ordered, shoving me aside. "What, because you're the star of the show you think you can hog the curtain?"

"I am *not* a stage hog."

"Yeah right, *oink, oink.*"

Madison pushed her tiny face back into the opening as I glanced around for Emily. She was seated on the floor, stage left, watching us. I smiled and waved her over. She actually twisted to look behind her as if she thought I was gesturing to someone else. Her eyes narrowed cautiously, then she slowly rose to her feet.

"You were really good," I commented as she trotted over.

"Thanks. You too." Her eyes were locked on the back of Madison's head.

"Looks like your fan club showed up." Madison sneered as she spun around.

"What are you talking about? Is my dad here?" Emily squeaked, hope in her voice.

"As if." Madison shrugged. "See for yourself."

Emily rushed to the curtain as Madison took a few steps back.

"*What's going on?*" I mouthed.

"Evan's here. And he's sitting right behind good ol' Mrs. Montgomery. What a coincidence," Madison snapped.

Emily's head flung toward us. She looked as confused as I did.

"Omigod," she gasped as she returned her stare to the audience.

"Yeah, I wonder if they drove here together. Maybe he's asking for her blessing," Madison muttered.

"Omigod," Emily choked again.

I paused, suspiciously, tilting my head. Then I placed my palm on Emily's shoulder and guided her away from the curtain. She didn't protest. She looked too stunned. I placed my eye in the velour gap and immediately located Emily's mom. Sure enough, right behind her was Evan Casey. And almost directly behind him was Eric—her mom's research assistant and Emily's secret date. It was a near perfect line of all the people causing drama in my friend's life.

When I glanced back at Emily, she was blinking rapidly and swaying on her feet. Madison glared at her without an ounce of sympathy.

We'd never confronted her about Eric; I had blurted out the Evan saga in the bathroom before we had had the chance. Then Emily stopped speaking to us. And at this point, I had no idea who was making her nervous—her mother, Evan, or Eric.

★ ★ ★

We were halfway through the final act. The production was going smoothly, and as I lay on the stage bed awaiting my prince's kiss, my body tingled energetically. I could hear Gabriel dancing with the Lilac Fairy as Carabosse (Emily) tried to prevent my awakening. I separated my eyelashes slightly and peeked as Emily furiously performed with her counterparts, her enormous costume swishing around her. I discreetly watched the scene until I heard an unusual shuffle.

At first, it sounded like Emily landing a jump, but then the noise continued—farther away. We had danced this piece so many times that I knew every bump and scuff the dancers made. Heck, I could have popped up and continued their parts effortlessly, I knew the production so well. But the sounds I was hearing were not part of our performance. The commotion was coming from the audience.

I secretly peered into the spotlights, but only saw white light. When I subtly shifted my gaze to Emily, panic was spread across her face. She was barely moving.

Finally, Gabriel approached my bed. It was time for my character's climactic awakening. I shrugged off my uneasiness and reconnected with Princess Aurora. I felt Gabriel's heat as he hovered above me, his lips never really brushing mine. It was not a very romantic Prince-Charming moment, but I played along and popped off the bed.

My fellow ballerinas flooded the stage for the wedding celebration. I soared through the movements, my arms locked with Gabriel's, until we unexpectedly almost smashed into Emily. She was standing at center stage long after she should have exited. Her character was supposed to die the instant the prince's kiss breaks her spell.

Ballerinas twirled awkwardly around her, trying to complete routines without crashing into the unwanted roadblock. Madison not-so-discreetly shoved her, only she didn't move. Emily just stared into the audience, awestruck, her feet refusing to budge.

Finally, Gabriel and I began our wedding dance and I attempted to launch into a series of pirouettes covering the length of the stage. I knew Emily was frozen in my way. I knew I was going to hit her if I didn't alter my path. So I focused on the far corner of the back wall and veered to the left of my friend, hoping my partner would notice my modified course.

Only he didn't have time.

Just as I detoured around Emily, she took a sudden step back and rammed into me as I turned. I immediately lost my balance, fell off pointe, twisted clumsily, and slammed onto the stage.

Everyone heard the pop.

Chapter 40

I had never been in a wheelchair before.

As soon as my body hit the stage, I clutched my contorted ankle. It was sore, but so were my muscles. I had thought I could work through it, I had thought I was fine. Only as I stumbled back to my feet, my ankle instantly gave way in a flood of hot pain. I yelped, tumbling onto the stage. A deep throb pulsed inside my foot.

Then everything moved in fast-forward. Dancers, parents, and audience members scurried around me, talking all at once. It was sudden, dizzying, and their horrified faces forced my tears to spill. I rubbed my eyes, clutched my ankle, and breathed harshly through my mouth. Before I knew it, my arms were wrapped around my father's neck as he raced me out of the theater. The car was no sooner parked at the local ER, than a team of nurses rushed outside with a wheelchair. I sped down a bright white corridor. The blazing lights whizzed past as my ankle sat propped on a footrest.

I was still in my tutu.

An hour later, after several agonizing tests, X-rays, a dose of Tylenol, and several cold compressions, I sat in a small hospital room waiting for answers.

"How are you feeling?" my mother asked as she rested beside my bed.

"Feeling like I wanna go home," I muttered as I stared at my red, swollen ankle.

The ice was making me as uncomfortable as the injury. I wasn't sure if my skin was pink from inflammation or from the cold. I adjusted the location of the icepack and rearranged the angle of my foot on the pillows. I winced the minute the joint moved.

"Well, we need to wait for the doctors," my mom said pleasantly. "Would you like some water?"

She gestured to the bubbling cooler beside her. She was already through her third cone-shaped paper cup.

"No. Do you think I'll be able to dance tomorrow?"

My mother said nothing and when I looked at her, she quickly painted on a smile and glanced away. There was a gentle knock at the door. I knew it was Lilly.

"*Hola*," she said as she entered. "How's the patient?"

"Bored," I moaned. "When can I get out of here?"

"I think your dad's talking to the doctor now."

"Well, why isn't the doctor talking to me?"

My mom patted my good leg. "I think I'll go see what's keeping them."

As soon as she closed the door, Lilly flopped against my bed with no regard to my elevated limb.

"Oh, sorry, Gimpy." She hid a smirk.

"Gimpy? Where did you get that from Miss *Puertorriquena*?"

"Vince. It's his new name for you. The Gimp or Gimpy, depending on the context."

"Great," I groaned. "Is he out there?"

"Are you kidding? Half the audience is out there."

I stared at her, my eyebrows scrunched in shock.

"Vince, Kyle, Alex, your uncles, your aunts, half the student body . . ."

"Shut up!"

"Okay, I exaggerated the last part. But you've got quite a get-well section. How do you think you got treated so quickly?"

" 'Cause I'm hurt." I shrugged.

"Yeah. Try because Uncle Diego called his neighbor who is an attending ER physician. Or something like that," Lilly said. "And Madison's father plays golf with the chief of staff."

"Mr. Jones!" It was all rushing back to me: the summer Madison, Emily, and I spent as candy stripers in the old folks' home. It was affiliated with the hospital. "Oh, man. I stocked magazines at this place! Well, not *this* place . . ."

"I know, Madison's out there reliving the glory days."

I paused, staring at my ankle. It was twice its normal size.

"Is Emily out there?" I asked softly.

"She's sitting with her mom. She's not talking to anyone. The girl looks like someone shot her dog."

"Really?" I felt a tinge of joy.

"Well, what the hell happened? She, like, freaked." Lilly shook her auburn locks.

"Don't ask me. She hasn't said anything?"

"Well, Madison started shrieking at her the minute you and your dad left. And Emily just stood on the stage like a mute. The *chica's* lost it." Lilly peered down at the linoleum floor. "Madison thinks she did it on purpose."

I already suspected as much. After she had "accidentally" tripped me during practice, it had occurred to me that our collision might have been intentional. But the thought of her purposely trying to end my ballet career was too much to absorb. Thankfully, my throbbing spasms gave me something else to focus on.

"Is it just her and her mom?"

Lilly cocked her head. "Yeah, why?"

"Right before the second act, we saw that college kid in the audience. He was sitting right behind Evan."

"Well, Evan's here."

"Shut! Up!" My eyes stretched so much my eyeballs felt a gush of cool air. "Who's he with? Emily or Madison?"

"Right now, Vince. Your brother is pretty much putting on a one-man show. He's got an endless supply of fraternity tales to entertain the masses."

"Leave it to Vince." I laughed.

Just then, my father walked in with the doctor at his side. My mom strolled a few feet behind them, her face still wearing a fake smile.

The doctor headed straight for the sink, pushed up his lab coat sleeves and washed his hands. His salt-and-pepper hair was full and straight. He was older, maybe in his late forties, but he had that handsome Richard Gere–distinguished look going for him. I was guessing he had a very pleasant family back home. Once his hands were dry, he calmly strolled toward me and lightly touched my foot.

"Does this hurt?" he asked as he outwardly rotated my ankle.

"Eh, a little," I said, eyeing him cautiously.

Then the doctor delicately rotated my foot inward. I instantly yelped and shot upright.

He sighed. "Mariana, the good news is you don't have any broken bones."

My face lit up. No cast. No permanent damage. I'd be dancing by morning.

"The bad news is, you have a pretty bad sprain and . . . it's going to take a while to heal."

"So, what? Ice and Tylenol?" I nodded. "Can I dance tomorrow?"

He shook his head as if he thought I had trouble comprehending the language.

"Mariana, this a grade-two sprain. You've torn several liga-
ments. I'd like to put you on crutches for at least three days.
We'll give you an air splint. . . ."

"What? A cast?"

The image of me hobbling around in a tutu and crutches
flashed in my brain. The air sucked from my lungs. A sprained
ankle, big whoop. Kids sprain things all the time. How could I
not be able to dance? It wasn't broken.

"I hear that dancing is important to you . . ."

"Doc, I was brought here in a tutu." I gestured to the costume on the chair beside us. A nurse had mercifully given me
a pair of scrubs to change into.

"It's going to take about four to six weeks before you can
return to normal activities—"

Four to six weeks? The second performance was tomorrow. Teresa's wedding was next Saturday. My stomach simultaneously tightened and gurgled.

"Can I walk on it?"

"In a few days, you'll come back in. We'll see how you do
with a castboot. It's a 'walking cast,' if you will . . ."

There was that word again: cast. My eyes narrowed as if I
thought this was all his fault—the enemy with X-rays and a lab
coat.

"I talked to your parents about getting you some physical
therapy. If you rest, and follow my instructions, you should be
able to return to ballet in a couple of months—"

"Months!" I choked.

My mom rushed to my side and grabbed my hand while
Lilly backed toward the door. I wanted to run out with her.

★   ★   ★

I left the hospital room on crutches. I was supposed to keep my foot elevated above my head (or rather, my heart) for two days. That included Christmas. All the while my ankle would be locked in a nifty plastic air splint with only over-the-counter drugs to ease my pain (yeah, the same stuff I used for a headache was all I needed to dull the millions of throbbing needles in my ankle). Oh, and I had a wonderfully uncomfortable set of crutches in case I dared to rise from my bed rest to pee or something.

"This sucks," I whined as Lilly and my mom helped me toward the waiting room.

My mother insisted that I thank my visitors for their support. Even with a swollen ankle and crutches, she still expected me to be polite.

As I turned halfway down the corridor and saw the glass waiting room ahead, I immediately realized why my mother was so adamant. The room was filled with helium balloons. Blue, green, and silver "Get Well" wishes hovered near the ceiling, each attached to healthy wrists. My entire ballet company was present, in costume, each with a bouquet of flowers. They had to have cleared out the gift shop.

"Wow, I should break a leg more often," I joked as I walked through the automatic door.

Everyone giggled. Madison rushed over, her stage makeup still thickly applied. It was humorous seeing all these made-up characters in such a serious setting.

"They wouldn't let me see you!" Madison hollered. "They said I wasn't family. Like, *whatever!*"

She hugged me carefully, so as not to damage me further. "You okay?"

I shook my head. "Looks like I'll be celebrating the holidays in bed. But I should be fine . . . in a few weeks."

Everyone gasped, then Madam Colbert stepped out from behind a crop of ballet pupils and hesitantly walked toward me.

"Miss Ruíz, I'm so sorry," she said, her face tense.

"It's okay. You didn't do anything. I'll be fine. I should be able to dance again . . . soon."

"He said she'll need physical therapy first," my mother added sternly.

"Apparently, my foot can no longer hold my weight. Good thing I'm skinny," I murmured under my breath. "But, I'll be fine."

I scanned the faces in the crowd; they looked worse than I did. I noticed Alex standing toward the back, avoiding my glances. Then Vince barreled forward, Kyle, Evan, and Bobby by his side.

"Well, maybe you can find something cooler to do than ballet," Vince piped up as he handed me a bunch of balloons.

I looked up and noticed that two said "It's A Girl" and one had a stork carrying a blue bundle.

"Very funny," I muttered.

"What? Bobby picked those out." He elbowed my locker buddy, who winced with embarrassment, shaking his head.

"I did no such thing."

"Hey, what's a little immaculate conception between friends," I joked.

"Watch it," my uncle Diego warned, as if taking the Lord's name in vain was actually on my list of things to worry about.

"I'm glad you're okay," Bobby offered.

"I'm glad I've got such a big fan club. Who knew? I thought Lilly was the only one with followers."

"Yeah, well, my fans are all in the A.V. club." Lilly giggled.

"Don't knock the A.V. club!" Bobby defended.

Everyone laughed and then slowly took turns offering me

well wishes. The company couldn't believe I wouldn't be attending tomorrow's performance and swore they'd dedicate the show to me. Madam Colbert, racked with guilt, informed me that my understudy would be taking over the role.

My understudy was Emily.

And she approached me last.

The entire room cleared when it was her turn to speak—even my parents stepped outside (as if they all expected a scene that they were too embarrassed to witness).

"Hey," I said. She stood several feet away, a long sober look in her eyes.

"Mariana . . ." She paused, then stared at the floor. "Mariana, I'm so sorry."

Her voice cracked. I could tell she had been crying.

"What happened?" I asked, unconvinced by her apology.

She covered her face with her hands. "I don't know."

"Em, you were supposed to leave the stage. Why were you there? Why didn't you move?"

"I don't know. I'm so sorry. I never meant . . . I mean, I didn't do it on purpose. Really."

She wiped at the streams of tears pouring down her cheeks.

"So you 'accidentally' didn't leave the stage?"

I adjusted the crutches under my arms. They almost hurt worse than my ankle, and the sight of Emily was creating a sick twinge in the pit of my belly.

"I looked into the audience . . . and I just freaked."

"You saw Eric," I said bluntly.

Her face closed up, her watery green eyes blinking rapidly.

"Em, I know all about Eric. So does Madison." Maybe it was the pain or maybe it was my utter exhaustion, but I had lost the capacity for bullshit. "I saw you two at McCormick & Schmick's a couple months ago. I was there with my family. And I texted you and you lied and said you were with your dad . . ."

"You were there?" Her thin lips parted as her eyes got very wide.

"Yeah, with Lilly."

"Why didn't you say anything?"

"Because I was waiting for you to fess up. Then all the crap started with Evan. . . ."

"I'm not interested in Evan. At all," she said assertively. "I just, I just thought Eric liked me. Then we saw him with that girl . . ."

"His girlfriend?"

"He says she isn't. But . . ." She stared up at the ceiling, tears welling again.

I couldn't tell if she was crying out of guilt for what she did to me, or out of her own hapless romantic situation. And that doubt caused anger to drum in my ears.

"Stop crying," I ordered. "You don't get to feel sad here. This isn't about *you*. Maybe if you weren't lying all the time . . ."

"I'm not a liar!" she cried.

"Then why did you ignore Madison when she honked at you a few weeks ago? I know you saw her."

"Because I was hoping she didn't see Eric! I didn't want to draw attention to the situation or make him feel weird. He already hates the fact that I'm in high school. I like him so much," she moaned.

My hands felt icy as they clutched my crutches. I couldn't believe I was standing here, broken, and she was talking about her problems rather than mine.

"Em, I'm sick of this! I'm sick of you acting like this. Why does everything have to be some big secret with you?"

"Because he's my mom's assistant. And he's twenty-one! If she found out, she'd throw a conniption—"

"Isn't that why you did it?" I asked, cutting her off.

"I don't know," she said softly, closing her eyes. "I had no idea he was coming tonight. We've hardly spoken lately. I thought he didn't like me anymore and then, *bam,* he was there."

"Yeah, 'bam' is the word I'd use too." I gestured to my aching limb.

"My *mom* saw him," she said ominously, strangling back a sob. "Right before the finale. I heard the two of them arguing up front, and there I was on stage. I just froze."

"Until you rammed into me."

"I'm so . . . *sorry.*"

I was tired, and frankly I was getting a little tired of having to forgive Emily. I was tired of trying so hard to understand her, and tired of her self-made drama.

I moved my crutches toward the automatic door. "Have fun dancing tomorrow . . ."

"Mariana!"

"I gotta go. People are waiting."

When I left, Emily was still standing inside. I didn't turn back to say good-bye, and she didn't follow me. She didn't have a chance. Lilly was waiting in the hall to guide me to the parking lot.

"How'd it go?" she asked, her arm on my back.

"Long story."

The minute I stepped onto the icy curb, I saw that the crowd had yet to fully disperse. Madison was waiting for me, along with my mom, my brother, Bobby, Kyle, and Evan.

"Where's Alex?" I whispered as a cold wind brushed my face.

"Long story," Lilly whispered back.

"Dad and Alex went to get the car," Vince explained as he guided me to a snowy bench.

"Is everyone coming back to the house?" I asked, scanning the faces.

"Uh, no. I can't. I just wanted to make sure you were okay," Bobby confessed, his breath freezing in the air. "I should get going."

"Thanks for staying." I smiled at him.

He nodded and turned to the pack. "Anyone need a ride?"

I looked at Evan; he was the only infidel left in the bunch. I couldn't imagine why he was so concerned with my well-being or why he had come to the hospital (let alone the performance).

Then he clasped Madison's glove-covered hand. "Can you give me a ride to my buddy's house?" he asked, gazing at her. "I said I'd swing by . . . You can come too."

A glow filled my friend's already rosy cheeks. "Sure."

Holding her hand, he walked her to her car in front of everyone.

Chapter 41

After I spent most of the night whining that I was too un-comfortable to sleep (my foot had to stay atop a mountain of pillows), my mother secretly snuck me a Percocet left over from her recent root canal. I slept like a baby and almost forgot everything that happened until I woke up the next morning to find my ankle had swollen to a point that it no longer resem-bled a human body part. It was purple and puffy and created an odd ramp that morphed into a football-size foot.

The effort it took to hobble downstairs was enough to make me pop another pill. The over-the-counter drugs just weren't cutting it, but my mom's stash had me flying in the clouds so high I couldn't feel my fingertips let alone my injury.

"This stuff is *great*," I moaned gleefully, tapping my fingers against my thumbs. "I can't feel ma finggeerrrs."

I yawned, stretching back on the couch.

My brother and Alex sat on the floor playing video games, which wasn't easy considering a large evergreen was blocking half the TV. We were all supposed to decorate the tree last night after my performance. Instead, my mother had our maid rush over to toss up the ornaments while we sat at the hospital. The garland was sagging, the lights were bunched, and all the balls were hung in the wrong places. The brass bells with our names were supposed to dangle under the angel tree-topper, only Josephine must have shoved them somewhere else. I couldn't see them.

It just didn't feel like Christmas Eve.

Not that anyone expected me to be in the holiday spirit. It was pathetic that our festivities were kicking off with a sprained ankle and my brother pummeling our Puerto Rican guest in a boxing match that was surprisingly bloody for being computer-generated. It all just made me want to don a red furry hat and cheer "Ho! Ho! Ho!" (yeah, right).

I rolled over on the couch, knocking the ice pack off my ankle.

"Whoops," I said, shrugging.

I was sick of the twenty-minute ice intervals. They sent constant chills through my body and I couldn't comfortably sleep while frozen.

"You need to keep this on," Alex said, re-wrapping the ice in a hand towel and placing it on my instep.

"Maybe they'll have to cut it off," I moaned, yawning again.

"The first sprained ankle amputation in history," Vince joked.

He didn't pause the game while Alex tended to my ankle. He kept right on slugging the crap out of his computer character.

"Five more minutes, that's all you need," Alex told me.

"Like you know what she needs," my brother huffed.

"Where's Lilly?" I groaned, my eyes closing.

"She and Mom are baking you Christmas cookies. The good ones, not the Polish ones." Vince mocked as his fingers kept tapping on his game control.

"Oooo, chocolate chip," I moaned, my eyes resting.

"You should've paused the game while I helped her," Alex said. I heard his fingers move across the controls.

"Yeah, well, you should've done a lot of things."

"Oh, great, *that* again."

Their conversation drifted far away. My head sunk into the cushions, my body heavy.

"Just stay away from her, *dick*."

"You don't know me."

"I know enough."

When I woke up a few hours later, I was in my bed. Lilly was curled tight beside me, and my entire lower half was nestled in a ramp of pillows. My leg ached from being stuck in that angle for so long.

"Ugh," I groaned as I tried to twist my body into a more comfortable position.

That apparently was just enough movement to stir Lilly. She quickly shot up.

"Your ankle! Your foot! You okay?" she asked, checking to make sure my leg was still securely raised above my heart.

"How'd I get here?"

"Your dad carried you. It was kinda cute."

My leg felt locked. All I wanted to do was stand up and stretch, but I couldn't.

"Don't even think of moving," Lilly hissed. "Your mother will have my head."

"I'm not an invalid," I grumbled.

"Actually, Gimpy, that's exactly what you are."

I growled and flopped back on my pillow. I didn't think I was going to be able to handle two days of this.

Lilly patted my stomach and jumped out of bed on her two healthy feet.

"Now lemme get you downstairs. Do you need me to help you pee?"

I tossed my hands over my face and screamed silently.

An hour later, after three people assisted me down the stairs, I was finally back on the couch. I didn't need their help. I had spent more than a decade balancing on one leg (balancing on the tippy toes of one leg). There was a dressing room full of ballerinas who could attest for my balancing skills. Only right now they were too busy getting ready for our final matinee performance. I was missing the big holiday show. Months of practice and now Emily was dancing my part.

"Thanks for the cookies, Mom," I said as I gobbled down the warm maple-lace masterpieces.

"Anything you want, dear."

I smiled (I could seriously milk this).

"Can I go to the performance in an hour?"

"Anything inside the house," she corrected, adjusting my pillows.

"Yo, Ma! Can I get some more cookies?" Vince hollered from my father's den.

"Vince, I'm helping your sister!"

Apparently, my brother was not getting the "son-who-just-returned-home-from-college" treatment he was expecting. I found it rather amusing.

"Maybe I should break my leg," Vince huffed as he trudged into the living room.

"It's a sprain," I corrected.

He stuck out his tongue.

"Very mature," I snipped.

"At least I've got two working legs, Gimpy."

270 DIANA RODRIGUEZ WALLACH

I scrunched my nose as my brother trotted upstairs, skipping two steps at a time.

"So," Lilly interrupted as she plunked down on the love seat. "We have a whole afternoon of movie-watching planned. Since this is *Nochebuena,* we were thinking of an all-day Christmas spectacular. Everything from *It's a Wonderful Life* to *A Charlie Brown Christmas.*"

"I can't believe I'm spending Christmas Eve chained to a sofa." I sunk my head back, staring at the ceiling. The frown on my face was widening with each moment.

"It's better than spending it dancing! I mean, come on, who works on Christmas Eve?" Lilly popped in a DVD.

"We *dance* on Christmas Eve. It's tradition."

"Then why don't you do *The Nutcracker* or something?"

"We've *done The Nutcracker.* We can't do it every year, we'd go crazy."

"See, you admit it. Ballet makes you crazy. You'll be much happier now, trust me."

Lilly cued the black-and-white Christmas classic. I was powerless to stop her. I had no other means of entertainment at my disposal. I wasn't about to bust out a book. Reading, alone, on the holidays was just too depressing. My shoulders sunk toward my chest.

"Don't be so sad," Lilly said.

I suddenly sat upright. "Where's Alex?"

"Probably hiding in his room," Lilly muttered.

"What's going on? I could swear I heard Vince going at him before I fell asleep. Of course it could've been the drugs . . ."

"Nope. You were right," Lilly said as she pulled a quilt around her with one hand and held the remote in the other. "Vince has been all over Alex since he got back from Cornell."

"Why?"

"Yo no sé," Lilly muttered, before pressing "play" on the remote. "But Alex is just taking it."

His trip was almost over. Alex was set to return to Utuado after the New Year. After weeks of touring Philadelphia universities, he was leaning toward Haverford College—it was only a few miles away and barely had more students than my high school.

Bells rang out from the surround sound. I could recite every line in the movie. I loved it. It always made me happy. But I just didn't feel in the Christmas spirit.

Chapter 42

The next morning, my whole family had to wait to open presents until they maneuvered me down the stairs. Then I had to be carefully arranged on the couch (which smelled like I had spent twelve hours sitting on it yesterday, because I had), with my leg propped on four pillows and an ice pack placed on my swollen bluish joint. The whole scene screamed Christmas.

"Well, I think Mariana should open the first gift," my mother cooed, rising from the love seat to pull a box from under the tree.

This year all of our gifts were wrapped in faded green paper with straw bows and red-checkered gift tags. It was Martha Stewart's "country Christmas" look, which fit perfectly with our location—ten minutes outside of one of the nation's largest cities.

She rested the box on my lap and pulled off the bow. "Make sure we recycle these. They're all natural."

I opened the lid of the Bloomingdale's box to find a winter-white cashmere sweater. "Ah, thanks Mom."

"Thank Santa," she corrected.

We went around the room opening gifts for nearly an

hour. At the end of the ordeal, I had a new wardrobe, a new perfume set, a digital camera, a designer necklace with matching earrings, and a gift card to download music.

Everyone else was equally satisfied—even Lilly, who finally had enough clothes to no longer borrow mine, which was a blessing given that she didn't leave Puerto Rico with much of a winter wardrobe.

"I can't believe you did all of this. Thank you," Lilly said, staring appreciatively at her pile.

There was enough wrapping paper on the floor to fill a small landfill.

"Oh, thank Santa," my mom said as she darted into the kitchen for a garbage bag.

"Wow, is this what Christmas is like here every year?" Lilly asked.

"Yeah, why? What's it like in Utuado?"

"Did you see the necklace and watch my mom sent me? That's all I would've gotten back home."

I winced slightly. I guess I always took our Christmas bounty for granted. I couldn't imagine only getting two gifts.

Slowly Alex crept toward me. My parents had purchased him a new winter coat and a video iPod. He was stunned, but I had never expected anything less. My parents were generous even to virtual strangers.

"This is for you," Alex said, handing me a small present wrapped in newspaper.

Vince immediately smacked his lips.

I unwrapped the present, smearing the ink residue on my green and red flannel robe (I'd worn it every Christmas since I was thirteen).

Inside was a small silver locket, shaped like a heart. I clicked it open to find a photo of Alex and me taken in Utuado, our faces squished together. My unusually tan cheeks highlighted my pink nose and frizzy hair, and my lips were spread wide in a grin that almost looked unfamiliar. I was really happy.

"Thank you," I said, a lump in my throat.

"*De nada,*" he replied, kissing my hand.

I spied my brother glaring at us, his lip curled on one side. I grabbed Alex's hand.

"I have something for you, too." I pulled a gift from the side of the couch.

Alex tore off the snowflake-themed paper and slid off the lid. Inside was a crisp white designer shirt and black striped tie.

"It's for your admissions interviews," I said meekly.

Alex nodded and grinned, though his eyes seemed flat. I wasn't sure if he liked it.

My family ate Christmas dinner alone. No aunts or uncles visited, not even my friends stopped by—Emily was in hiding and Madison was going to her grandmother's. But at least she called with an update on the performance. She said Emily was a "subpar" understudy and that the dancers were scared to get near her out of fear of bodily injury. The audience was only half as large, no unexpected guests appeared (Evan, Eric, or otherwise), and the production was over in a flash.

After months of preparations, I didn't get to dance in both shows. I would never get that back (is it wrong that I secretly wanted Emily to fall on her face and the production to collapse without me?).

I gawked at my throbbing ankle, still propped on sofa cushions.

Just then, Lilly and Vince barreled into the living room with a full glass of froth.

"Mom and Dad are in bed, right?" Vince asked, his eyes shifting mysteriously from side to side.

"Uh, yeah. Why?"

"Well, then I've got a drink for you, Gimpy." He handed me a tumbler full of nutmeg-smelling liquid.

"Gee, egg nog. Thanks. Is it from Wawa?" I asked, rolling my eyes.

"No, it's the real deal," Lilly insisted.

"You didn't take a Percocet, did you?" Vince asked, raising a concerned eyebrow.

"No. Mom thought I'd had enough."

"Good. Drink up."

I moved the glass closer to my nose and sniffed. It smelled like egg nog. I took a sip. It was creamy, sweet, thick, and sprinkled with cinnamon. I swallowed. Then, I sensed the aftertaste.

"Whoa! What's in here?" I winced.

"It's *coquito*," Vince said with a wide grin.

"Little frog?" I struggled with the translation.

"It's Puerto Rican egg nog," Lilly explained as she plopped down on the love seat.

"She used three cups of rum!" Vince cheered.

"What?" I almost spit up my sip.

"It also has coconut milk and a boatload of calories." Lilly chuckled.

"And it's one of the few things left on the planet that still uses condensed milk," Vince added.

"We have condensed milk?" I asked, one eye squinted.

"In the emergency kit in the pantry. We'll now have to resort to bottled water if the world ends." Vince took a large gulp.

"I'd ease up on that. It packs a punch." Lilly took another nip.

I leaned back on the couch, my ankle twisting painfully.

The scene reminded me a lot of my first drink in Utuado—sitting on the porch with Alonzo, José, and Lilly, drinking piña coladas and trying to ease my sunburn. Though I wasn't so sure I was in the mood for medicinal alcohol this time. It just didn't seem Christmassy and the holiday was already ruined enough.

Alex bounded down the steps. He had taken a break from our family to call his parents. They had booked his return ticket to the island. He was leaving in two weeks.

"What's everyone drinking?" he asked.

"I made *coquito*," Lilly said with pride.

Alex immediately tore off for the blender.

"Yeah, drink up. Only a few more days to mooch," Vince huffed in a harsh tone.

"Dude, what's your problem?" I narrowed my eyes.

"He's a douche."

"Gee, that's persuasive."

Alex bounced back into the living room with a full cup in his hand. He plopped down on the floor in front of me.

"*Feliz Navidad*," he said, raising his glass.

"*Y prospero año*," I toasted.

Vince clicked on his new video game console and turned up the volume. I pinched the bridge of my nose. It was as if he was purposely trying to ruin any peaceful moments. My ankle was already aching; I really didn't need my head to as well.

"Hey, wanna help me upstairs?" I patted Alex's shoulder.

"You're going to bed!" Vince protested. "You barely sipped your drink."

"I think my swollen limb is telling me it's time to call it a night."

Alex rose to his feet. "Sure, I'll help you."

He slipped his arm around my back and under my armpits

as I placed my good leg on the ground. I shifted my weight as he pulled me to my feet. Lilly immediately handed me my crutches.

"See you *mañana*." I waved to Vince, but he didn't turn around.

Alex steered me to my room. I longed to stretch my legs before lying back down, but I knew if I even put an ounce of strain on my ankle, the pain would make me vomit. I sighed and swung myself onto the bed.

"Thanks for helping me."

Before I could react, Alex fell onto the bed, pushed his face against mine, and kissed me hard. Egg nog stained his breath and I struggled to shift my leg from out of harm's reach (he seemed oblivious to the throbbing joint between us). We kissed for a few moments—me pushing his hands away and him trying to force his body weight on top of me. It was more like a wrestling match than a romantic moment.

Finally, I placed my palms on his chest and pushed him off.

"I miss being with you," he muttered. "We're not alone enough."

I stared at him, cross-eyed. Sure, Alex and I didn't make out on a daily basis, but we kissed often. It wasn't like we were newlyweds living in our apartment. I had parents to contend with and rules to obey.

"Sorry if I'm not meeting your weekly targets," I huffed.

"*Qué?*"

I shook my head. It wasn't worth repeating. "I should rest."

"But your parents are asleep," he whispered, thrusting closer to me.

"And I'd like to keep it that way." I nodded to the door.

He sucked in his lips and shook his head in a snarky gesture that made my stomach lurch. I had just been to an emergency room; I had missed the performance that I had trained months for; I had spent my Christmas tied to a sofa; and he was going to give me grief for not "being in the mood."

"See you tomorrow," I said curtly.

Finally, he took the hint and left. As he closed the door, I flopped back on my bed, propped up my ankle and tried to block out the pain.

Chapter 43

Christmas break puttered by remarkably slowly given the speed that vacations usually travel. When your only opportunity to leave the house is to be fitted for a castboot, the days can be rather dull. There's only so much TV a person can watch before actually noticing the loss of brain cells. The only light at the end of the tunnel was Teresa's wedding. Tomorrow marked my one bonafide, doctor-approved outing (pre-school, that is). It seemed that once the academic calendar resumed, I would be miraculously healed and lifted from my house arrest to hobble around high school from class to class.

"So, the moment's almost here," Madison said as she pulled my long robin's egg blue dress from its garment bag. "But the question remains, can a walking cast be fashionable when paired with evening wear?"

I stumbled to my feet, dragging my heavy foot, and snatched the dress. Then I limped to my bathroom, my plastic boot thumping on the tile floor. I really didn't think a satin sheath would be forgiving with regards to a giant black foot device that looked more like a ski boot than a cast.

I struggled out of my sweatpants (the only things that fit around my new fashion statement) and pulled the dress over my head. I yanked at the zipper and then blinked at my reflection.

"I look like the foot of Frankenstein!" I whined, tossing open the bathroom door.

Madison eyeballed my silhouette, the material bumped and puckered around the boot. I had a black sneaker on the other foot—the only thing that could get me from points A to B with the cast.

"It's not that bad," she tittered, covering her mouth.

"We can tell everyone it's an alcohol monitoring device, like the celebrities wear," Lilly offered. "House arrest has become very fashionable."

"Ha, ha," I droned, trudging toward them.

I glared at my reflection in my full-length mirror. It was official. I was the Gimp.

"Okay, maybe we can dress it up," Madison offered. "We can pop some rhinestones on it . . ."

"You're gonna Bedazzle my foot?"

"If the infomercial fits." She giggled.

"At least it's black," Lilly offered.

She looked so much like me that I wanted to tear her healthy foot off and connect it to mine. It didn't seem fair. I spent a dozen years performing, keeping in shape, conditioning my body, and I end up broken? Shouldn't my ankle be more capable of taking a hit?

"Okay, we're thinking of this the wrong way," Madison pointed out.

She strolled to my side and lifted my hair in her fingers.

"If we can't hide the boot, then we'll just make people not wanna look down." She smiled wide at my reflection. "We'll make you look so fabulous that no one will care what's on your feet."

From the look in her eyes, I wasn't sure I wanted to know what she was thinking. Though I was pretty sure I didn't have a choice.

By the next morning, Madison had finagled an appointment for her and the bridal party (which really just included Teresa, Lilly, and me, but somehow Madison tossed herself into the category) at one of the most expensive salons on Walnut Street.

I was currently sitting in a stylist's chair as Albert decided how to "highlight" my best features. At this point, my opinions seemed utterly unnecessary. He and Madison were calling the shots; I was merely their Barbie doll.

"I think we should play up the red," Albert stated.

"Like a lighter auburn?" Madison asked as her stylist, Giuseppe, streaked a fresh coat of highlights onto her long blond locks.

"No, something richer. A little more 'winter.'" Albert tousled my hair in his fingers. "We wanna keep the length, right?"

I stared at him. Silence.

"Oh, were you asking me?" I muttered.

"Of course, sweetie, who else?"

I grunted quietly. "Yes, we're keeping the length."

"Okay, I'm thinking a single process. Maybe a step darker . . ."

"Not even a few highlights for dimension?" Madison asked as she handed Giuseppe bits of foil to wrap her hair.

"Nope. I think the natural red and copper are enough. . . ."

"Copper?" I choked.

"It's gonna look fabulous. Alicia, come here daaarling." He beckoned to his assistant, who immediately scampered over with a pencil and notepad.

Albert spouted out a series of numbers and fractions that sounded more like the formula for a chemical weapon than hair dye. I took a deep breath and accepted my fate. I had never dyed my hair before. I didn't think I needed to. There weren't many women with natural red hues. But apparently, according to Albert, every head of hair needed enhancing. When he lifted a lock and placed it against my root, for the first time I could see that my hair was drastically different colors.

"That hair on the end is more than two years old, sweetie. The sun has done its work. Now, I have to do mine," he cooed.

How could I argue with that?

I glanced around the salon and glimpsed Teresa. She was getting a few highlights near her face before her stylist, Sasha, would be creating her "magnificent bridal look." Teresa brought in a picture of Jessica Simpson's wedding hair, but apparently, Sasha had other plans. She desired something "a little less windswept" that would be more "age appropriate" for a "mature bride." Teresa was thirty-five.

Nevertheless, my *tía* agreed. We had both spent our entire lives with our natural hair, but at this point we were convinced they knew more about our follicles than we did. And about two hours later, we realized they were right. Anyone who saw us enter the salon surely wouldn't recognize us exiting. We were transformed.

I reached for my face, but Madison batted my hand away.

"Felicia just spent thirty minutes putting on that makeup, don't you dare touch it now!" she hissed.

My eyes squinted at my reflection. My hair was a deeper shade of reddish brown, not fake or "out-of-a-box"-looking, just rich and expensive. And it shined. I had never seen my hair with such a glow. The light practically bounced from every strand, which were each perfectly maneuvered into a loose, wavy do. The hair around my face was swept up in such a natural way that from a distance it almost looked like not a single bobby pin was inserted. And my makeup was so light I could hardly feel it, yet it took nearly a half-dozen brushes to apply. I looked like I had spent a day at the beach. My freckles showed, but under a skin highlighter that made them look "fresh" and "adorable."

"No one will be looking at that castboot now," Madison confirmed, who was equally elegant in a simple chignon and smoky eyes.

"No offense, Mad. But this beats the heck out of my Sweet Sixteen look."

"Hey! These people are professionals," Madison whined. "I'm still in training."

I giggled.

"Qué bonita," Lilly whispered, strolling over.

She opted to go for highlights that made her brown eyes nearly pop off her face. For the first time since I met her, we looked completely different.

However, Teresa took the cake. Her dark auburn hair was pulled high off her neck in waves pinned "to show movement." Her eyes sparkled under eye shadow that ranged from burgundy to taupe, and her lips were the perfect shade of bridal pink.

"Ay Dios mio," Lilly mumbled.

"You like it?" she asked, patting at her hair.

"You look amazing," I cheered.

"Perfecto," Lilly added.

"Madison, I don't know how to thank you. I was just going to do my hair myself . . ." Teresa smiled at my friend.

"Consider it your wedding gift," Madison said, tossing her father's credit card at the cashier. "Now let's get out of here. We have a wedding to go to."

We stepped out onto the city streets and were greeted with a world of white. It was snowing on New Year's Eve.

Chapter 44

The crowd had already arrived. Even Uncle Diego showed, which I gathered from Vince's text that, "The Puerto Ricans are in the house." There was only one person missing—the mother of the bride. Her flight was cancelled the night before, and she had to depart this morning. At last check her plane had landed, but we were stalling the evening ceremony until her cab arrived. The pianist had already been playing for twenty minutes.

"We can't start without her. We just can't," Teresa said frantically as she paced in the bridal suite.

Lilly was strolling beside her while I rested my ankle on a banquet chair. The more the clock ticked the faster Teresa moved.

"She'll be here. The airport said the plane disembarked. She's on her way," Lilly told her.

Too bad the woman didn't have a cell phone. A little bit of modern convenience would do wonders right now.

"Teresa, you look beautiful. Just look at yourself." I pointed to the mirror. "This day is going to be perfect. Trust me."

"Pero mi mama no está aquí!" she shrieked.

The more nervous she got, the more she reverted to her native language. It was giving my rusty Spanish skills a work-out.

Finally, I heard a knock on the door.

"Maybe that's her!" I smiled hopefully.

But when the door opened, my father emerged.

"Everything all right?" he asked.

"No! No, nada está bien!" Teresa hollered.

"We're waiting for her mom," I mouthed.

He nodded, then rubbed the back of his head—his think-ing face. "You know if you want to start, I'd be happy to walk you down the aisle."

I nearly gagged on my tongue. I stared at my father, my heavily made-up eyes stretched wide. "Whoa."

"Lorenzo," Teresa whispered, her face just as stunned. "I don't know what to say . . ."

"I don't want you to feel like she's the only family you have here," my father continued.

It was the greatest wedding present he could have ever given her. Teresa's eyes formed tiny puddles. *"Gracias,"* she whispered. *"Gracias."*

Just then, the door to the bridal suite flung open. *"Estoy aquí!"* shouted a portly gray-haired woman as she barreled in. "Teresa! Teresa!"

The woman's eyes darted around the bridal room, then stopped on her daughter. *"Ay, Teresa. Mija,"* she said lovingly, before rushing toward her with her arms spread.

She looked very different from my grandmother. Her big hips and full chest contrasted starkly with my grandmother's barely hundred-pound unshapely frame. She yelped loudly as she hugged her daughter, while my grandmother hardly said a word. And she was dark, her skin even more tan than my grandfather's, while I clearly credit my grandmother for my milky fair skin.

I watched them hug for several moments, then I noticed my father staring as well. He didn't look sad or angry to see her, this woman responsible for so much of his family's damage. He looked curious, as if he were trying to find her life's history written on her face, as if he was trying to locate what, exactly, his father saw. Finally, Teresa pulled away and glanced around the room.

"*Mama, esta es Mariana, y Lilly . . . y Lorenzo.*" Teresa pointed to my father cautiously and the old woman's eyes fixated.

Neither said a word. It was as if there was so much to say that they couldn't pinpoint any one thing. They simply stared, each acknowledging the other's existence.

The piano music cued and I hobbled down the aisle. I had practiced a step-shuffle that I thought better hid my limp, but I still felt like the hunchback of Notre Dame (just with a better makeover). I smiled at my relatives and spied Madison sitting up front. Evan was at her side, Bobby beside him, and Emily beside Bobby. It was as if the wedding had wiped the slate clean. I took my place at the altar. Carlos was already there, his brothers at his side. His graying hair was slicked back and his lips stretched across his face.

Lilly quickly joined me and we waited for Teresa. The pianist switched to Canon D and the banquet doors swung open. There stood my *tía*, gleaming in white, her mother holding her arm. I heard a collective gasp.

My uncles had been warned that she was coming; they were even instructed not to attend if they couldn't control themselves, but I didn't think that they were truly ready for the sight. It had been thirty-five years since she stood naked on their front lawn, screeching the details of her affair with their father, her belly swollen and pregnant, for all of Utuado to see. That was the vision they held of her, and Teresa was the reason they left.

I held my breath and slid my eyes across my family's faces. Aunt Joan angrily shook her professionally styled hair, my uncle Roberto glared at the wall as if his eyes burned to look at her, and my uncle Diego focused on the hands clenched tightly in his lap. I could see his nostrils flare and his shoulders heave as he struggled to breathe calmly. Then my aunt Joan discreetly reached out her manicured hand and grabbed his. His breathing soothed the minute she touched him. It was the first time I ever felt love between them.

The wrinkles on my forehead relaxed.

I turned my gaze back to Teresa. She was glowing.

The ceremony moved quickly. Without a Catholic service, there really wasn't much for the justice of the peace to say. Vince chimed in with a Shakespearean sonnet but, fittingly, Teresa's son wailed the entire time. Not to be out-done, my brother "accidentally" hissed, "little twerp," into the microphone. I'm not sure who was more mature, he or the two-year-old.

Twenty minutes later, the pianist broke into the "Wedding March" and my *tía* and her groom raced down the aisle. I followed them out, clutching my white roses and nodding to guests. Then Lilly grabbed my arm and helped me limp to the reception.

"Open bar on New Year's Eve, Gimpy!" Lilly cheered as she ordered a glass of wine.

Our faces were so full of makeup that the bartender didn't question our age (I'm sure the bridesmaid gowns didn't hurt either). Lilly tipped back her chardonnay as my relatives and friends piled in.

"Hey." I nodded at Emily. "I heard you made a good Princess Aurora."

She smiled faintly. "Not as good as you . . ."

"Well, I'm glad you remembered the routine. It would've sucked if they'd cancelled . . . because of me."

Emily nodded and took a step out of our circle. According to Madison, she was the last to arrive at the ceremony. Given that her father's hotel was only a block away, she didn't have much cause to be late. But I was surprised that she had attended at all. We hadn't spoken since the night she forced a cast onto my foot, and a family function wasn't exactly the best time to clear the air.

Alex walked over and wrapped his arms around my waist. *"Qué bonita,"* he whispered into my ear.

I pulled away, unwrapping his hands. I was never big on public displays of affection, especially in front of family. Bobby immediately shifted his eyes from me.

"So everyone seems to be getting along," I noted, glancing around the room.

Teresa's mother was keeping her distance from my uncles. I assumed she had been fairly warned. As long as we could keep my uncle Diego's drinking to a minimum, I thought we could avoid a spectacle. Though from the way my father was purposely inserting himself in front of my uncle's line of sight, I was guessing he wasn't so certain he could depend on his brother's good behavior.

Vince suddenly rushed over, Kyle on his heels.

"Let's do shots!" Vince cheered, pumping his fist.

"Are you nuts?" I asked.

"Come on! The bartender said he can't serve shots, but

he'd pour me a whiskey with a few extra glasses." Vince patted his own shoulder. "I'm so slick."

"Why not rum?" Alex asked.

"Because in *America*, we drink whiskey," Vince spat.

"Count me out," I huffed.

"Mariana, we have to celebrate the fact that I didn't fail out! I survived the semester!"

"Wow, you didn't waste forty-grand of Mom and Dad's money, drink up!"

"Well, I'm in." Alex stepped toward my brother.

"Great," Vince said gruffly before turning to my friends. "What about you guys? A little SoCo? Some JD?"

Bobby leaned back. "I think I'm with Mariana on this one."

"You suck."

"I'll do it," Lilly said, dashing to Kyle's side.

"See! Lilly knows how to have fun." My brother patted her back. "How about this? Anyone who's not a *loser* step forward. Oh wait, Alex, you stay there."

I looked at Alex sympathetically. His face resembled a scolded puppy's.

"I'm in too!" Evan cheered.

"Wait for me," Madison hollered as the group took off.

"Mad!" I shrieked.

"What? I'm just gonna watch."

"I'll watch too," Emily muttered, trudging after them.

"Traitors," I griped as I stood, deserted, with Alex and Bobby. The air felt heavy. I shuffled my feet.

"You know, I think I'm gonna head to the restroom," Bobby mumbled, turning away.

"No, don't!" I squeaked too quickly. "I mean, I'll come with you."

"To the men's room?"

"No, I mean, to the ladies' room. I'll walk with you." I smiled at Alex. "I'll be right back."

And with that, Bobby and I hobbled out of the reception.

"How's the foot, Gimpy?"

"Oh, just peachy. I hear castboots will be all the rage on the runway this year," I joked.

"Oh, really? Well, you're always ahead of the curve."

"You know it."

We walked quietly down the corridor a few paces before I broke the silence. "I saw you sitting with Emily at the ceremony."

"Yeah, I was. And you know? It actually wasn't that weird despite our parental issues."

"I wish I could say the same. Ever since she went all Tonya Harding on me, our relationship's been even more strained," I confessed.

"You don't think she did it on purpose, do you?"

"No . . . not really. But the girl's become an international woman of mystery."

"Hey, don't knock it. That can be very attractive."

"I wouldn't know."

Bobby swiveled to face me. "Well, I think the straight-up girls are much more appealing."

I stopped walking, absorbing the comment. Bobby quickly halted. The bathrooms were only a few feet ahead, and I didn't want to reach them. I didn't want to end our walk.

I looked at Bobby, my eyes sliding toward his lips. He brushed a stray hair from my face.

"You know, you clean up real nice," he said softly. "I hardly noticed the cast. I was too busy looking at the rest of you. . . ."

For the first time since Cornell, I realized how much I

wanted to kiss him. In that moment, I brushed away every logical reason why I shouldn't and reached for his lips. He didn't resist. He grabbed my head and held on, his hands warming my cheeks. The butterflies in my stomach overtook the pulsing from my ankle. I dug my fingers into his hair.

Finally, Bobby pulled away. "I never thought I'd be able to do that again."

It was then that I noticed Madison.

"Whoa, uh, sorry to interrupt." Madison's head jerked back. She sucked in her lips to hold back a smile.

I blinked at her, startled, saying nothing.

"I was just . . . um, looking for Emily," she mumbled, still trying not to grin. She abruptly spun back toward the reception.

"No, wait!" I called out. Madison stopped. "I thought Emily was with you."

"She never showed up at the bar. Everyone did the shots without her. I thought maybe she went to the bathroom." Madison's eyes flicked between Bobby and me.

"Well, I didn't see her pass us," I said.

"Sure you would've noticed?" Madison pumped her eyebrows.

"Yes," I stated firmly, my cheeks flushed. "Give me a minute. I'll help you find her."

Madison headed back to the party as I turned to Bobby.

"I should go." I gazed into his azure eyes.

"Yeah, definitely." Then he grabbed my face and kissed me once more.

My stomach turned cartwheels as our lips moved. Then, Bobby slowly pulled away.

"So, um . . . What about Alex?" he asked tentatively.

I stepped back. The moment was officially ruined. Reality was mentioned.

I shifted my weight. "I'll tell him. About this. Tonight. After I find Emily."

Bobby's face erupted in bliss. "Well, all right. Go! Find her!" He pushed me toward the reception, and I giggled as I limped away.

He stood there, watching me, and when I turned back, he was still glowing.

Chapter 45

"So, oh my God!" Madison shrieked as I approached our table. "You and Bobby!"

"I know." I smiled so wide my cheeks felt strained.

"Well, what does this mean? What about Alex? Are you and Bobby together now? Did Alex do something?"

The boys were still at the bar for another round of shots. This time Alex had joined them.

"I don't know. I was kissing Bobby because I wanted to," I confessed as I dropped into my seat. "It had nothing to do with Alex."

"But what about Emily and her mom and . . . like, every-thing?" Madison asked, shaking her freshly highlighted hair.

"What about her?" I stared at my castboot. "She doesn't seem to be thinking about any of us lately."

Madison nodded. "Very true. Anyway, I don't think it'll matter. You and Bobby aren't just hooking up. It's, like, for real. And their parents aren't even together. She'll understand."

I watched Madison shift her salad on her plate. I didn't think she'd eaten a single leaf of romaine, which only meant one thing. "So how are things . . . with Evan?"

Lately I could tell her relationship status by the food on her plate. The more conflicted she and Evan got, the less she consumed.

She stared off toward the bar where Evan was downing whiskey. "Good."

"It seemed at the hospital that you guys were a done deal . . ."

"Yeah, I know. It's just . . . I still feel weirdness, you know?" She looked down at her untouched food.

"So I take it you found Em. . . ." I raised my chin toward her empty seat.

Her eyes shot up. "Omigod, no." She peered around the banquet room. "I got all overwhelmed with you and Bobby."

I looked toward the reception door. There was no sign of her. I glanced around the compact room—nothing. If she was present, I would've seen her.

"Do you think she left?" Madison jumped up from her gold-trimmed chair.

We sped to the ladies' bathroom—actually Madison "sped," I hobbled. She wasn't there. We immediately moved to the elevator and down to the lobby. There was no sign of her.

"She had to have gone back to her hotel," I reasoned.

Madison whipped out her cell. "She's not answering."

We plunged into the snow-covered streets, my cast foot leaving a trail behind me. Emily's hotel was only a block away. We dove inside the warm lobby, which was packed with travelers in formal evening wear hurrying off to New York's celebrations. We weaved through the crowd and entered the elevator. I pressed the button.

"Have you been here before?" Madison asked. "Because she's never invited me."

"Once," I told her. "Lilly and I showed up unexpectedly." I took a deep breath. "Em had a guy hiding in the bathroom. She denied it, *of course*, but I swear I could hear someone."

"Omigod! Why didn't you tell me?"

"Because when I asked her, she lied. Like she always does. So then, what was I supposed to tell you? That I'm paranoid? I didn't know who was in there."

"I think we do now."

Only I didn't want to tell her that, at the time, I was concerned it was Evan.

The elevator stopped, and I limped toward Emily's room. Madison quickly pounded on the door.

There was rustling inside, but no one responded.

"Em! Em! We know you're in there! We can hear you!" Madison cried.

Footsteps quickly padded across the floor, then we heard the faint sound of whispering. Finally, the door creaked open.

Emily stood before us, her dress from the wedding twisted, her hair sweaty and her cheeks flushed. Madison pushed the door open and stormed inside. She glanced into both bedrooms. One was perfectly made with the turndown mint on the pillow. The other was worn, rumpled and sunken in the middle.

Madison swung her face toward Emily. "So where is he?"

"I don't know what you're talking about," Emily mumbled, staring at the patterned carpet.

"For the love of God, Em! Do you think we're retarded? Where Eric?" Madison glared at the bathroom door. "Get out here, wu! Or, what, are you too embarrassed to be seen with her?"

Madison pounded on the bathroom door. When it squeaked open, Eric entered bare-chested and in a pair of jeans.

"You're pa'tc!" Madison shoved her finger in his pale face. "What are y like, eighty? And you're cheating on your blond-bimbo coll with a high school sophomore?"

"I'm twenty-one," Eric stated calmly. "And Emily and I aren't exclusive."

"So exactly how many people *are* you sleeping with?" I gestured toward the bed.

"We're not having sex," Emily mumbled.

"God, you work for her mother. What's wrong with you?" Madison asked, disgusted.

"I was about to ask the same question," said a stern voice from behind me.

I didn't need to turn around—the sound triggered a gag reflex, and she wasn't even my mom. She was Emily's. We had left the hotel room door open.

Eric quickly darted to where he left his shirt (like that was really going to make a difference at this point).

"You know, when your father told me that you were dating a boy named Eric, I thought 'it couldn't be,' " Emily's mom said calmly as she pushed past me and headed straight for her daughter. "Of course, I also didn't think your father could be such a cliché that he'd sleep with his secretary. But he did. I'm sure you know that by now."

Mrs. Montgomery stopped a few feet in front of Emily, her eyes shifting to Eric.

"But when I saw you at my fifteen-year-old's ballet performance, I was sickened. The two of you lied to my face . . . not that I should be surprised. Your father taught you well."

I grimaced. Emily's eyes flooded with tears.

"But when I told your father what was going on, I *honestly thought* he would keep you two apart. Really, I did. Then, I sat in those divorce proceedings today and heard that he's been living at *Candy's* house! Since November!"

My palm shot to my mouth, and Madison darted to my side. It was very uncomfortable, under normal circumstances, to watch a friend get yelled at by her parents. In this instance, the scene was downright torture-chamber worthy—but it was also so twisted that we couldn't help but watch.

"You've been living here, in this hotel suite, *alone*, for two months!" her mother shouted. "Oh, wait, you weren't alone. *Eric* was with you."

"I wasn't living here," Eric said meekly.

"Don't you dare speak to me." She pointed a bony finger in his face. "I haven't decided if I'm gonna call the cops yet, so I suggest you shut the hell up before you make my decision easier."

For being a poetry professor, in that moment Mrs. Montgomery scared the crap out of me.

"I can't believe you would be so stupid, Emily!" she hollered.

"*I'm* stupid? Why? Because I'm dating someone you don't approve of? Gee, like you and Dad have room to talk!" Emily shouted.

"Yes, I had an affair. But that was long after I found out about Candy. Why do you think it was *your father* who moved out?"

My head jutted back. I hadn't thought about that. We all just assumed that Mrs. Montgomery was the bad guy (or bad woman, in this case). It didn't dawn on us that she wasn't the only one who'd destroyed their marriage.

"Dad said that Candy wasn't an issue when you guys were together," Emily defended.

"That's because I looked the other way! For *your* sake." She drew a slow breath. "But that doesn't matter now. What matters is that my teenage daughter has been living unsupervised. And you know what? That's going to stop right now. I just came from my attorney's office. Your father gave me full custody—"

"What?" Emily shrieked.

"Are you *surprised*? He and Candy are going to start their own family."

"I'm still his daughter!" Emily snapped, tears flowing freely.

"And you're my daughter, too."

"Well, which guy are you sleeping with now? Maybe you should update me before you drag me back to that hell hole!" Emily was crying harder with every word. I knew she didn't mean what she was saying. She just couldn't comprehend how she had been so wrong.

"Emily, I'm not seeing *anyone*! Yes, I was with Jim. And I'm sorry about how that came out. But I *loved* him," her mom's voice cracked slightly. "But none of that matters now. It's over. I haven't seen him since your film thing . . ."

"What . . . what about that guy we saw you with . . . at the Constitution Center?" Emily sniffled, gasping for air between sobs.

"He's my *lawyer*, Emily! My *divorce* lawyer." She waved at Eric with disgust. "You didn't have to do *this* to get back at me."

"We didn't *do* anything," Emily whispered, wiping at her tears. She lazily looked at me as I leaned against a wall, relieving the weight from my throbbing foot.

"Why didn't you tell me any of this sooner?" Emily sobbed, turning to her mother. "I've ruined everything. I practically broke my friend's foot!" She flung her arm toward me. "She thinks I did it on purpose! Everyone does! I'm . . . *pathetic*."

"Em, no!" I blurted so suddenly that the sound of my own voice startled me. "I don't think . . . I don't think you did it on purpose. Really."

Mrs. Montgomery tossed up her hands as if to signal that I had spoken enough. I flinched, my shoulders rising.

"Eric, I think it goes without saying that you're fired," she said through clenched teeth. "I will be reporting you to the dean. And I will be making sure you *never* work near children again. Do you hear me?"

"But—" Eric started.

"I can still call the police . . ."

Eric grabbed his wallet off the nightstand and rushed past us. I grabbed Madison's hand. *"Maybe we should leave,"* I whispered.

When I turned back, Emily's mom was holding her daughter as she cried. It was definitely time to go.

I stepped into the hotel corridor, Madison closing the door behind us. Then, we trudged toward the elevators.

"Wow, that was intense," I muttered.

"Seriously, I can't believe that Eric stood there the entire time. I really thought her mom was gonna kill him. There was a whole *CSI* scene running through my head where you and I ended up covered in blood splatter evidence," Madison huffed.

The elevator chimed as it neared our floor and the doors parted. Only it wasn't empty.

"Evan? How'd you know I was here?" Madison gasped.

He tentatively stepped out. "Um, uh."

"Wait, how do you know where Emily lives? Were you looking for her?" Madison took a few steps back, nearly banging into a decorative table.

"No, I wasn't. I mean, yes. I mean . . ." Evan stammered.

I took a seat on a dusty hall chair. I had a feeling this might take a while (seriously, who was going to show up next? Tupac? Elvis?).

"Omigod!" Madison cried. "You really do have a thing for Emily, don't you? How many people is she hooking up with?"

"What? Huh? No." Evan rushed toward Madison, who had backed herself against a wall. "I saw you guys jet out. I realized

I hadn't seen Emily in a while. I thought you might've come here. I thought something happened."

"How do you know where Emily lives? Have you been here?"

Evan shifted his weight. "Yes."

I rolled my eyes.

"Omigod," Madison moaned again.

"But it's not what you think. . . . We're friends."

"You and Emily?"

"Yes."

"Since when?"

"Since she moved to the city."

"Why in the world do you care about Emily Montgomery's living accommodations? You never cared about her when she lived in Spring Mills!"

"That's because *I* don't live in Spring Mills," Evan stated softly.

Now that got my attention. I sat up straight.

"What?" Madison croaked.

Evan sighed and tossed his head back.

"My parents split up, like, over a year ago. My house in Spring Mills is empty. They're fighting over it. My mom's living in our shore house and my dad moved to Manhattan. I've been living with my *nana* since last Christmas. That's why you guys saw me with her at the ballet . . . a couple months ago," Evan confessed.

"Holy shit." Madison's head jerked back.

"She lives in one of those new condos. I ran into Emily at Starbucks." Evan tossed up his rough, wrestler hands. "I mean, how many people do you know going through the crap that we're going through?"

At this point, I think I knew too many.

"So Emily and I started driving in together. I mean, we

were both living the same lie!" Evan shrugged. "But that's it, really. We're just friends."

"Why didn't you say anything?" Madison asked.

"Because I'm embarrassed. I'm living with my grandma, my parents couldn't care less about me, I could get kicked out of school . . ." He closed his eyes. "I begged Emily not to tell anyone."

He pulled his heavy eyelids apart and glanced at me. "I knew it was making problems for you guys. But I thought if you knew"—he gazed back at Madison—"you wouldn't like me."

He reached for Madison's hand.

"You were worried I wouldn't like you?" Madison squeaked, her voice hopeful.

"Well, yeah. Who wants to date a loser living on his grandma's couch?"

"I do."

And with that, she kissed him.

Chapter 46

After their lips unlocked and we all realized we still had a wedding reception to attend, we raced back (as quickly as one good leg could take me). By that point, Vince and Kyle were screeching a slurred rendition of a Bon Jovi classic into the DJ's microphone (I was fairly certain that no one in my family had much of an appreciation for the New Jersey hair metal band, though it did oddly make me like Kyle more).

I scanned the reception for Alex and Bobby. Neither one was in view. I stared at our table; Alex's digital camera was resting at his place setting. He couldn't have gone far. I trudged over and plopped down. My chicken with raspberry sauce was still untouched. I lifted a fork, but caught a green light flickering out of the corner of my eye.

Alex had left his camera turned on. I reached over to click it off, but as I held the heavy equipment in my hand, a memory flashed. The last time I had touched his camera was when I had seen the hidden pictures he had taken of me in Puerto Rico. I couldn't help but wonder if he'd erased them. Something deep inside my gut told me to check.

I stared at the tiny digital screen and clicked through his shots of Teresa's wedding. He had captured my walk down the aisle, the look on Carlos's face when Teresa had appeared, their first kiss, their first dance. My *tía* was going to love them.

Then, my heart seized.

The next photo, the last photo he had taken prior to the wedding, was an extreme close up of passionate female eyes. Only they weren't mine. A stormy gray gaze stared back at me. I clicked the next photo. It was Mali sprawled on my family's couch, giggling suggestively. The next showed Mali grinning, her lips closed and dewy. The last was a close up so tight, I could only see the perfect tan skin on the crook of her neck and a slight hint of the top of her chest.

I dropped the camera on the floor. Its weight clanked so loudly that heads turned at nearby tables. My heart pumped in heated pulses all the way to my fingertips. A high-pitched buzzing filled my ears.

Before he even said a word, I felt his presence. I slowly peered up through my lashes and spied his petrified black pupils staring back.

"What the hell is wrong with you?" I rose from my chair.

Alex clutched my arm, hard, and dragged me into the hotel's corridor—out of sight of other guests. After everything he had done, he cared more about what others thought of him, than how I felt.

"I'm sorry," he barked, still gripping my biceps.

I yanked my arm away, stumbling onto my bad foot. "I *saw* the pictures, Alex! Of Mali! How could you? *When* could you?"

"Mariana, I was going to tell you . . ." He rubbed the back of his neck, staring at the floor.

"Oh, my God! You *hooked up* with her." My hands balled into fists as the hairs rose on my arms. I had known it was a possibility. I had even accused him of it. But when he'd denied it, I believed him. Or, at least, I chose to.

"It's just, you were so distant. You were never around . . ."

"So this is *my* fault. You hooked up with my brother's girl-friend, in my parents' house, and this is *my fault*. . . . My parents invited you into our home, they gave you a place to stay, they let you borrow their car, and date their daughter, and you hooked up with Vince's girlfriend! *And* lied! *And* photographed her! What the hell is wrong with you?"

My fingernails were digging so far into my palms that I felt them break skin.

"We just . . . messed around," he mumbled.

And that was when everyone else appeared. It was like his admission was a beacon for the rest of the party. Vince, Bobby, Madison, Evan, Lilly, and Kyle emerged in the corridor, their jaws collectively scraping the carpeted floor.

I snapped my face toward Vince and thrust an angry finger toward my former boyfriend. "He and Mali. *He and Mali!*"

"I know," Vince said calmly, stepping toward Alex, their eyes locked.

Bobby ran to my side.

"I found the e-mails," Vince spat, his dark eyes shooting lightning bolts. "You are *such* a tool. '*Mi amor*, I miss you so much.' '*Mi amor*, I can't wait to see you again.' '*Mi amor*, I miss your *touch*.'" Vince shot out the last word so harshly, spit splashed on Alex's cheek.

My heart drummed with such fury that sweat formed on the back of my neck. My jaw clenched. Alex said nothing.

"I've been wanting to tell you." My brother looked at me, his face suddenly soft. "But I didn't want to do it over the phone with him living there. Who knows what the perv's capable of? And then I got home and you ended up all gimpy. I didn't want to add to your shit. I mean, you *liked* the dude. . . ."

"Well . . . about that," I muttered. Bobby rested his hand on my shoulder.

I caught Madison smile as everyone else leaned back.

I glared into Alex's crumbling face. In that moment, I couldn't see what I had ever found appealing about him. He was so fake and superficial. All he cared about was the chase, about the "score," about the physical connection. He probably didn't even remember the name of my ballet performance, or the title of my role, but I was guessing he knew every scene where my butt flashed from under my tutu.

"I can't believe I ever liked you," I hissed. Then I grabbed Bobby's hand. "But you know what, it's over. It's been over since before you got here. So go stalk Mali, or whomever else you want. I don't give a shit. I've found someone better than you'll ever be."

Alex snorted, shaking his head as he sneered at Bobby. "I knew you were after her. What, you think you've won now?"

"Actually, I don't think it's a competition," Bobby rebuffed, tightening his grip on my hand. "But if it were, then you're the big loser. In *every* way."

Vince jumped on his toes, extending his arms overhead. "I knew it! I knew you couldn't like this asshole! You know, Alex e-mailed her just yesterday?" He glanced at me. "I still have Mali's password. I have a total online revenge scheme planned. . . ."

"Well, you should see the photos he took of her," I huffed.

"You've gotta freakin' be kidding me." Vince spun toward Alex. "You know, I guess since everyone knows what a piece of crap you are, there's really nothing stopping me from doing this . . ."

My brother pulled back his arm and swung his closed fist directly into Alex's jaw. He dropped to the floor, moaning and clutching his bleeding mouth. There were tears in his eyes. I stared at him, bloody and cowering, and felt nothing.

"We're over," I hissed as I pushed my brother to the side

and glared at Alex. "Seriously, get out of my face. . . . *And* my house."

Alex squeezed his eyes closed as a tear dripped down his cheek. He stumbled to his feet still rubbing his jaw and charged down the corridor. No one ran after him. He was lucky he wasn't lynched.

Chapter 47

When we got back to the reception, my family was still celebrating, completely oblivious to the bizarre turn of events that had just taken place tonight. My mind cartwheeled in circles as Lilly and I plopped down at our table. Everyone else immediately headed to the bar.

"Wow." It was all I could think of to say.

"Seriously," Lilly added, grabbing a sip of water.

"Alex and Mali. I can't believe it. How could he? He lied to my face!"

"Mine too," Lilly added, staring at me. "I asked him, you know. He told me he never touched her. He swore. . . ." She tapped her fingernail on her dripping water glass. "I would've told you if I knew something. You know that."

Actually, I didn't. But I did now.

I looked onto the dance floor and spied my uncle Diego gyrating, like a wildman, beside my father and my uncle Roberto. Teresa and Carlos were spinning arm and arm in the center, as if they were the only ones in the universe, while Manny ran circles around the floor, shrieking.

"Am I going schizophrenic or is that scene really happening?" I asked.

"Oh, wait. You missed *a lot*," Lilly explained. "Teresa's mom stood right next to your uncle Diego and ordered a rum and Coke, and he said nothing. Absolutely nothing. It was like divine intervention. I mean, I saw his fingers cringe like a cripple, but he kept his mouth shut."

"Are you serious?"

"Yup. But when she walked away, he turned to your uncle Roberto and said, 'I will never speak to that bitch.' And your uncle Roberto said, 'Fine, you don't have to. Just don't make a scene. Not today.' And that was it."

"Holy crap." My jaw swung open.

"I know!"

"The man had no problem ruining Vince's going away party, my birthday, Thanksgiving dinner, but now . . ."

"Maybe he's changed?"

"Or maybe somebody slipped him a Xanax." I giggled. "It's like the entire wedding switched to Bizarro World."

"Well, maybe it's better this way. We can all start the year fresh." She gestured to her watch. "It's almost midnight. I can't believe I have someone to kiss."

"Like you were ever lacking dates in Utuado."

"No, but they don't count. Kyle's different." She gazed meltingly as Kyle wobbled at the bar, knocking back another shot. "He's a 'real' someone. . . ."

"Your first boyfriend," I stated simply. "You're so grown up!" I nudged her shoulder, giggling.

"We both are. You sure let Alex have it."

"Well, he deserved it." I shook my head at the memory of the scene.

"What do you think he'll do now?" Lilly asked, staring at the ice cubes in her water.

"Let him go back to Puerto Rico, where I should've left him to begin with."

"It wasn't all bad. . . ."

"You'll have to excuse me if I find it hard to remember the good at the moment." I sighed. "And that's what sucks. I've ruined the memory of one of the best summers of my life."

"Hey! You still have me. I was a part of that summer, too!" Her eyes were wide and offended.

"This is true." I nodded. "I'll just focus on those memories."

"Or you could make new ones. Maybe work on having one of the best winters of your life." She gestured behind me.

I twisted my neck and smiled as I caught Bobby's eyes gazing down at me. I quickly stood.

"You didn't leave," I said. "I was worried you might've run off screaming."

"It takes more than a little physical violence to freak me out. You know, I'm very tough. I could've taken him." He flexed his barely there biceps as he chuckled.

"Of course. You're very frightening." I grinned. "You should consider a career as a bodyguard. Forget the whole film thing."

"Exactly. I might look into that." His eyes twinkled. "Besides, I couldn't have left. I've been waiting too long for this."

"For my *tía*'s wedding?"

"No, for you."

And with that, he grabbed my hand and led me onto the dance floor.

A few minutes later, the lights in the banquet room turned black. The waitstaff entered with a wedding cake illuminated by dozens of sparklers, which they quickly passed out to guests along with metallic cardboard party hats. I placed a red sequined triangle above my perfectly coiffed hairdo and secured the elastic strap below my chin.

"You ready for the new year?" Bobby asked as he slipped a glittering black top hat above his mop of curls.

"Hell, yeah!" I laughed.

I watched as my *tía* slid an engraved silver knife into her three-tiered cake. I waved my sparkler in the air, cheering, and the DJ quickly boomed into the mike, preparing to lead the crowd in a midnight countdown.

I glanced around the darkened room. Madison's face glowed from the light of her sparkler. Evan's arms were wrapped around her shrinking waist. Kyle gazed at Lilly as he whispered something that I couldn't overhear, but it made my cousin giggle. Vince high-fived my father, who was standing strong alongside my two uncles as they clapped politely for their half-sister. They looked truly happy for her, and not one of them sneered at her mother who stood proudly at her daughter's side.

"A new year," I muttered to Bobby. "Can't imagine it could be any more eventful than the past one."

"Oh, you never know."

The crowd chanted *"three, two, one"* as Bobby held my face and kissed me.

Catch up with Diana Rodriguez Wallach's first book,
AMOR AND SUMMER SECRETS,
available now from Kensington.

Chapter 6

As soon as I opened the heavy red door to our house, I was struck with an eerie vibe. There were no strange noises or items out of place—the knickknacks were where they were supposed to be, the furniture was dusted and fluffed—but something felt off, like that moment right before the guest of honor realizes there's a houseful of people waiting to yell "surprise!"

"Mom? Dad!" I shouted as I walked into the marble foyer.

I wiped my sandals on the doormat, walked toward the spiral staircase and yelled up. "Vince, you here?"

No one responded.

I walked through the living room and glimpsed the spotless kitchen ahead. There were no dishes in the sink or seasoning scents in the air. It didn't make sense. It was six o'clock, my mom should be cooking dinner. She cooked every night at this time. She loved to cook.

I continued toward the back porch and gazed into our freshly landscaped yard. There sat my brother, my mother, and my father on the wrought iron patio furniture drinking iced tea like a cheesy commercial. I tilted my head as I slid the glass door open.

"What's going on?" I asked as their heads swiveled to face me.

"Mariana, sit down," my dad said, patting the navy blue cushion on the chair beside him.

My brother was smiling—not a happy smile, more like a sneaky "I know something you don't know" grin.

"Okay, what's up?" I asked, my eyes darting from side to side.

"Iced tea?" my mom asked, grabbing the crystal pitcher and a tall glass from the bamboo tray beside her.

"Um, okay. Uh, will someone please tell me what the heck is going on?"

"Dad and I came to an arrangement," Vince said as he stared at his designer sneakers.

"You're going to Europe!" I squeaked, my hand shooting toward my mouth.

"Not exactly. But I *am* traveling."

"Okay, then what? Where are you going?"

I grabbed the glass of iced tea from my mother.

"Lemon? Sugar?" she asked in her sweetest voice.

"Sure."

My mom was smiling so wide that it almost looked robotic, like her face was programmed to stay in that position. It wasn't a good sign.

"All right, why are you all being so weird?"

"We're not being weird," my mom said in a flat, peaceful tone. She was bracing herself for an argument. I could tell. She was setting a mood.

"Look, Mariana. Your brother and I talked," my dad started. "I knew he was serious about wanting to travel. But I didn't think it was safe for him to be so far away unchaperoned. So I came up with a compromise."

"I'm spending the summer in Puerto Rico," Vince interjected, glowing.

"That's awesome! Good for you!"

My mom and dad exchanged a look.

"I still have family there," my dad added slowly. "And an aunt and uncle of mine have agreed to be hosts for Vince . . . and you."

"And *me*! What do you mean, *and me*?" I coughed as I choked on a gulp of sweetened tea.

"I thought it would be a good learning experience for both of you," he stated as he stared at the recently manicured bushes rather than my horrified eyes.

"What? What are you talking about? I don't want to go anywhere."

"Mariana . . ." my father continued sternly.

"Don't *'Mariana'* me. Didn't it occur to you to ask me first? This is ridiculous. *Mom!*"

"Honey, look, it'll be fun," she offered. "You'll get to go to the beach. You'll meet your relatives, be in a different country."

"But I have friends *here*! I have Madison's party! I can't miss that. I *won't* miss that!"

"Your friends will still be here when you get back," my dad added gruffly.

"Dad, are you nuts? I can't do this to Madison. She's counting on me!"

"She has an entire staff to count on," he huffed.

"That's not what I meant and you know it! It's her sixteenth birthday! That's a once in a lifetime thing. I have to be there for her. She's my best friend!"

"Mariana, I realize you're upset now," my mother cooed. "But once you get to Puerto Rico, you'll forget all about this and have fun. Really, you will."

"You honestly think I want to *forget* all about my best friend? Are you mental? Have you ever had a friend in your life?"

"Oh, come on, Mariana! You're missing some stuck-up, superficial party for a spoiled little rich girl. Who cares? You're better off." Vince pumped his eyebrows.

"I don't care what you think of her. Like you have room to talk. Trust me, I could say a lot worse about *your* friends," I snipped, my eyes frozen. "Madison's a good person. And she's my best friend. This party is the most important thing in her life. I'm not going to miss it. Why the heck am I even being dragged into *your* mess?"

I jumped up from my chair and swung around to face my parents.

"I am *not* going."

"Mariana, you have plenty of summers and birthdays to spend with your friends. It's not the end of the world," my dad said unsympathetically.

For the first time, I understood just how Vince felt when he fought with our father; Dad didn't hear a word we said, nor did he care what we thought. His mind was made up before our mouths even opened. We were in two totally different realities.

"You really think this is just a birthday? No big deal? God, you really have no idea what goes on in my life! What type of parents are you? I've done nothing wrong!"

My dad blew a puff of air from his cheeks and glared at my mother, the vein pulsing on his forehead. She immediately stood up and rested her hand gently on my shoulder—a move I've seen her do a thousand times.

"Mari, it'll be fun. Trust me. A tropical island. Your parents nowhere in sight. You can hang out with Vince. You'll do all kinds of stuff, *together* . . ."

A spotlight suddenly lit up in my brain. I finally under-stood what was happening here. I *had* to go with Vince, but not as his traveling buddy. I was his fifteen-year-old watchdog.

"Oh, this is great! You act like an irresponsible idiot and now I have to go babysit you from across the ocean! Thanks for ruining my life, Vince!" I screamed.

"You are *not* babysitting me!" Vince jumped to his feet.

"Like hell I'm not!"

"Mariana, listen to me!" my father shouted, slamming his hand on the iron armrest as he stood. "You are going to Puerto Rico with your brother. It'll be safer if the two of you are there together. Plus, your Spanish is better."

"Says who? I got a 'B' in Spanish last quarter." Tears filled my eyes. "And you never even talk about Puerto Rico. You don't speak to anyone from there. Since when do you care about any of those people? I care about my friends *here*."

My father looked into my teary eyes. He paused for several seconds, and I actually didn't think he was going to respond until he added, "You have a lot of family there you should meet. I probably should've gone back, with all of you, a long time ago. I think this'll be good for all of us. At the end of the summer, your mom and I will come visit. We'll all travel back together. Mariana, it's done. It's settled."

I swallowed a knotted lump in my throat. He already had the plans made. He probably had them made before he even told Vince. Anything I said at this point would be futile. My father had no intention of taking my feelings into account. He didn't care about my friends or Madison's party or what I wanted. I had no choice. He was sending me off to slaughter (or Puerto Rico) whether I wanted to go or not.

And here's a look at Book #2,
AMIGAS AND SCHOOL SCANDALS. . . .

Chapter 1

"**A**re you sure you wanna do this?" I asked as I piled clothes into my jumbo-sized suitcase.

It was officially my last night in Utuado, the tiny mountain village in Puerto Rico where I had spent the summer. I was going back to Spring Mills.

"Of course," Lilly answered as she scanned my tenth grade schedule.

My mom had snatched it from the mail before she hopped on the plane to the island, and I was incredibly grateful that she did. Not that I didn't already know which classes I'd be taking, but it was nice to see the schedule in its official form. Now I knew which teachers I had, which electives I got, and how my day would be laid out. I loved the predictable, comfortable order of home.

"Wow, that's a lot of classes," Lilly muttered.

"It's the normal course load. You get used to it."

I tossed my bathing suits into my luggage. I wouldn't be breaking them out again for quite a while. There was something sad about packing up a swimsuit for the season, as if it signified the end of fun.

"So, how are your parents dealing?" I asked.

"Eh, they've mellowed a bit. I know they want what's best for me, and to be honest, I've been thinking about it ever since you and Vince got here. . . ."

"Switching schools is a big deal."

"I know." She nodded. "I just see your dad and . . . I want more than this."

She waved her hands around my bedroom. I guess it wasn't really my bedroom anymore, if it ever really was. I glanced one more time at the rock-hard mattress on my twin bed, the powder blue walls, the cement floor, and the stained white window shade. I was going to miss it. I was going to miss all of this.

Alex stood before me, his eyes smiling. He kissed me every time my parents weren't looking. They probably looked away on purpose, so they could deny any evidence of my emerging love life. Though I doubted one semi-boyfriend really counted as a love life.

His lips pressed against mine. I wanted to lock the feeling into my brain, soak it in one last time, but before I could, my father subtly blew the car horn. Alex pulled away. His brown eyes looked dull, and his eyelids drooped slightly. A lump pulsed in my throat.

"So, you gonna meet some other American tourist tomorrow? Take her salsa dancing?" I asked with a nervous laugh.

"Absolutely. I've already got one lined up. Only she's Canadian," Alex replied with a grin.

"Canadian, eh?" I mocked, tossing in the one bit of slang I knew from our neighbors to the north. "Well, be careful. They might look like us Americans, but they're a whole different breed. Bad weather, hockey, bacon . . ."

"I like bacon."

He smiled and hugged me tight. I let my head fall on his shoulder. His shampoo smelled like oranges.

"Mariana, it's time to go," my father said, exiting the car.

I paused and stared at my great aunt and great uncle's mountain house one last time. The blue concrete façade I'd dreaded with a passion two months ago now seemed like home. Uncle Miguel, Aunt Carmen, my cousin Alonzo and his "friend" José—who were gathered on the bright green grass watching our family load up the car—now felt like family. In some odd parallel universe, I could almost see my life fitting in here, but instead, my brother and I were headed back to our normal lives.

Well, almost.

Lilly pushed the porch door open and propped it with her newly purchased—courtesy of my father—travel bag. Her auburn hair was pulled back in a high ponytail, and two duffle bags hung from her shoulders—she looked a lot like I did when I first arrived. She paused to wipe the sweat from her freckled brow, and I could tell she was trying to mentally block the Spanish mumblings of her parents. They were chasing after her, rambling on, with their faces tightly twisted in worry. Lilly had spent the past few days reassuring them, in every way possible from conversation to pantomime, that this was *exactly* what she wanted.

She was moving to the States.

Once my dad realized how advanced Lilly's bilingual skills were and how dedicated she was to her education (she got straight A's at her English-speaking school), he couldn't help but offer her a chance to learn in Spring Mills. He wanted to give her the opportunity his parents gave him, and Lilly jumped at the offer. The girl had been riding on a bus for more than two hours each day just to get to and from school. (Meanwhile, Vince and I complained when there was no parking in our school's private lot and we had to walk an extra ten feet.)

"Will somebody please tell my parents that I'm doing the right thing, because I don't think they can actually hear the words coming out of my mouth. They're acting like the universe is going to explode if I step foot off this island!" Lilly exploded as she yanked her suitcase from her father and hauled it across the lawn.

My dad immediately darted toward Lilly's parents. They knew she was in good hands. She was going to be with family (even if we were distant cousins who were totally unaware of each other's existence until a few weeks ago). Plus, my dad had covered every detail of his plans with them numerous times. Within three days, he managed to enroll Lilly in Spring Mills High School (conveniently, the dean went to our church and played golf with my dad on weekends), have the housekeeping staff prepare one of our spacious guest bedrooms, and book all of my cousin's last-minute travel arrangements. He then kindly traded in Vince and my first-class tickets for three coach seats. (He and my mom still planned to take advantage of the plane's luxury accommodations without us.)

Lilly's parents were thrilled at my father's generous offer, and they knew it was a life-changing opportunity for her. They had agreed to the move days ago, but still, Lilly was their only child. She was fifteen and had never traveled farther than San Juan. Now she was moving to Pennsylvania, where she would attend an American school, and meet new friends and boyfriends, and live in a world completely separate from theirs. A world full of posh amenities they'd never even contemplated.

She was moving to Philadelphia's Main Line—a far stretch from the mountain town where she was raised. There would be no tropical rain forests, exotic birds, wild chickens in the backyard, or laundry duty at her grandfather's run-down hotel. Soon her biggest worry would be which marble bathroom to shower in and which gourmet meal to order from takeout.

"So, are you really ready for this?" Alex asked as my cousin trudged over.

"Are you kidding? A chance to be rescued from the island? I think I've been waiting for this since birth," she joked as she dragged her luggage to the back of the car.

Alex hurled it into the already packed, shiny new SUV, which stood out drastically on the mountain road.

"Ya gonna miss me, Alex?" Lilly asked with a big grin.

"Funny, I was wondering the same thing." I smirked.

"Oh, really. Well, I'm sure he'll miss you more, even though I've known him my entire life. Apparently years of friendship pale in comparison to a few weeks of smoochy, smoochy."

"Hey!" I screeched, my cheeks burning.

"I will miss you both," he replied, squeezing my waist a few times.

I giggled and squirmed as he pulled me tighter.

"See! You two are disgusting! Vince, can you see this?" Lilly asked my brother.

He had been sitting in the car and ready to hit the road for more than a half hour. His escape to Cornell was merely days away, and he couldn't wait to detach himself from our parents.

"I prefer to believe my sister is asexual," he said flatly, leaning out the window of the car. "Mom, are we *ever* gonna get out of here?"

My mother was seated patiently in the passenger's side. I could tell the week-long trip had been a whirlwind for her. Not only could she not speak Spanish (and thus not understand a word anyone was saying around her), she was forced to drink rum (I had never seen her sip any alcohol other than a crisp white wine), shower in moldy accommodations, and succumb to the humidity-induced frizz in her blond hair. Her locks were currently tied in a sloppy ponytail akin to my own. It made me realize just how similar we were.

"We're gonna leave in a second. Let your father smooth things over with the Sanchezes. Lilly, why don't you go over there and help?" my mom suggested.

Lilly groaned.

"It *is* the last time you'll see them for a while," I reminded her.

"I know, I know. I guess I need to pretend that upsets me."

"Lilly, you are going to miss your parents," Alex stated plainly. "I don't think you realize how different Spring Mills is going to be."

"Are you kidding me? I know all about Spring Mills. She hasn't stopped talking about it since she got here. 'Back in Spring Mills, back in Spring Mills.'" Lilly nudged my shoulder as she headed off toward her parents.

They were engrossed in conversation with my father. But I knew he'd have the final say. He always did.

A few hours later, we boarded the plane headed back home. I was squished between Vince and Lilly. Since Lilly was technically our "guest" (even though we were still on a plane and not yet on American soil), I felt compelled to offer her the window seat. Vince's extra inches of leg won him the aisle, leaving me stuck in the middle for four straight hours.

I sipped my tiny bottle of water and fought my brother for the armrest. The elbow war was the only thing distracting me from my impending Madison and Emily drama. I knew they wouldn't let my MIA status this summer drop easily. They hadn't returned any of my e-mails from the past week, and they still had no idea I was bringing a five-foot-four, redheaded souvenir back from the island. But they were my best friends, my only friends before Lilly. They couldn't hate me forever.

"Hey, you thinking about Alex?" Lilly asked, looking up from the gossip magazine she'd purchased at the San Juan airport.

She wanted to brush up on Hollywood celebrities before she landed, which I agreed was a virtual necessity. If she didn't know Tom and Katie's latest relationship woes, there would be no way she'd fit into Madison's world.

"Nah. We'll keep in touch. Or at least I know you guys will, so he can't exactly drop off the face of the Earth—"

"Are you kidding?" Lilly interrupted. "Trust me, you have a better chance of hearing from him than I do. I wouldn't be surprised if he goes to college in the States next year just to be near you."

"Oh, please! Like that would ever happen! I wish I had that much influence over boys."

"You do. . . ."

"Whatever," I scoffed, readjusting the hairband holding back my stringy red mop. I flicked my eyes toward her. "You scared about moving?"

"A little," she said with a sad smile. "I'm excited, scared, sad, and happy all at the same time."

"I still can't believe you're really doing it. There's no way I'd be able to up and move. I mean, you've got your whole life back in Utuado. . . ."

"Yeah, and if I didn't do something now, my life would always *be* Utuado. My parents have never left the island. Ever. I don't wanna be like that."

"Still, it's a pretty big leap from traveling to moving." I pumped my eyebrows.

"I figure I'll give it a year and, if it doesn't work out, then I'll just go home. What's the worst that could happen?"

I stared at my hands. "You could be away for so long that your whole life evaporates. You could come back to a world that's completely different. . . ." I said softly.

"I have a feeling you're not talking about me," Lilly said with heavy emphasis. "Lemme guess, the infamous Madison and Emily?"

I shrugged with a knowing nod.

"You think they'll hate me?" she asked.

"Well, right now they hate *me*," I mumbled.

"If they're half as good of friends as you say they are, they'll get over it. And if not, you've got me, *chica*."

Just then Vince turned toward us and unplugged his earphones. We had only been on the plane for an hour, but already his dark brown locks were disheveled from the headrest.

"Hey, I just remembered that when we were on the plane to Puerto Rico, and you were sulking like a baby, I bet you that you'd be crying when we left. And that you'd have fun this summer. I *so* won that bet."

"Too bad we didn't put money on it," I snipped. "Besides, I'm not crying."

"I think I saw you shed a tear. 'Oh, Alex, I'm gonna miss you *so* much.' Mwah, mwah, mwah," he teased, planting exaggerated noisy kisses on the back of his hand.

"I don't sound like that!"

"Sure you do," he mocked with a crooked grin.

"I wasn't talking to you anyway."

"No, but I heard you. You're acting like Madison and Emily will never speak to you again. I thought they were your *best friends*," he whined, wiggling his fingers.

Then he plugged his earbuds in and turned his attention back to his iPod.

"They'll speak to me again," I muttered under my breath.

At least I hoped they would.